The Coming of Noah's 2nd Ark

Apocalypse & Hyperspace Jumping

MATTHEW ILAYATHU

THE COMING OF NOAH'S 2ND ARK:
Apocalypse & Hyperspace Jumping

Copyright © 2016 Matthew ilayathu

All rights reserved.

First Published 2016

Ernakulam, Kerala, India

No parts of this publication may be reproduced, stored in a retrieval system, or transmitted in any form or by any means, electronic, mechanical, photocopying, recording, or otherwise, without the prior written permission of the copyright owner.

This book is sold subject to the condition that it shall not, by way of trade or otherwise, be lent, resold, hired out, or otherwise circulated without the publisher's prior consent in any form of binding or cover other than that in which it is published and without a similar condition including this condition being imposed on the subsequent purchaser. Under no circumstances may any part of this book be photocopied for resale.

This is a work of fiction. Any similarity between the characters and situations within its pages and places or persons, living or dead, is unintentional and co-incidental.

Cover design: Amal Arts, Kochi.
Printed & bound by: CreateSpace, Amazon's Print On Demand service.

ISBN-13: 978-93-5267-506-7
(Amazon Ebook ASIN: B01LWB1G1U)

DEDICATION

Motivation to write this book:

- Albert Einstein and his theory of general relativity.

- Stephen Hawking's intellectual lectures in the fields of cosmology, general relativity and quantum gravity, especially his ground-breaking ideas about black holes.

- All scientists and Organisations conducting research on Global Warming & Climate Change.

- Sci-fi writers who fuel our hopes of interstellar travel in search of habitable planets. If we can overcome the current speed restrictions in interstellar space travel, the whole Milky Way galaxy will be open to us to explore.

♣ ♣ ♣

CONTENTS

CONTENTS

PREFACE

The Relevance of Noah's 2nd Ark

Noah's Ark in the biblical story may be the maximum criticized item from any religious scriptures the world over. However, it'll be good to take the moral of the story.

Noah's Ark is a beautiful concept where even though God wants to punish the world when it's becoming evil and destructive, still He wishes to preserve the life on Earth.

Let's now compare the evils of Noah's time to the modern-day human's evils where we exploit the Nature and its resources indiscriminately, causing global warming.

Noah's Ark hints that when our evils grow horrendously and we don't pay heed to the warning signs from heaven, God or the Nature punishes us with all his fury. He does this to rearrange everything in an orderly manner or say, to renew the life cycle.

In today's world, the change is clearly visible- unreasonable ways of industrialization, deforestation and modern lifestyle have given rise to huge CO2 emission, pollution and degeneration of Nature. This paved way for global warming & climate change.
We face untimely rains, droughts, flash floods, massive earth quakes etc. It'll be intriguing to imagine what will happen if Earth's surface and atmospheric temperatures rise like this continuously.

If we live in the hostile conditions of Mars for a week, then we'll know the blessings we have on Earth – even the air we breathe, the water we drink, the greenness and life giving environment around us will look like golden treasures!

The hardships we face to live on Mars will be an eye opener. After returning from Mars for a week's stay, anybody will become an advocate for environmental protection.

Life is precious and Earth with its inhabitable condition is a very rare phenomenon in the Universe. So far scientists watching the Milky Way galaxy haven't found any planet as pleasant and life giving as Earth. We'll have to preserve it lest the future generations may find it difficult to pull on. Stopping over exploitation of the Nature will help the flora and fauna to peacefully coexist.

It's high time to think if climate change is growing beyond our control. If so, the fury of nature may come upon us as it happened during Noah's time! We'll have to either correct our wrongdoings or face the doomsday. Only hope is that we may get a last straw to safeguard life as happened during Noah's period.

This book is a humble attempt to explore that idea of the coming of a 2nd Ark for saving the precious life amidst the chaos.

BOOK – I

MISSION MILKY WAY & LIGHT-SPEED BARRIER

Code To Build The New Ark Revealed To Mankind

"And God saw the earth, and behold, it was corrupt, for all flesh had corrupted their way on the earth. [13] And God said to Noah, I have determined to make an end of all flesh, for the earth is filled with violence through them. Behold, I will destroy them with the earth. [14] Make yourself an ark of cypress wood...This is how you are to build it: ..."
Genesis (6:12- 15)

1 OUTFOXING THE SUPER COP

An important global science communication summit was held at the NASA centre in the New Orleans City of the state of Louisiana, United States of America. The absence of Mohammad Franklin at the summit was seen as a shock to the scientists, especially the cosmologists and astrophysicist.

Mohammad Franklin is an associate professor of astrophysics at the University of Southern Mississippi. He looked very peculiar and was different from other professors in his mannerisms and behaviour. He used to talk to himself, and sometimes walk around in deep thought and that time he won't recognize anybody around him. Some people used to say he's crazy. Outstanding personalities are sometimes considered eccentric because we fail to recognize the greatness in their thinking, general manners and behaviour.

Prof. Franklin is a very intelligent astrophysicist who has been conducting research on space exploration, rocket propulsion systems and light speed travel. It was known to the scientific community that Franklin achieved a breakthrough in crossing the light speed barrier. He was due to present a paper at the NASA convention. Nobody has any clues about Franklin's theory as he's a lone person and conducted research on his own without keeping assistants.

The coordinators were very busy arranging everything as the delegates started arriving at the convention hall. The NASA convention featured a three-day program with several academic papers presented. It's the last day of the meet. Participants were given the agenda papers, and other info sheets at the convention hall.

The chief coordinator Prof. Nelson Thomas was worried as he didn't get a confirmation call from Prof. Mohammad Franklin to attend the meet. The VIP for the day is Prof. Franklin as he will be presenting an important theory paper.

Prof. Thomas is now trying the fifth time to contact Franklin on his mobile. Prof. Franklin's mobile has been switched off. Thomas is sweating profusely now. He could have met Franklin yesterday itself; he cursed himself for the lapse on his part. He never thought Franklin will be this late as he used to be very punctual.

There is not much time left now. Almost all VIPs have arrived; only a few are left who're on the way. Prof. Thomas called his assistant, Ryan and barked, "Go urgently to Prof. Franklin's suite and bring him straightway here."

It's just a 10 minutes drive and Ryan reached Prof. Franklin's suite within 5 minutes. He reached for the front door and hit it urgently. He rang the bell. Nothing. Again. Still no answer. Ryan now felt uneasy. He banged on the door and pushed it with his shoulder. The door flew open and he stormed in. There was complete silence, and nobody was there.

The convention proceedings started and Prof. Franklin's seat was vacant. During the tea break, some scientists gathered around a table.

One scientist aired his displeasure openly, "Why didn't that Prof. Franklin show up to the meet today? I came just to listen to his new theory." Another delegate said, "I too was expecting a great research paper and a possible discovery from Franklin." All of them at the table exclaimed, "Why do the coordinators keep mum?"

Some of them were banging on the table in disappointment. The convention hall reverberated with questions like: "Why Franklin was absent?; why didn't he turn up?" The NASA convention thus ended with dissatisfaction and murmuring.

Franklin was also absent without leave from the University of Southern Mississippi. His parents came to know about the situation only when the University had informed them. Because of his eccentric behaviour Franklin never used to come home daily. Sometimes he would be away on research and science tours etc. So his parents didn't take his absence seriously. But one thing confused them; Franklin's usual messages to his mom are missing. He used to call or message frequently whenever he was away from home.

So, when Prof. Franklin's parents heard about the issue from the University, they straightaway lodged a missing person's report with the local police authority. The New Orleans Police Department (NOPD) conducted preliminary enquiries. They concluded that the case was a serious one and might have direct bearing on national security. NOPD promptly reported the matter to higher authorities and soon the Federal Bureau of Investigation (FBI) took up the case of Mohammad Franklin.

FBI special agent David has been given the charge of Franklin's missing case enquiry. He was told to finish the preliminary enquiries within a week as the case has high priority.

David normally only receives the most important cases. He is known in FBI as Mr. Fox! This is not just because he's very cunning. He has certain gestures and special mannerisms while concentrating on an investigation. That time he assumes certain facial expressions that vaguely resembled a fox, hence the nickname Fox.

David scrutinized the FIR registered by NOPD and understood that it's not an ordinary man missing case.

David took an appointment with NASA.

He went there and met a scientist and an administrative officer in a secret meeting room.

David said to the admin official, "As you're aware, I have come here to know some facts about Prof. Franklin."

"Welcome Mr. David, I'm Peter from the admin office, and he's Astrophysicist Joshua at the Space Science Department. Please proceed."

David just wiped his face and while doing so, he closely observed the walls ceiling and the door. He was happy that there are no windows in the room because he thinks it's a vulnerable point. "I want to know what type of research Pro. Franklin was doing here and which research paper he was due to submit," David asked.

"Franklin was a brilliant scientist and his research paper would have become a turning point in human history. It was about crossing the light speed barrier," Astrophysicist Joshua said.

"Was it related to a missile or other weapons, and if not, was it something very important?"

"It was not any missiles, but a spacecraft that can travel at the speed of light. Achieving light speed is important because we can't move out of our solar system within a life period with the with the 50 Mach maximum rocket speed available now."

David was considering the kidnapping angle in the case and then Joshua came up with the investigative thread.

"One can assume that Franklin's possible invention of crossing the light speed barrier has far reaching implications for the whole human race. This made his absence a serious issue. If some terrorist organizations or countries take away his theory paper and formula, then it could be catastrophic to the whole world.

"If Franklin's invention is used to make spacecraft that can attack with lightning speed, then they can target any country from anywhere in the world within a few minutes. And think about this spacecraft carrying nuclear warheads. It can be used against the US interests."

David sighed in relief and whistled gently. Joshua and Peter looked at him curiously, but David never bothered even though his expression betrayed a fox's face. He burst out, "Thank you sir for giving valuable info. Good bye."

David quickly left the NASA office and reached his den. He wrote all clues and suspected individuals in his diary. After thinking deliberately for some time, David wrote two names in the diary and went out. It could be another interview session. His interviews with the accused are well known. Nobody could hide anything from him.

Like a psychiatrist hypnotizing a patient, David could extract all required info from the people he interrogated. That made him a very successful and much feared investigator among the criminals.

Detective agent David went to see Franklin's parents. It was not a very posh apartment. David rang the calling bell and waited. A respectable woman in her 50's opened the door. After showing her his id card, David said, "I'm from the FBI. I need to talk to you about Prof. Franklin."

"Come in," she said in a polite but uneasy voice and added, "Mohammad Franklin's father is bedridden. He's suffering from Alzheimer's disease. I'm Martha, his mother."

"Oh, I see. I'm David, and I just want to collect some information about your son. We're here to help you out in this difficult situation," David said in a soothing tone.

He pushed on, "When was the last time Prof. Franklin talked to you? And did he say anything unusual?"

Martha wiped tears down her face as she tried to recollect when Franklin talked with her last time on phone.

"No, he didn't elaborate anything that time when he called. He just said he may be away for a while for the NASA convention."

David then asked Martha, "Can you please show me his study room?"

Martha reluctantly agreed as she know there is no other option.

David entered Franklin's room and looked around. In the bookshelf, he found some new books by the side of the old bunch.

He just picked up one of the new ones and gone through the contents. Martha flushed a little because she knew that Franklin has of late developed a new habit of reading those books.

David read the expression on Martha's face before she could assume normal looks.

Fox David also has his hands on Franklin's personal computer. However, he found that all data was deleted from the system. But David knows what to do in such circumstances; he can extract data from the hard disc.

He said, "I need to look into the hardware and so I'm taking it. Here are the required papers signed to complete the formalities."

During the ensued dialogues, David understood one thing that Martha is very reluctant to disclose the fact her husband's paternal grandparents had migrated to the U.S. from Iran. Their father Mustafa Mohammad was a trader and he had married US citizen Josephine. Mustafa Mohammad had adopted the name Mustafa Franklin, and thus the family has Franklin as the surname.

They never talked about their family's Iranian connection to anybody in the neighbourhood – may be because of the not so good relations between U.S. and Iran.

In his office lab, David could extract what he wanted from Franklin's laptop as he is also a computer expert. After extracting the data, David scrutinised it. On the screen, there displayed Franklin's regular communications with his cousins and other parental relatives in Iran.

Franklin's recent internet downloads also show radical Islamic speeches and other documents from fundamentalist organizations.

Now David could guess what actually happened to the missing professor.

He checked flights from the U.S. to countries in the Middle East region from one week prior to the start of the NASA Summit. Yes, David was correct. Franklin had travelled to Pakistan.

David promptly informed the Central Investigation Agency, and CIA checked with Pakistan authorities.

Franklin had fled to Iran!

The explosive information about Prof. Franklin created havoc in the higher rungs of power in the United States.

Member organisations of the United States Intelligence Community are always proud to hear that their Nation is the super cop of the world. Their high-tech surveillance of people within the U.S. and of the outside world is said to be the most powerful security intelligence tracking in the world. Irrespective of all those feathers in their cap, an ordinary university professor has outwitted them!

A high level meeting was scheduled at CIA headquarters. The White House Chief of Staff would be attending, showing the urgency and importance of the situation.

2 ESPIONAGE

Franklin's case is handled directly by the Director of the CIA. While enquiring about Franklin's parents, it was revealed that his mother is an Indian origin US citizen (a Malayali, native of Kerala state in India). Upon enquiring about Malayalis, the CIA Director came to know that they are spread all over the world, and keep a common identity and help each other, irrespective of religion, caste or profession.

So the CIA Director decided to try playing the Malayali card to impress Franklin's mother.

Somehow he has to make a link to Franklin who fled to Iran. Because the United States has no diplomatic relations with Iran, extradition is not possible, even if they could prove he had committed a crime. The only option to gather information is espionage and infiltration.

The CIA Director has checked the presence of Malayalis in Defence Service, and Space Research Departments. The idea is to recruit someone capable of understanding Franklin's scientific theory, as well as being able to conduct an espionage mission to Iran.

The shortlist contains four people, which was further narrowed to two candidates. The first one is US Air Force pilot, Sam Ananthan, 27. And the second one is a NASA scientist and cloning expert, Dr. Mary Koshy, aged 24.

Sam came from Kakkanad, Ernakulam District in the Kerala State of India. He was a fighter pilot in the Indian Air Force (IAF) and had come to the United States on deputation for a UN mission. He'd later joined the US Air Force service after resigning from IAF. Sam was a very professional test pilot. What made him unique was the fact that he was also an efficient aircraft mechanic. Normally pilots with their busy flying schedule never shown interest in the repair and maintenance of aircraft. While serving in IAF, he had learned Russian and Arabic as per service requirements. He held black belt in Karate. And with his stylish hero looks, no one could detect him as a military man. CIA Director thus saw many plus points on Ananthan.

Mary Koshy's parents came from Kottayam in the Kerala state. Mary was born while her parents were working in Dubai, UAE. She studied in Dubai till 10th grade, as a result she was fluent in Arabic before her family migrated to the United States.

Mary gained the highest marks in her year for her Pre-Medical exams. After completing the MD program, she had enrolled for a PhD in cloning research then joined NASA after successfully completing the PhD through Medical Scientist Training Program. At present she is conducting research regarding the scope of cloning in space. Mary had travelled to the International Space Station and was willing to take more space expeditions for her cloning research.

Other than the Malayali card, another reason to select Mary was that she and Sam looked as if they could be a couple. They even shared the hobby of martial arts. Like Sam, Mary also looked like a model or film star. It would be easy to introduce them to a third person without arising suspicion about their military background.

The CIA Director had invited them to the important meeting scheduled at his office.

Sam and Mary reached the CIA Director's office for the high level meeting with the White House Chief of Staff, the Deputy Secretary of Defence, Joint Chiefs of Staff of U.S. Department of Defence, NASA Administrator, and the CIA Director.

The White House Chief of Staff first read out the US President's message. He further said, "The President has instructed that we get back the invention Professor Franklin might have made while working here. He has ordered us to plan an operation accordingly. The President wants everything to be done confidentially and has also asked us to conduct an inquiry into the missing professor to check if any security lapses occurred."

Next the Deputy Secretary of Defence addressed the meeting, "FBI and CIA's confirmation about the incident of an astrophysicist defecting to Iran after formulating a theory to cross the light speed barrier has stunned our defence establishment.

"The invention could enable Iran to make hyper-speed missiles or even spacecraft. This will prompt them to attack the United States of America because they think we're the main force behind UN sanctions against them.

"We'll have to make changes to our defence systems in such a scenario of light speed spacecraft carrying nuclear warhead targeting us. We should not allow our enemy to develop a formidable weapon jeopardising the security of America. I therefore invite CIA Director to explain how they plan to handle this high risk security breach."

The CIA Director was checking some papers and writing here and there with a pencil. He looked busy and engaged in deep thought. As the Deputy Secretary of Defence signalled him to speak, he kept the notes aside, and looked at the audience as if to read their thoughts.

He began in a shrewd voice, "We have selected suitable agents to infiltrate and gather information. All plans are made to hijack the missing professor or to get the blueprint of his invention. We've the operation moving on a war footing."

There was a small interval for tea and refreshments. The CIA Director looked very active; he talked with everybody in a thrilled voice as they sipped the tea.

Next turn was of NASA Administrator. He looked serious and concerned. He started to talk as everybody sat attentively and there was pin-drop silence in the room.

"The disappearance of Prof. Franklin assumes great importance as he might have invented a formula by which human can create a spacecraft and travel at the speed of light. If he didn't flee to Iran, it would have been a time for celebration.

"As you know this important invention could now become a curse for humanity. There are chances that Iran or some extremist organizations may misuse it. Not only they can attack us, but our satellites and space program could also be targeted.

"Moreover, the spacecraft travelling at faster than light speed will be invisible too and our stealth radars won't be able to detect it! Imagine such a situation- it'll be catastrophic."

Listening to the possible consequences of Prof. Franklin's defection, the Deputy Secretary of Defence became restless.

You can see anxiety written all over his face at the thought of Iran developing a formidable weapon. He intervened, " Let me ask one thing. Could Iran make such a sophisticated spacecraft? Won't our satellites detect it if they test fly it on Earth or in outer space?"

"If they succeed in developing the prototype of the spacecraft, they can take help from some allies to produce it," the CIA Director said.

The NASA Administrator nodded, "Yeah, you're correct. And if they make it, we're not sure whether we'll be able to detect it.

There are peculiar things associated with light speed travel. The spaceship may turn into energy form at light speed and special magnetic sensors or spectroscope will have to be developed to keep tracking it."

The White House Chief of Staff then asked the NASA Administrator, "How important is this invention for America and the world as a whole? If their spacecraft prototype is destroyed in our commando operation, will it be a great loss?"

"Yeah, it's going to be a loss for everybody," NASA Administrator said. He added, "Achieving the speed of light will be a pivotal moment for humanity; everything will then change phenomenally. And we could expand our horizon not up to stars, but even up to galaxies and beyond! The survival of human species actually depends on it. Climate change and global warming could make the Earth uninhabitable. So we need to find out another planet quite like Earth- and for that, it's a must to travel at faster than light speed."

When everybody finished talking, the CIA Director stood up and said," I'm thanking each one of you for participating in this discussion. Proper briefings will be given as per procedure about our commando operation in Iran. From my part I assure you that destroying the invention will be our last option. I'll be eager to break good news to you in the near future. Once again thank you, and let me conclude this meeting."

After the dignitaries departed, the CIA Director conducted another round of discussions with Sam and Mary.

CIA Director, "Listen carefully; the Iran operation will be called Operation Milky Way (OMW) and you will also be known by codes. Ananthan will be SOM-001, and Mary Koshy's K will be added to get KOM-002"

It was a thrilling experience for Sam. He always wanted to be part of a live military ops. And now a beautiful girl is there as part of that mission. It's going to be a thriller one, Sam thought. His thoughts were interrupted as the CIA Director continued the instructions.

"You will not talk about this operation to anybody. Both of you will be reporting to me only and that too not directly. You won't be meeting anybody from the CIA or other police or defence establishment. This is to maintain the secrecy of the mission. No spies should get any clue; remember our enemy is Iran. We don't have any diplomatic relations with them, and their punishments are barbaric and on the spot."

Sam and Mary looked at each other. Sam expected fears in Mary's eyes, but they were calm.

The CIA Director further said, "FBI agent Mr. David has a role here too! We'll open a bank locker with a nationalized bank where only you two and David have access. You will put any messages in the locker and David will scrutinise it before passing it to me. In the same way, my messages to you will be dropped in bank locker by David.

"Your employment details will be removed from all US Air Force and NASA records so that even hackers won't get access to your original whereabouts."

Mary couldn't digest it fully. She asked, "Are these steps necessary and are they adequate to hide us?"

"This is necessary because once you start the operation, spies may track your movements. And we can assume that with our current security measures in the Air Force and NASA, both of you were inside several security layers, and not visible to any foreign agents."

Sam and Mary nodded, and took a five minutes break to attend their missed calls. A new sense of urgency and responsibility reflected in their body language. They realized that motivation and alertness have become part of their thought process. Mary laughed and talked enthusiastically over the phone. Sam noticed her feeling of excitement.

When they returned, the CIA Director was busy with his laptop.

Sam asked Mary, "How do you feel it?"

"I have certain interest in this mission, so I'm ready to face any difficulties," Mary said in a determined voice.

"Nice to know that, same here too."

As they were talking, the CIA Director came back and said, "Ok, guys, just one more thing. The complete records about the mission and the information about both of you commandos will be kept in a physical file format at my office. Everything will be top secret.

"Your appointment letters as commandos for Iran operation will come through the President's Office, and I'll personally sign it. Henceforth you will be acknowledged only as SOM-001 and KOM-002."

Sam and Mary confirmed their willingness to participate in the dangerous operation. They affirmed that they will prevent Iran from attacking the United States using Franklin's invention.

Finally the CIA Director stood up to shake hands, "All the best Mr. Ananthan and Ms. Koshy, take a week's rest before you join Fort Drum Military Base, Jefferson County, New York."

3 AT FORT DRUM MILITARY BASE

After getting appointment letters as commandos for Milky Way Mission Iran operation, Sam and Mary went to Fort Drum Military Base, Jefferson County, New York for two months' commando training. They are known with only the code words AOM-001 and KOM-002 in CIA records that were forwarded to the military training base.

Fort Drum, a United States Military Reserve, was home to the 10th Mountain Division and consisted of over 107,000 acres.

Selected combatant members of Army, Navy and Air Force used to go for training at Fort Drum Military Base. Because of the need for maintaining confidentiality, nobody was required to introduce himself/herself in the training squadron.

People come and go after the top rated training - neither friendships made, nor addresses exchanged at the base… This was beneficial to Sam and Mary because nobody seriously enquired about them and they didn't have to struggle to keep their Milky Way Mission a secret.

The aim of Fort Drum Military Base was to produce daredevil commandos who will be able to reach anywhere in the world and conduct espionage missions independently. Only highly capable, talented and strong people are drawn from the defence forces, CIA and police academy to this special training programme. Sometimes participants of top secret missions were also trained at the military base.

The training was tough, really tough!

In addition to strict physical training, the trainees were given practical lessons on handling live arms, ammunitions and improvised explosive devices etc. No dummy practice - commandos will have to attend live diffusing of IED's and other bombs. This was to instil a jungle instinct, and awakening of the sixth sense in the trainees.

Daily health runs in the morning and evening, and full day exercises in addition to educational classes were the daily norms.

Field survival practice, mountaineering, running sprints, running uphill, jumping, and repetitive impact exercises, ice skating, skiing, swimming across river, speedboat controlling, and more such items were included in the course run by ground training faculty. The faculty consisted of a team of highly qualified and dedicated instructors.

No priorities were given to anybody. Only the fittest and smartest were allowed to pass out and be given the certificate of completion.

The first day of training proved very hard for Mary. Even though she practised martial arts during her college days, she left everything after starting research on cloning.

In the morning health run, she was feeling dizzy after 2kms run. She sat down for a few minutes and Sam waited with her while the others continued running. The ambulance service for the sports ground came by and Mary was given Oxygen and energizer. She regained her strength soon and both of them started walking towards the Physical Fitness training ground.

It was the first day of the training course, so there can be excuses...but henceforth, no more considerations...Frog jumping, crawling, push-ups till you crash, and so on – there were no dearth of field punishments for the trainees.

There is about a walk of 10 minutes to the PT ground. Mary and Sam have a nice chat while walking.

Both are adventurous and the current mission of espionage and the possibility of travelling with the speed of light have equally thrilled them.

If the spacecraft can travel with the speed of light, Mary sees amazing possibilities for fast and efficient cloning. This could be human's first step towards immortality. If organs and even a child could be cloned in a fast pace inside the light speed spacecraft, then even if somebody dies, she/he can be resurrected within a few years.

However, if the light speed travel invention by Prof. Franklin reaches the hands of terrorists, it will have disastrous out comes.

Positivity could turn into negativity for humanity. There should not come such a horrible situation in the world. That's why Mary volunteered to participate in the mission. And she is ready to sacrifice anything and do any hard work for it.

And for Sam, there are more reasons to be happy. If the operation of fact finding and retrieving the professor becomes unsuccessful, they'll have to infiltrate into the professor's research team. He can help their technical team to design a prototype of the spaceship using Prof. Franklin's theory.

The distant possibility of piloting a spacecraft that travels with the speed of light is so thrilling that Sam wanted to go for the mission at any cost. Because of his expertise in the aviation field, Sam is confident that he can impress and win the confidence of Franklin if somehow they can get in touch with him.

While they walked, Sam asked Mary, "What about your hubby and family?" He was not sure whether to ask that question or not, but that was the only thought that came to his mind.

Mary flushed.
She said with a mild smile,
"Not yet married…actually couldn't find time for it because of studies and research. Papa and Mamma are now hinting and I was just thinking to give my nod as they always preferred an arranged marriage as customary in India.
"And then came this big mission. Such a thrilling opportunity comes once in a lifetime and so marriage can wait."

Sam wondered, "Oh, Is it? Same here too! I came to America just two years back. And I'm only 27, not late for marriage, isn't it?! So the mission is more important, I can also wait."

The morning air was so fresh and they felt energetic. They enjoyed the warm Sun and mild breeze.
Sam continued, "I'm an orphan and was brought up in a Christian orphanage in Kerala. I was the pet of Fr. John, the father in charge there. So I got good care and studied well.
Father John is my only relation, no idea about parents. He's very old now and leading a retired life. I told him to come to the U.S., but he wants to die in his native place.
"Fr. John jokingly said that he had nuns and the orphan children to look after him well there in Kerala…if he came here in the U.S., he asks, who'll take care of him, as I'll always be in the sky flying jets."
"Am I boring you, Mary?" Sam iasked, just to know her mood.
"Oh, come on, you're very interesting…Please continue."
They have sufficient time to continue the chat as the PT ground was not at sight.

"Thanks. Fr. John wants me to only marry a girl from Kerala. He told that I was born a Hindu. When they found me near the orphanage, there was a cloth bundle by my side and it contained a small gold idol of lord Ganapathi.

"When I was selected in the National Defence Academy as a trainee pilot, Father gave me the Ganapathi idol and a little crucifix.

"He told me I could live as a Hindu or a Christian, but that I should always be a good human being and should do good things to the poor and orphans. So I'm keeping both the idols and believe in the good points of both the religions."

Mary smiled at him, "That's a lovely story and you're lucky to have such independence and freedom on religious matters."

Shortly, they reached the PT ground by foot. Both of them felt good to be developing a friendship with each other, even if it was more than a friendship of necessity.

While talking to each other, they didn't even notice the passing of time. Maybe the challenges of the mission and the hardships ahead might have made them happy to stay close and share their feelings.

May be there are other factors too - both were engaged in professional matters till that time and now they had a chance to mingle with somebody from outside their sphere of work.

The training was very hard. The Ground Training Instructors (GTI) were merciless and enjoyed harassing the trainees- at least the trainees felt like that.

Punishments like crawling, frog jumping, and running/frog jumping with rifle over the head were routine affairs. No complaints were entertained and reporting sick was practically illegal except for serious illnesses.

If two people bunk out on weekends, i.e. go outside the camp without permission, and if you're caught, both of them were forced to pour water on each other's dress for half an hour at night 11 o clock in front of all trainees.

During night roll call, everybody will be talking and standing in a relaxing way (stand on one leg etc.), suddenly you'll hear a heavy "THUD-THUD" noise from the back and everybody will stop talking and stand properly. Source of the heavy noise: some unlucky fellow at the back got a heavy beating on his back by the GTI for talking or standing improperly.

One GTI used to tell trainees to take push up position and rub their noses on the ground.

There was a tree standing far away from the parade ground, which was named "Darling!" So any loose movement on the parade ground would get punishments like, "Run baby, run backwards, touch the Darling and come back in under a minute!"

Crawling with rifle in hand, reverse parade (putting on clothes inside out & doing heavy and mock drill on the ground), gardening in hot sun, and many more - harassments galore....

Even if you die during the training process, the GTIs won't be blamed- that was the situation... this was to instil a fear psychosis among the trainees and thus make them rough and tough daredevils in real combat.

Mary at many times thought to abandon the mission, but the presence of Sam gave her the strength and courage. One reason for both of them becoming too close during the training period was the hardships and insecurity prevailed in the training centre.

It was more than a friendship of necessity, but there was some spark of love also prevailed there.

Being together, they felt like they can do anything, cross any obstacles, and go to any distant corners of the Earth... Yes, a bond was developing, that of love, necessity and trust... and it would help them greatly to pursue the mission in hostile conditions in Iran and beyond, may be!

The two months' commando training thus went ahead with memorable events and finally they completed it with much struggle.

Both Mary and Sam knew that the training has made them powerful and smart.

After completion of the course, they returned to their respective new offices to pursue the Milky Way Mission. They will be working from different offices and won't be meeting each other openly to maintain secrecy.

Mary took a short leave and went to her parents' house on the outskirts of New York to spend the holidays.

Because of the oath of confidentiality, she didn't tell anything about the commando operation planned at the treacherous land of Iran. However she couldn't hide her friendship with Sam while her newfound love was at full sail!

And her papa and mamma were very happy to hear that...

4 IN THE SHADOW OF DATE PALM

A date processing plant at a remote area in North-eastern Iran has been taken over by Iran Govt. From outside, it looked like any date processing factory as the processing and packing is going on there and the secret govt office has been run in the warehouse area.

The date factory workers have no access to the govt office area and most of the people even don't know such an office existed underground because the entrance to the warehouse is from the other side and not visible to them.

The management of the date processing unit just has a vague idea that some medical equipment production is going on in the warehouse. As the police department had given them strict warning not to disclose or talk about the govt office, nobody enquired about it. No one has any idea what's going on there...and nobody dared to ask also.

The govt office uses vehicles with the same logo and design of the processing factory and so even satellite images couldn't find anything suspicious there.

This medical lab has been converted as the new operational unit and research centre for Prof. Mohammad Franklin. He and five other scientists and some visual artists are working on the spacecraft project. They rarely went out.

The underground warehouse has elaborate accommodation with all the facilities of a four star hotel.

One fine morning, some decision makers of the Iran government assembled there for an important meeting. Iran President's envoy, Ministry of Intelligence representatives, Minister of Communications & IT, Space Agency Chief, Chief of SAVAK (secret police force & intelligence wing), Defence rep from General Headquarters of Armed Forces are the dignitaries.

After greeting everybody, Mohammad Franklin addressed the gathering. The blueprint of the spacecraft was on a projector. What made everybody spellbound was the peculiar shape of the spacecraft. It's very different from the conventional designs. The spacecraft prototype has a disc shape which will allow it to move in a spiral trajectory.

"You're probably wondering at the shape of the spacecraft. The disc shape is actually the best model for a spacecraft to travel at high speeds equivalent to that of light. A disc shaped spacecraft travels in a spiral movement achieving maximum speed. I have all the theoretical evidence to prove it. This information and the theory and formula by which we can cross the light-speed barrier are stored in my laptop. In order to open my laptop, my finger touch is required as is the password. These security measures are provided to avoid the Americans or their partners hijacking my invention.

"The main challenge we face here is to create a prototype for my spacecraft. We don't have such spacecraft design companies in Iran. We'll have to do it with the help of Russia or India. We can also consider the USA and the European Union as a last resort. The Ministry of Intelligence representative can give a briefing in this regard."

The ministry rep raised his hand and nodded. There were two oval-shaped tables in the room and the dignitaries were sitting in one side. The projector and the speaker's dais were on the opposite side.

Franklin said, "Even if we're successful in creating a robust design, there are difficulties ahead such as launching and test flying the spacecraft. Hope we will be able to overcome all those hurdles, Insha'Allah.

"So the first step is to create a blue print of the spacecraft and then manufacture it. I'm indebted to the Islamic Republic of Iran and the officials for giving me these facilities within a short time of my arrival here. The astrophysicists and the technical team working with me are superb performers. Thank you all. Sukran."

The next speaker was the representative of Ministry of Intelligence.

"Thank you for explaining things, Prof. Franklin. Taking help from a foreign country is a risky business. If we approach European countries, the news will surely reach the United States of America. Then come Russia and India - here also we can't rely on them 100 percent as they may hijack this important discovery from us. I'll discuss this serious issue with the Minister and other sources and will take a final decision soon and will let you know at the earliest. Thank you very much. Kheily Mamnoon."

When the Ministry of Intelligence rep took his seat, the Space Agency Chief asked Franklin, "What type of rocket engine are you planning for the spacecraft, Professor?"

Franklin got up and went to the dais to explain further. He has to convince the Iranians that his theory is valid and has great importance.

"That's an important question, sir. I have gone through all the latest theories and concepts in rocket propulsion such as the Ionic Propulsion, Nuclear Thermal Propulsion, Nuclear Pulse Propulsion, Fusion Rockets and the Laser Sail. Ionic Propulsion and Nuclear Thermal Propulsion systems were discarded as they can't give the required speed for 4-D space-lift for my spacecraft.

"The Laser Sail concept is very promising. In this theory, as you know, they plan to use a powerful and focused laser beam to propel the spacecraft forward through the interstellar space with almost half the speed of light. However, it aims only to fly Nano, wafer like sailing spacecraft whereas I wanted manned spacecraft. The laser beam concept could be used on my spacecraft, maybe at a later stage when the technology becomes effective and fully under control."

Franklin glanced at the audience to see how they are digesting his ideas. The Iran officials were fully convinced; it was evident in their facial expression. Their astonished gestures indicate that they highly valued the invention brought by him.

Franklin enthusiastically explained his theory.

"Finally, I have decided to go with Nuclear Fusion technology. Fusion is the natural nuclear force that gives immense power to the

Sun. In this rocket technology, deuterium and helium-3 pellets are used as fuel. These nuclear elements are joined using the fusion technique and the high energy gas generated is utilised to propel the spacecraft. As we have the technology to make a smaller, lighter fusion reactor now, it can give much higher speed to the spacecraft in deep space.

"A two-stage fusion rocket will give enough thrust for my spacecraft model to achieve about 10 Lakhs Kilometres per Hour. Travelling at that whooping hyper speed, the spacecraft will eventually accelerate into the speed of light (1.08billion Kms/hour) due to its peculiar shape and special design features. Inshallah."

The Space Agency Chief cried, "Let it be so! That's a fantastic theory, Professor."

Franklin thanked him, and then turned to the defence representative, "Will there be any problem in acquiring nuclear fusion rockets for the spacecraft?"

The Defence representative replied, "That won't be an issue. We have strong ties with Russia for nuclear fuel transfer. Once you give us the specifications for the Fusion Rocket, we can acquire it from Russia within short notice. Russia already has large-scale manufacturing units for nuclear rocket propulsion systems."

"I'll give the blueprint and required measurements for the Nuclear Fusion Rocket by tomorrow. Please start the procurement procedures today," Franklin said.

The Space Agency Chief nodded. "We'll give you one of our spacecraft engineers for a few days to assist you in generating the specifications for the Nuclear Fusion rocket. We'll also work with the Ministry of Intelligence to get you a brilliant spacecraft designer for your phenomenal spacecraft."

Franklin smiled broadly. "Thank you everybody for the help and support. Goodbye."

When the speeches and discussions were over, everybody, except the Chief of SAVAK (secret police force and intelligence wing), left the place saying Khoda Hafez.

The Chief of SAVAK said to Franklin, "I know that your movements in Iran are restricted... and you may be feeling isolated in this remote location after coming from the lavish lifestyle in the

United States. Please adjust with the new situation. Because of Allah's desire, Muslims will rule the world and your position in that new world order will be a majestic one. Insha'Allah. So be patient and do your duty. Professor Franklin, you'll have to disguise yourself when going out from this place, otherwise the spying eyes of America will track you down.

"The agents of SAVAK will be accompanying you wherever you go. Your security and safety is more important to us. In this underground warehouse, some other govt offices are also working. You need not to look into those areas. Never try to mingle with anybody. Speak to me or use the hotline numbers given to you in case of urgency."

Franklin said, "That's ok. I'm not much bothered about security and going out. I have an important mission ahead. It calls for much hard work and concentration. That's my first and last priority. The Islamic Republic of Iran has provided all facilities for that. That is good enough. Thank you, bye."

The Chief of SAVAK nodded, "All the best, Professor. Good bye. Khoda Hafez."

After the Chief of SAVAK has also gone, Franklin talked to his team. He asked the visual artists to make more models of his spacecraft with the aid of computer art.

Franklin worked with them and explained the concept of intergalactic travel by bending space-time:
"The stories related to warp travel are going to be reality.
"First we'll have to achieve light speed travel, and then things will evolve further... like stretching the space-time in a wave and then riding the wave to travel thousands of light years between the galaxies in a matter of months, weeks or even days."

Franklin urged the scientists to put their full effort to convert the imaginations of the Star Trek creators into a real life event. "God has given the hypothesis from which I was able to make the theory and formula. Now it's everybody's duty to help me make a spacecraft that can achieve faster-than-light speed.

"Now we are living through the best time to think big and explore the Universe. The modern science has smart technology and equipments to do any research and experiments.

"A devastating calamity like a huge Sun flare, catastrophic climate change or a gigantic asteroid hitting our Earth could send us back to the Stone Age!

Everybody in the room looked at Prof. Franklin with a feeling of awe as he slowly slipped into a prophetic mood. They paid full attention to him as he was talking no nonsense.

"So the need of the hour is to invest all our energy into this light speed spacecraft project and make it a reality. There will be at least a handful of planets in this Universe where our future generations will be able to go and live in happily ever.

"Some lovely Gardens of Eden will be waiting there for the arrival of humanity. Inshallah."

Everybody said, "Inshallah."

5 DECODING EFFORTS

One day, Mary Koshy went to see Franklin's mom, Martha. The purpose of her visit was to befriend with the lady because she is the only source that might lead Sam and Mary to Prof. Franklin. Martha is a Malayali and Mary started talking to her in Malayalam to have a warm and affectionate approach.

Malayalis all over the world are known to like and help each other, and they take pride in speaking in their own language.

This way Mary was able to influence Martha. Mary told her that she is a researcher in cloning technology and when heard about Franklin's studies about space exploration and high speed travelling she was impressed and want to know more.

Mary convinced Martha that Franklin's invention, if true, could drastically change her research on cloning and bring amazing benefits for humanity.

Martha liked Mary very much. She said, "I'm much worried about my son. I have no news about him since he went missing. . The police questioned us, but they didn't reveal anything about Franklin."

"I'll surely find him out. In fact, I must meet him to continue my research. Now, knowing your predicament, Aunty, I take it as my duty to search for Prof. Franklin," said Mary.

"Police searched Franklin's room and took away his computer and other things. I don't know why they treat us like sinners. We're now completely isolated from the society as people think our son has acted against the interests of America," Martha sighed.

They moved to the kitchen. "I'm very pleased to see you. At least there is somebody who understands us," Martha smiled.

Martha started preparing coffee. Mary looked around. The kitchen was well arranged and looked perfectly clean.

Mary consoled her, "Sure, aunty, I'm with you. Together we can get some clues regarding the whereabouts of Franklin."

"We're under constant police observation, and our internet and mobile calls are trapped. You know Mary, my son Franklin is a very decent gentleman and won't do any wrong things. I'm very fond of him and miss him very much. I can't survive without talking to him,." Martha opened her mind.

She poured a cup of coffee for Mary.

Martha said, "Yes, I had seen some changes in Franklin's behaviour for the last two or three months before he went missing. He was worried. He said some people are cornering him in the university due to his religion…But I never expected that things will take such a turn!"

Tears fell down from Martha's eyes.

Mary patted her on the shoulder, "Franklin's point is correct, I know it, aunty. I also feel racial discrimination in my profession. I can fully understand Franklin now. In fact, I'm thinking of following his course of action."

"Never say like that, Mary. Can't you see what trouble we're in? Don't let your thoughts go out of way; never talk about such things to anybody. Don't make such a horrible situation for yourself."

"Ok, sure, aunty. I won't talk this to others. I'm eager to do my experiments and Franklin's invention will help it a lot. Collecting

DNA samples and doing cloning thrill me a lot. The Nature has so many secrets we're yet to explore."

Mary talked further about her research to make Martha comfortable and to affirm that she is really a scientific researcher.

She added, "One curious thing I want to tell you is about mosquitoes. While collecting their DNA, I just noticed their survival instincts. With human beings who have hands and easy access to every part of their body, the mosquito evolved a new trick to bite them. Have you noticed that, when you go behind a mosquito and try to kill it, it just disappears from your view. It achieves this invincibility by quickly gliding through the air and suddenly changing the direction of flying that can cheat our eyes."

Martha's mood slowly changed and she said, "Good observation Mary...I too noticed it."

"To outwit the mosquito, I contacted an optician who makes Augmented Reality (AR) spectacles. Without disclosing the actual requirement, I told him the approximate specifications of an eyeglass that'll help me to closely watch flying insects. After much design trials, he was able to produce a sort of Laser EyeTap (Generation-4 Glass) for me. You might have heard about Google Glass and Microsoft's HoloLens that use augmented reality. My pair of spectacles was something similar to a device that adjusts the light rays from the object coming towards your eyes."

Martha is curious now. "Have you tried the eye glasses to watch mosquitoes?"

Mary smiled to see her enthusiasm. "Exactly, aunty. I used those specs in a room where there were a few mosquitoes. When disturbed, they tried to evade me with the gliding trick, but because of the new eyeglasses they couldn't cheat my eyes. I could easily catch them as they didn't disappear from my view."

"I'm happy to know your capabilities and interest in cloning and related research, Mary. I now understand your eagerness to use my son's invention to further advance your research."

Mary thanked Martha and gave her the mobile number and address to contact her. Mary also explained to Martha the way to the Church where she goes every Sunday. Martha has agreed to inform her if she gets any details about Franklin.

Mary was thrilled to make that much progress in the very first meeting itself with Martha. Even though she is acting and spying, Mary has nice feelings for Martha. She loved her innocence and caring attitude.

A few days passed by without any turning point and on a fine Sunday morning, Mary was surprised to see Martha at the church. She came and sat near Mary's seat. While making the sign of the Cross, Martha secretly put a piece of paper inside Mary's jeans pocket.

Once the holy mass was over, and people started moving out of the church, Martha whispered to Mary, "I got that chit yesterday while shopping at a super market. That'll lead you to Franklin. Read it and do the needful, and keep everything secret. Police agents are following me, so let them not see us together, I'm going now. See you later."

Martha came out of the church and straightaway took a taxi and went away. She knew that somebody was following her. It's intriguing to feel followed...

You can't see who's following, but you can always sense it when being followed by somebody... Such a horrible, haunting feeling it is!

Mary is in seven clouds now because she has a chit from Martha. She is very eager to read the message, but she knows it's not advisable to read it openly. While returning from the church, she parked her car near a shopping centre. She took out the slip, while her heart kept thumping. It pounded harder as she read it. "Send me mail to: ..... Franklin."

"Wow, what a turning point for Mission Milky Way!" Mary exclaimed.

There was also a chit written by Martha that read: "Please come to the Palace Restaurant at Church Gate tomorrow 11 a.m."

Mary went to Palace Restaurant the next day morning. As there was rush in the restaurant, they could seat safely in a corner without noticed by anybody. Mary thought everything is happening like a dramatic sequence - pre-planned and fast. She couldn't believe things will turn out this fast in favour of them. She felt there is a divine hand moving things behind the scene...

They ordered ice cream, and Martha said, "Mary, I told you to come here because I knew that somebody was following me to the church yesterday. So I thought they should not see you too.

"I know your interest in Franklin's research and your eagerness to meet him; same way I too want to hear about my son. I can't survive without him. So we can move together, helping each other."

Mary nodded in agreement. "Did you know the person who gave this to you? Did he speak anything?"

"No, I don't know him. I hardly saw him. Just seen a slip pushed towards me from behind a clothes hangar. I was frightened when I saw it, but I regained balance within seconds... Deep in my mind I was always expecting something to come like that, so I just took the piece of paper and put it into my shorts pocket. Thank god, nobody noticed. I literally ran away from the shopping centre, not even bothered to look back at the person who gave the slip."

The bearer brought their ice cream. They ate it while closely checking if anybody observed them.

"So, please write a mail to Franklin on my name. If I write, the police will get hold of it somehow. But they won't suspect you. I'll give you some info that Franklin and I only know. Use it as code words, so he'll understand that it's me."

Martha then told Mary the codes and soon they left the restaurant one after another.

6 MY HEART WILL GO ON AND ON...

A discussion is going on in a conference room at the Directorate of Intelligence and Analysis (DA), under the CIA. The room is small and slightly cramped, but it's soundproofed and well appointed. The technical equipment and other accessories are up to date. The coffee and snacks table and leisure chairs are arranged neatly.

Two DA officers are discussing Mission Milky Way. The first officer who looks senior with a determined and authoritative expression is explaining things to his junior.

"Due to the secret nature of Mission Milky Way, the records of commandos Ananthan and Mary should not be seen in the Air Force or NASA records. If any mole or computer hackers find out their details in the enrolled list of Air Force and NASA, and transfer it to Iranian spies, then that will be the end of the mission. The commandos will be at the mercy of the Iran security agencies."

"Yea, I understand Sir. The commandos will have to infiltrate Franklin's network and introduce themselves as science enthusiasts without leaving any suspicion about their military and NASA background," the junior officer said.

"So, collect the orders from CIA Director's office. Mr. Ananthan will be transferred to the New York office of the

Federal Aviation Administration (FAA) and his service details at the Air Force records office are to be shifted to the data bank of the CIA."

"It'll be done, Sir. Where do we put Mr. Ananthan at FAA?"

"Create new records at FAA computer database showing Ananthan working there for the last five years. Induct him into the Quality Assurance (QAS) section of the Aviation Admin Dept because it's an isolated supervisory section, which doesn't have much contact with other sections and offices- the situation is ideal for him to operate without being noticed by others."

The junior intelligence analyst noted the points on his laptop.
"In a similar way, the lady commando, Mary's records are also to be shifted from NASA to the CIA. She's to be inducted into the New York City Health and Hospitals Corporation, our largest public hospital system.
"Records are to be amended to show that she has been working there for the last four years. City Health and Hospitals Corporation are associated with the New York University School of Medicine, so Mary can be appointed as Senior Field Researcher at the School of Medicine."

"Sure Sir. We'll ask the authorities to set up her office in a comparatively isolated corner and as it's a research section, nobody would have much interaction there."

"Ok. Liaise with concerned departments to make the transfers completed within one week. That's all for now."
"Done, Sir."

Mary and Sam are in New York but at different locations. They don't use internet or mobile phone networks of private service providers to communicate with each other. In order to maintain secrecy, they used teleconferencing via the direct satellite communication system of US Defence Department.
After flying to New York City, both of them collected identical letters via the bank locker system from The CIA Director. It was commonly addressed to them.

Hello Commandos Ananthan and Mary,

Best with your new appointments and collect your new ID's.

As you know you have very little time to accomplish the mission; also its scope is limited because your destination is the inaccessible Iran where we have no diplomatic influence.

Franklin and his team in Iran may implement his findings anytime and develop some spacecraft or missile that travels with light-speed. Once they succeed, nobody will be able to stop them from conquering the world. So, you have to act fast.

The only chance is that even if Franklin has made his final discoveries, Iran may not have the latest technology to develop the spacecraft. So there is hope. But Iran can always get help from Russia or other allies.

You'll have to sweat to reach Iran and take home the blue prints of Franklin's spacecraft project. If your mission doesn't bear fruit, you should not allow Iran to use the new technology – rather you'll destroy the project and shoot the defector. But you should resort to that final step only if everything fails because the discovery of light speed travel would be a remarkable achievement for humanity.

In fact, it'll be a giant leap for mankind through which humans can escape from the Solar system if climate change makes living impossible on Earth.

In this situation, sending an intercontinental missile and destroying Franklin's project site will be a very distant and unlikely option the US President will entertain. You'll have to go and find Franklin. Accomplish the mission fast; use your license to kill efficiently.

It's decided that Ananthan will be given advanced training on space travel and launching mechanisms. Theory papers of piloted flight of spacecraft, and practical classes on simulated space-pilot training are the areas stipulated for the coaching.

Meanwhile Mary will try to make contacts with Franklin by befriending his mother or by other tactics.

Both of you should keep in touch with mission planning and report progress regularly via satellite conference.

All the best.
Director

Sam was very much interested in the space travel course and the training has been going on well.

Even though he's very busy, he used to have daily talks with Mary. And Mary also finds time to call back.

On one occasion, Sam was not able to make contact as he went for a space mission for four days. Sam felt awkward as he couldn't contact Mary.

Sam looked back at Earth while travelling through space...It's such a fantastic sight to see Earth from space when you are about 300 kilometres above the surface. During the day, major landforms were visible and at night, you see the cities twinkled. Earth looked so beautiful and memories of Mary rushed to Sam's mind.

Memories then slowly turned into romantic songs and Sam used to sing them.

As the space station passed the moon (about 380,000 kilometres away), Earth looked like a bright ball in space, somewhat similar to the way the moon appears from Earth. He then started seeing the shadow of Mary's lovely face on the Earth. Then the slides of spacewalking with Mary flashed through his mind.

The love music of the movie, Titanic was one of those songs hummed by Sam while in space. He felt that the song echoed everywhere in the void outer space. And for him, it looked like Mary was singing the song, "My Heart Will Go On..."

●●●　　●●●　　●●●

After the meeting with Franklin's mom Martha, Mary went to her office. There was no contact with Sam for the last four days, so she couldn't share the new development with him.

Once she reached her office, Mary has tried to contact Sam through teleconferencing. Sam is not picking up the phone. She shook her head "no" and looked at the phone impatiently.

Mary understood that she is getting tensed and angry. It's a strange feeling hitherto unknown to her! She's very eager to speak to Sam.

After trying for two minutes, she dropped the phone and sat silently for a while with folded hands. And there came a ring. She picked it up with a flash movement, her breathing quick and uneven. She took a deep breath as she heard Sam speaking at the other end.

Mary said, "I'm so happy to hear you after some days, Sam. I have missed you dearly."

Sam replied, "Is it so?! Same here too- Every minute I was thinking of you, and missed you for the past four days."

And then Sam slowly sang the second stanza of Titanic love song.
And Mary also sang the next lines.
And both of them sang together the first few lines.

It was like one of such sweet moments when lovers forget the world and indulge in their own sphere of love and care, completely isolated from others, lovers will stay unto themselves for so long…
A few moments passed by and suddenly Sam and Mary woke up from the binding garlands of love…
How it all happened they don't know… but they realised that they have openly admitted and expressed their love, it was the first time both accepted it openly even though both of them knew they're in love.
Things have become easy now, no more inhibitions and tensed expressions to know the mind of the other person - so much the better.
But they are commandos, not just lovers...
Soon they woke up from the bond of love and started talking Mission matters.

"Mary, what's the progress on Mission MW?"
"Great news, Sam- I got the E-mail contact of Franklin in a surprise move." Mary then narrated the meeting with Franklin's mom, Martha and the events that followed.
So, the next step is to write an E-mail to Franklin. They discussed it in detail; written the mail, corrected it and then rewritten…
Finally Mary clicked the send button.

Sam further said, , "I'll be busy for a few more days. I've got some more practice on the spacecraft simulator and will be going for some more space walks. Also, there are technical maintenance classes and some theory papers on astrophysics and cosmology. If we happened to see Franklin's theory papers and blueprint, it's good to know how to handle them.

"So, continue with managing the contact with Franklin. Try to make some progress, but be careful with your dealings. Think twice before making any commitment. There are chances that Iran spies in the U.S. may try to find you. Take care."

Mary nodded.

Sam then said laughing, "The new turning point, the Titanic song in our relation; let it remain a secret. What do you say, dear?"

"Oh, sure," Mary said smiling.

"When I'm in space, I imagine the spaceship to be the Titanic. And feel like you and me enacting that unforgettable moment when Jack takes Rose to the ship deck and on top of the railings and says "Open your eyes," and Rose says, "I'm flying, Jack!"

"And then in place of Jack, I sing slowly for you as happened in the Titanic movie: "Come, Josephine, in my flying machine, going up, she goes up, up she goes."

"And then we kiss, as they did, so passionately, so violently— are you listening, Mary?"

"Hmmm..."

"Oh Mary, how I wish to be by your side now."

"Oh, Sam, you're so magnificent; so romantic... I too wish you're here now," Mary whispered.

"Sam, Titanic was a love tragedy, why do we continuously talk about it...? Tears fall down my eyes whenever I think about that movie."

Sam consoled her, "Be courageous, young lady! Our space ship travel and Titanic have similarity only about the deep love of Jack and Rose, not the tragic fate of the journey. We'll see the beauty of twinkling little stars at night as we fly on our spacecraft. Our new mission will take us to bright star worlds and we'll nestle somewhere there to keep us warm."

Mary quickly said, "My romantic hero, no; we won't stay there. We'll come back home; come back to our beautiful Earth where all our friends, relatives, and all these lovely flora and fauna exist."

"Let it be so, cute girl; take care, bye for now."
"Bye, Sam- take care."

After Sam went offline, Mary kept on thinking about their conversation. Things are happening unexpectedly and taking turns surprisingly.

She talked to herself: "Never thought that I'll have such a love affair with somebody. And when it came, love feels so fantastic. It's divine indeed. It can make you fly… you'll start talking and laughing in silence and everything appears to be pleasant and sweet when you're in love…It's also painful, the pinching pain in your heart, when your lover is away, is suffocating…

"Love is like moonlight- so calm, pleasant and beautiful. A moonlit night can make the lover more affectionate, and melt her like wax in a burning candle… and the souls fly aboard the cool moon light beams, dreaming all the way…

"But I'm not just a lover; the world expects heroic acts from me. I have the responsibility to ensure that Franklin's invention is used for the betterment of the society. It shouldn't fall into the hands of terrorists…

"And I'm a commando on an espionage mission to one of the most hostile countries in the world – and so, not just a lover."

Mary repeated the words, 'I'm a commando' several times to get away from the lunatic spell of love.

And a beep heard from her computer.

It was the alert for receiving a new email. She checked the mail box, and uttered a loud cry to see a reply from Franklin to the fake e-mail id that she created for Martha. Mary was surprised; she didn't expect a reply so fast.

When Mary opened the mail, there was another surprise. It was not addressed to Martha, but to her! She read it within seconds. And then sent a message to Sam.

Franklin said in his mail to Mary: "I know mom has not written it, but the codes are correct, so I believe you, Mary. But I need confirmation from mom that everything is fine. So, the following mail is for mom; please take a printout of it and give it to my mom. Let her sign the mail and give it to an agent in the supermarket from where she got my e-mail id last time. If it's found to be her original signature, then I'll accept that everything is fine, and I'll believe you, Mary.

"And Mary, I'm impressed that you are interested in following my path, and that you also feel isolated and cornered in the United States. After I get my mom's mail and once it's verified, I'll write to you in detail."

Mary printed Franklin's mail and put it in an envelope to give to Martha. She locked her office and left the building. Mary parked her car next door to Martha's villa. After checking her old lady disguise was in place, Mary got out of the car. She locked the car, crossed over to the next lane and took a taxi.

The old woman wearing a long coat reached Martha's home and rang the door bell. Martha looked through the spy hole, but didn't open the door. She asked the guest through the side window, who she was...

7 COOKING UP THE PLOT

Franklin has been engaged in his spacecraft research work at the secret lab, which is located at the date processing plant in North-eastern Iran. One day, police CID, Saleh Hameed and his assistant came to visit Franklin.

Franklin had earlier informed Saleh about the turning point in contacting his mother who is in the United States. He also revealed the surprising lead to get in touch with cloning scientist, Mary.

So Saleh came to discuss the matter further. His assistant, Nissam, is a religious scholar and social media expert. His main job was to influence Muslims in the U.S. and European countries and turn them against the governments and people of other religious faith in those countries.

Franklin said to them, "There are two important things in this matter. The first one is that Mary has great interest in my mission and so we can persuade her to follow our path. She is a cloning scientist. She is studying the possibility of conducting cloning on human and other species in the outer space.

"If cloning can be conducted inside a spacecraft travelling at the speed of light, then it's possible to transfer all the species on our Earth to a distant solar system where there is an Earth-like inhabitable planet."

Nissam wondered, "That sounds amazing. One more Earth in this universe! We can make it a promising land for Muslims, and thus make Allah very pleased But how'll you trust this Mary? What surety is that she is a doctor conducting research on the said topic?"

Franklin affirmed, "We can fully believe Mary. I have verified the things she told to my mother. My mom also went to her office in New York University to see everything physically. Mom had seen Mary's DNA collections of different animals, birds and human beings. Mary has become a good friend of mom. Mary told mom that she felt isolated in America and that she wanted to follow my footsteps. Mary might be more impressed about my invention of light speed travel.

"But we have to be very cautious with the Americans," Nissam uttered while glancing at a designer's computer screen where spacecraft models were displayed.

"Moreover, Mary comes to meet my mom disguised like an old lady, which means she also fears the American police. I strongly believe that we can trust her fully," Franklin urged.

Saleh kept mum and was observing everything in the lab. He suddenly asked, "Ok, agreed, and what is the second thing, Professor?"

"Second thing?! Oh, Yes, the second important matter I mentioned is the requirement for finding a spacecraft designer who can transform my scientific ideas into an illustrated design format like that," Franklin said pointing to the designer's computer system. "We don't have experts here to do that."

"Why don't you tell Mary to find a suitable spacecraft designer from America itself?" Saleh asked.

Nissam interfered, "Sir, won't it be better to wait for some more time to ask for such favours? First let her become a close friend of Dr. Franklin."

Seeing their confusion, Franklin assured them, "It won't be difficult to get going with Mary. She already has a liking for my attitude with the U.S. people. Now we need to educate her more with our religious teachings to make her closely linked to our faith - for that I need your support."

There was a broad smile on Nissam's face.

Saleh knew that Nissam is very happy to do such a job. "Nissam, you may e-mail Prof. Franklin some of the religious materials and also give the DVDs of preaching by our scholars. Franklin can use them for convincing Mary about the supremacy of our religion."

Nissam responded with enthusiasm.

Franklin also showed his satisfaction. "Sure, using those religious talks, I can now explain to her why I left the United States of America. She already has strong feelings against the colour discrimination, and injustice meted out to the second degree citizens.

"Once she knows my situation clearly, I'm sure she can be convinced to find out a spacecraft designer from the U.S., which is critical for the success of our space project."

"Great to know. Carry on Professor with your fantastic work. khoda hafez," Saleh said while shaking hands with Franklin.

Franklin smiled, "khoda hafez."

When Saleh and Nissam have gone, the executive secretary of Space Agency Chief, Riaz Mohammad, and two other officials came to meet Franklin and his team.

Soon everybody assembled at the conference hall.

Franklin addressed the gathering and spoke about the progress in his spacecraft project.

"We're going very fast as per everybody's expectations. The team here is an excellent one consisting of very hardworking and talented professionals. We have successfully cracked a few deadlocks in the hypothesis of my diagram and developed some additional procedures for the theory to attain the speed of light."

Everybody had tea and snacks while the meeting was on.

Franklin stated, "We're going on full swing with the theory papers and I hope it'll be completed within a few weeks, Inshallah. The next step is to make a prototype of the spacecraft, and for that we need a highly capable design engineer…"

Riaz Mohammad then replied to Franklin's comment, "We're working on war footing to find out somebody for making the sophisticated spacecraft design. We have some Russian engineers here who're doing servicing and modifications on Sukhoi Su-24 fighter jets we bought from Russia. We have discussed with them some spacecraft design matters without disclosing our actual light-speed project. We are also on the lookout for some people who are working in the civil aviation industry in Russia.

Franklin listened to him curiously as Riaz continued, "And for piloting the spacecraft, we have shortlisted some of our smart fighter pilots and their security verification processes are getting completed. We hope that some solutions will arise soon, Inshallah. So, let your research continue with full steam…"

After the conclusion of the meeting, Franklin personally told Riaz, "Happy to inform you that I'm also trying to find out a spacecraft designer from the U.S. If it succeeds, then no tensions, we'll reach our goal faster, Inshallah. I have informed about it to the assistant of Police Chief. They will inform you about it. So see you- Shukran."

Riaz bid good bye, "Shukran, Ma'assalama."

●●●●   ●●●●   ●●●●

Mary has made tremendous improvement in her acquaintance with Franklin. Both of them have had specific agenda in the present case that each one successfully hid from the other. But they also have some common points of interest that nurtured their good relationship. They exchanged e-mails daily.

Mary was happy to receive the mails from Franklin. Getting befriended with Franklin is the only way to push the Mission further.

Franklin's mails were lengthy ones. They depicted his thoughts as a scientist and a common Muslim religious thinker. He is very hopeful of fulfilling his scientific theory into developing a spacecraft that can travel with the speed of light.

Franklin at the same time also expressed his wrath against the Americans who treat Muslims as second class citizens and terrorists.

Mary wondered how a brilliant scientist like Franklin can be so religiously sensitive. It seems that he has been misguided in religious and social matters concerning the Western countries and the Muslims settled there. He might have got Nobel Prize and other accolades if the invention was made public in the U.S. He could also have availed all the technical assistance from NASA for completing his light-speed theory. Alas! Now he's sweating with the primitive facilities available in Iran.

Mary thought that genius personalities differ greatly from common people. They used to have special mannerisms and thought processes which sometimes are mistaken for eccentricity.

Great minds sometimes are isolated in a society, and their married life also gets affected due to this Albert Einstein was an example for that. this. His personal life was full of problems associated with marriage and and other social issues.

Einstein had taken an important role in the making of America's first nuclear bomb, but later he was worried sick to hear about the Japan bombing in the 2nd World War. When the U.S. and its allied Nations had almost dismissed the idea of making a bomb using Einstein's mass and energy formula, $E = MC^2$, Einstein had personally written to US President Roosevelt about the possibilities... Then the Briggs Committee was formed and subsequently the nuclear bomb was developed.

It's said that Einstein was very much disturbed to see that his invention was used for making weapons of mass destruction. What Einstein thought was that the weapon will act as a deterrent for Hitler and his hardcore Nazi henchmen. He never assumed America will do such a massive and horrible killing using the atomic bomb. Einstein realized his blunder late and was haunted by the guilty consciousness in his last years.

Mary just compared Einstein's situation with that of Franklin. Franklin, the great scientist, couldn't realize the real aim of the religious chauvinists behind him. He simply blames America without concrete reasons. Somebody has doctored his mind-somebody with vested interests.

Of course, Franklin is a gentleman and doesn't want to hurt people. But he never thinks about a situation when Iran gets a spacecraft that can travel with the speed of light. There is no guarantee that they won't use it to destroy Israel and, America and its allies. It can create havoc in the whole world. From space they can target any country with lightning speed and nobody will be able to target them because they will be in the light speed travel mode and mostly invisible. It's a pity that the genius mind in Franklin doesn't realize such simple things. If Iran makes such a spacecraft and decides to attack its enemies, the destruction will be much higher than that of the 2nd World War nuclear bombings of Japan.

Mary had vowed to avoid such a horrible situation by all means. She decided to convince Franklin about the issue and discuss the matter in detail at a later stage.

Mary was thinking about all these topics while going to her office one day. After reaching her cabin, when she opened the e-mail system, she saw a mail from Franklin.

She quickly read the mail.

"Hello Mary, how are you? I'm writing this mail to inform you how sorrowed I'm to see the cruelties done by the Americans and their allies to Muslims around the world.

They told there were weapons of mass destruction in Iraq and attacked the country, but could not show a single such weapon there. They simply destroyed Iraq and people had become refugees. Same way, they only created the revolution in Syria...

If you know who the actual people behind ISIS, then you'll realize the cruel face of America. If ISIS is was a Muslim movement, they would have destroyed Israel first! I have attached some documents which were hacked from CIA by Iran intelligence. Read them and you'll realize the American devil

People from Syria and Iraq who lost everything are seeking asylum in the European countries. But those nations simply shoot at those refugees travelling by the Mediterranean Sea. Muslims around the world are undergoing such cruelties and living in inhuman conditions.

These issues are never discussed in the United Nations – even many people are not aware of this grave situation. The international media never bothered to talk about this because they are bribed and just favours the Westerners. They are just 'presstitutes' who misleadingly tailors news to suit the partisan agenda of Europe and America. .

Again, there occurs lot many riots and racial killings in America and European Union, which do not get any attention and nobody cares... However, whenever a Muslim is involved in some killings, they give it international attention and say all Muslims are terrorists. Simply Ridiculous.

Do you know why they hate Muslims? –

It's not just hate, actually they fear Muslims because Islam is the religion of peace and Muslims are the blessed ones. We live strictly according to Allah's scriptures, and our salvation is guaranteed. The westerners are jealous about us, and look forward to our destruction. But God is with us, and He protects us. The Americans and their friends lead a life of chaos- no religious discipline, and no moral or social values… they just want to enjoy life like animals. So, they don't have peace. They fear that one day lot of people will convert to Islam seeking peace of mind, and so the rest of them will be doomed. That's why they hate us and target us.

But can anybody act against the will of Allah?! At the time of Earth's destruction, Muslims only will get the blessings of Allah. So Mary, think again, and again. Start reading the holy Quran.

Mary, I'm happy to take you to our spacecraft mission. Meanwhile, read the attached files which contain preaching of learned men about Allah's doctrines and rules. If you have any doubts about the scriptures, promptly e-mail me and we'll help you.

Once you're in our fold, you can carry on with your cloning research. We'll collect the DNA samples of all the flora and fauna and implant them into another liveable planet, and thus create Allah's world there.

Wow, think Mary, it all looks fantastic.

Good Bye,

Franklin

P.S.: Hi Mary, I was about to send the mail and there came a technical meeting of our spacecraft project team. Iran Space Agency Chief's staff came to discuss some points with us. The main discussion was about getting a smart spacecraft designer for the project. Do you know anybody in the US who's associated with aircraft or spacecraft prototype designing? The person should be likeminded as you and me. Never disclose about our project unless you're sure about the person. Otherwise things may backfire. Beware, there are spies all around.

F.

Mary was just wondering how to include Sam in her dialogues with Franklin, and lo, here comes the answer. What a coincidence. This is why Mary thinks that there is a subtle divine intervention in everything that's happening in their Mission Milky Way.

Mary wrote a reply e-mil to Franklin then and there.

Hi Prof. Franklin,

Good day.

Thank you for that long mail and explaining everything where the U.S. and Europe put a stigma upon the global Muslim population, especially in the Middle East. I agree with you that the Westerners are hypocrites. They have double justice- one for their citizens and another one for Asian expatriates. That's why I've decided to follow you.

Moreover, your invention of crossing the light speed barrier will help me to optimise my space cloning research.

From your mails, one thing I could analyse that your BP is getting high when you talk about the injustice meted out to the Muslims by Americans and the Europeans. It's good to leave the Americans and concentrate on your dream project. You should take care of your health too.

Do you know that scientists and thinkers are more prone to getting affected by diabetes, high blood pressure, and heart ailments? They do lot of brain storming activities and work on the computers...but their body mechanism considers only the actual physical activities they do when deciding upon the quantity of food requirements for the body. If you are not going to the gym regularly, the body metabolism just recognises that you do some finger exercises only while typing on your keyboard- no other vigorous physical activities.

Being a human being you take normal food, but the mechanism of digestion and absorption of food in the human body thinks that you are a very inactive or a sick person due to less bodily activities and burning of calories. The body then mess up with the abundance of food intake. This paradox in the biological process leads to high or low blood glucose levels, cholesterol issues, obesity, and heart diseases.

Read it fully, this is going to be my next thesis paper to cure diabetes and cancer etc.

The human metabolism still has the basic tendency to store lot of fat in our body for survival in case of starvation or famine. But the issue is that in modern times, we take plenty of food items rich in calories, which the body tends to store in fat cells as excess caloric energy for future use – though no starvation or famine time comes these days. Thus the bio mechanism in our body wrongly interprets that starvation will come in the future and stores up unwanted fat. This leads to obesity and many other health issues.

The genes should understand that a scientist or a computer software engineer is producing more quality work output than a carpenter or a body builder. And the digestive system should consider a person's mental activities also as work/exercise and so digest more or less the same amount of food considered necessary for physically active people...

A kind of Darwin's evolution is required for our genes to understand that rather than manual work, modern humans are required to do more brain work. When the genes started realising it, many life style related diseases will disappear.

Currently I'm doing some experiments to alter the genetic sequences in the DNA of liver and pancreas cells in rats so as to change the way their genes interpret insulin production to control blood glucose levels, and store body fat for future use.

The rats will be kept in an environment where there is food abundance, which is accessible without much labour. They will also undergo stress, strain and mental activities with the help of video games and other radio magnetic signals. This is to mimic the situation of modern humans. If I can succeed in rewriting the genetic codes, then those altered cells can be cloned to produce new organs like liver, pancreas etc.

This way we can prevent diabetes and all those unwanted heart diseases due to inherent fault in our body metabolism which fails to interpret socioeconomic and environmental changes.

All these experiments and the cloning procedures can be conducted on a superfast pace while travelling at light speed. And it will pave way for some breakthroughs in human cloning. That means, Prof. Franklin, your invention will also enhance my research and do wonders for the mankind, in addition to the big leap you have provided for humans to conquer the space-time.

And all our achievements will be for the benefit of humans and other species on Earth.

Thank you for your time.

As you have called for, I'll start searching for a spacecraft designer from today itself. I take it seriously and will do my best to find out somebody here in the U.S.

Take care.

Bye,
Mary Koshy.

♣ ♣ ♣

8 ENCOUNTER AND DUETTING

Mary and Sam were discussing the progress of the mission sitting in the entrance room of Mary's flat on the 10th floor. Franklin's latest mail was the subject matter of discussion. Sam wants that the Mission should go fast forward now. There are many obstacles to cross, and whenever the situation is ok, it's good to take advantage of it and move ahead.

Mary has prepared breakfast and lunch for Sam. After lunch at 1.30pm, they sat in the living room to visualize further action plan for Mission Milky Way. The operation scene would soon be shifted to the Republic of Iran…

Mary said that she has taken Franklin into confidence and can now trust him without any fear. She has a soft corner for Franklin, may be because of his innocence and open-mindedness as an individual, his brilliance as a scientist and his stupidity as a religious person in blindly following the fanatics.

Mary also assured Sam that she will never become a follower of Franklin's fanatic believes. But she sees great hope in improving her cloning research in space and is confident of getting a breakthrough if they could conduct the experiments at "travelling at the speed of light" conditions.

Again, Mary supported Sam's view that if things go wrong in Iran, they'll have to shoot Franklin and his research team and escape to Saudi Arabia (via Kuwait), possibly with the research papers and prototype of Franklin's spacecraft.

Sam said while doing something on his mobile, "You have to be very careful in dealing with Franklin. One wrong step can spoil the whole results achieved so far. In your next mail, write to Franklin saying that you fully agree with his religious views and are very much interested in Islamic faith."

"Of course Sam, it'll be done. And tell me, how should I introduce you to Franklin?"

"Yes that's to be done in a perfect way without giving any room for doubts! We should not disclose our intimacy…"

Suddenly Mary interrupted Sam before he can conclude! She saw the shadow of a man in the balcony.

Mary got up and pointed towards the balcony. Sam sprang into action and ran towards the door. Before they could intervene, the spy just took back the digital camera which was recording Sam and Mary's conversations, and jumped out of the balcony.

"Sam, the guy recorded our talks and the action plan, we have to catch him at any cost, otherwise all information will reach the enemy," Mary shouted.

Sam took his revolver and looked down from the balcony and saw the spy going down through sunshades and concrete projections. Sam told Mary to reach the ground floor and come to the backside of the building with her car.

Sam fired at the spy and then followed him climbing down through the pipelines and sunshade slabs. They are on the 10th floor, and it's not easy to go all the way down from that height. Sam followed the spy closely. He shot at him, and the spy returned the fire. This firing made their journey down very difficult and slow. Sam thought his karate practice has come handy to climb down a building in this dangerous way. One slip can be fatal. It looks like the spy is quite experienced and going down smartly. Sam followed him at close heels.

By that time, Mary locked the flat and ran towards the lift. She also called their CIA contact point by clicking the single key emergency access . She entered the lift and pressed the ground floor. If the spy gets away, he'll pass the vital information to Iran, and that'll be the end of Milky Way Mission! Franklin will understand that I'm part of the American mission to hijack their spacecraft project, Mary thought.

Before reaching the ground floor Mary got a call from the CIA officer. She said, "We need to intercept a spy… it's so important and urgent. Arrange an aerial surveillance helicopter at the earliest, and also send a police team to the highway near my apartment"

Mary knew each second is vital in such a situation. If the spy escapes with the evidence of their involvement with CIA, then there will be little hope to pursue the mission. No more dialogue will be possible with Franklin and he won't be available for any future contacts.

As soon as she reached the ground floor, Mary took her car and drove it to the other side of the building where Sam and the spy are getting down. From a distance, she saw the spy mounting the boundary wall of the apartment building and running towards his car. Sam is close behind.

The spy managed to get to his car and drove ahead. Mary stopped her car for Sam to enter and take over the driving then they chased the spy closely without giving him any time to send messages to his agents in Iran. They also exchanged fire. The spy's Land Cruiser has the speed advantage and so Sam couldn't puncture his tires. But they kept the spy fully engaged moving nose-to-nose with the pursuing vehicle.

Mary contacted the CIA officer and gave him their location specifications and the spy's Land cruiser number while Sam was busy on the dog chase.

The CIA officer said, "Helicopter service will arrive within 5 minutes. But you'll have to prevent the spy from sending messages to his source in Iran. For that, continue the dog chase very closely with rifle firing so the guy won't get a chance to message them."

Sam said, "We can't overtake him with this posh car of yours. Anyway I'll cross its maximum speed now and going to puncture his tires...because of its high speed his vehicle may crash. So we won't be able to catch him live."

By that time, a helicopter came hovering over the highway near to the car chase location. It spotted the spy's car and started firing at it. The spy was forced to reduce the speed with the unexpected aerial attack. He may want to change his route to escape from the aerial attack. And Sam took advantage of the situation and shot at the Land Cruiser's tire and punctured it.

The Iran spy's car jumped in the air and overturned two three times then crashed on the roadside barrier. It caught fire instantly and exploded. Sam stopped their car at a safe distance and watched. The Land Cruiser became a fireball and there is no point in waiting there. The spy is dead for sure.

"So, did he mange to send message to Iran telling about us?" Mary asked.

"No, there is possibly no chance for that. We didn't give him enough time to send the recorded video message of our conversation. And his mobile phone and digital camera might have been burnt by now, and so we'll have to wait for the CIA squad to check the SIM cards to confirm whether any messages have been sent within half an hour," Sam sighed. .

Sam rang up the CIA officer and told him to do the necessary things to check the SIM cards of the spy's mobile and other electronic gadgets.

"Let's go back to my flat now. If any messages have been passed to Iran, we have no scope of continuing the mission. Everything was moving ahead quite comfortably and even luck was favouring us till now. Who might have thought somebody will climb up to the 10th floor and spy on us?" Mary exclaimed.

They went to Mary's apartment.

"Does Iran have the network to field such capable spies on the soil of United States of America?" Mary murmured while entering the apartment.

"The refugees who come to Europe and US are routinely abused by the international terrorist organizations. They use the refugees for spying, terror attacks etc. Some people within the country are also supporting terrorism and religious fanaticism. So there is a wide network of active and sleep agents here," Sam explained and sat down on the edge of one of the tall gift chairs in the reception room.

"People fleeing crises- the asylum seekers and refugees- are a concern for the local population in Australia and Europe also. They think this is an unwanted and awkward situation forced on them without any wrongdoing on their part. They see the refugees as the main source of terrorist attacks. See this social media post by one Mr. David Butler which gives another dimension to the refugee crisis, Sam has shown the post to Mary on his mobile phone.

Mary read the Facebook post.

"They're not happy in Gaza ..
They're not happy in Egypt ..
They're not happy in Libya ..
They're not happy in Morocco ..
They're not happy in Iran ..
They're not happy in Iraq ..
They're not happy in Yemen ...
They're not happy in Afghanistan ...
They're not happy in Pakistan ..
They're not happy in Syria ..
They're not happy in Lebanon ...

SO... WHERE ARE THEY HAPPY?

They're happy in Australia ..
They're happy in Canada ..
They're happy in England ..
They're happy in France ..
They're happy in Italy ..
They're happy in Germany ..
They're happy in Sweden ..
They're happy in the USA ..
They're happy in Norway ..
They're happy in Holland ..
They're happy in Denmark ..

Basically, they're happy in every country that is not Muslim and unhappy in every country that is!

AND WHO DO THEY BLAME?

Not Islam.
Not their leadership.
Not themselves

THEY BLAME THE COUNTRIES THEY ARE HAPPY IN!

AND THEN- They want to change those countries to be like, THE COUNTRY THEY CAME FROM WHERE THEY WERE UNHAPPY!

Excuse me, but I can't help wondering...
How frigging dumb can you get?
Everyone seems to be wondering why Muslim Terrorists are so quick to commit suicide.

Let's have a look at the evidence:
- No Christmas
- No television
- No nude women
- No football
- No pork chops
- No hot dogs
- No burgers
- No beer
- No bacon
- Rags for clothes
- Towels for hats
- Constant wailing from some bloke in a tower
- More than one wife
- More than one mother-in-law
- You can't shave
- Your wife can't shave
- You can't wash off the smell of donkeys
- You cook over burning camel shit
- Your wife is picked by someone else for you
- and your wife smells worse than your donkey
- Then they tell them that "when they die, it all gets better"???

Well No Shit Sherlock!....
It's not like it could get much worse!"
[Facebook post dated August 5, 2014]

Sam said, "It may be little bit sarcastic, but shows how people in the West look at the refugee issues...Their concern is evident from the reactions to the post on Facebook. It has around 4.3 K Likes and 329,303 Shares!"

Mary said, "Yes, it's a strong post depicting the real situation- it really hits the refugee mentality where it really hurts. Please send me a copy of the post."

Mary continued, "In espionage cases, if things continue to move quite comfortably for some time, then it can be assumed that there may be an invisible noose slowly tightening on the secret agents. And this saying has come true for us. Anyway, if we're lucky this time, we won't give another chance to their spies. Now let's write a mail to the CIA Director explaining everything regarding the spy attack."

Sam agreed. "Yeah sure…That's ok. After reaching your flat, write a mail to Franklin also, and wait for his response. If the spy had succeeded in sending a message to Iran about our mission, then there will be some difference in Franklin's behaviour, even though they won't show it openly."

Soon they sent a detailed message to the CIA Director.

Then Mary wrote a mail to Franklin:

Dear Professor,

I fully agree with your religious views. I have read all the documents and sermons you sent. It has drastically changed my views on god and the religion. I'm grateful to you for all this. I'm interested to know further. I would like to come to your place. I want to listen directly from you on those religious matters. Also, I need to further develop my research on cloning…

Then listen, there is good news. As you have asked for a spacecraft designer, I enquired about it and stumbled upon somebody. He's a distant relative of my father, one Mr. Sam Anandhan. He's a test pilot in the civil aviation department in New York. He's also an aircraft and rocket design engineer. He had also taken part in NASA's space missions- a very suitable person for our mission. Today I met Sam and had discussion about my cloning project to be conducted in space. Sam can be trusted because he's a distant relative and he's crazy about space travel, space walking and all those stuff. Being an Indian, he's also like me, doesn't have any sentimental feeling towards USA. I didn't tell him about you and your spacecraft project, but I'm sure he'll join us.

Now what's next step? Waiting for your response.

Regards,
Mary.

After sending the mails, Mary sighed in relief. "Sam, now it's a long wait for the crucial replies from both the CIA office and Franklin. It's just boring to wait…I can't sit here idly, and handle the tension. Can we visit my papa and mom now? I can introduce you to my parents too. Mom has already told me to bring you. They are eager to see you. Tomorrow is Sunday. They'll be free."

"Ok, dear, let's go. Everything is part of the mission- and now we're on duty- though this is a marriage mission."

"hmmm…" she flirted and looked at Sam through the corners of her eyes.

Sam smiled while admiring her attractive looks.

Mary readied things for one day stay at her papa's home…

Sam continued, "Even if the killed Iran spy managed to send some short message to Iran, he might not have passed the video recordings of our talks to his Iran source. There was no time for connecting the cables of the digital camera to his laptop or smart phone. Now Franklin will be reading the mail you sent today. Even if Iran security people got a quick SMS from the spy, they will think it's a false alarm, because of the mail you sent today hinting your interest in Islam."

"Hmm... let's hope so.

Anyway, thank you for your interest to meet my parents. You're so caring, Sam. It's just one hour drive to my parents' villa. We'll be going through a farmland in the countryside. It'll be such a calm and quiet journey, enjoying the nature. I simply love those journeys whenever I go to visit my parents. Ok, let's move…"

They started the journey at around 6pm… Mary drove the car. There was very less traffic and the natural sceneries were very beautiful… The atmosphere looked romantic too… the sweet-smiling villages appeared so refreshing.

They saw that the birds and grazing animals on the pastures were all in a happy and lively mood… Pretty villages passed by…

Behind the village houses, there were rolling farmlands, pastures and meadows… the cooing and chirping of birds, melancholic songs of skylarks, the buzzing of bees, the trilling sounds of crickets, katydids, cicadas, grasshoppers etc. from the shrubby fields- all have created a cool, natural rhythm in their minds.

Mary tuned the car stereo to Radio Mirchi, the Malayali radio channel. The program being aired at that time was Hindi romantic duets.

Sharman Joshi and Zarine Khan were singing the famous lines, 'Tumhe Apna Banane Ka' love song from the movie: 'Hate Story 3':

"Tumhe Apna Banane Ka Junoon, Sar Pe Hai, Kab Se Hai
(I have a strong passion/desire to make You mine, since a long time)

Sam asked Mary, "Do you know Hindi?"
"Hmm...," she replied.

"Just think about the meaning of those lyrics... do you understand it?"
"Hmmm..."

"Isn't it about us?!" Sam asked cunningly.
Mary said automatically, "Hmmm..."

Sam laughed, "Is it really? Are we the lovers?"

"Hmmm... errr, NO! You cheat, I was just listening to the tune and you made advantage of it! The duet was sung by lovers in the movie, not by us, or about us," Mary said giggling.

There was more giggling, and Mary once more sang the duet lines sweetly: "Tumhe apna banane ka junoon, Sar pehai, kab se hai..."

So, they pursued the ride to parental home listening to songs and then imagining themselves as the star pair in those love songs.

Love is such a fantastic feeling... it creates romantic emotions in the mind irrespective of colour or creed.

It's such an incredible energizer which activates each and every cell in our body.

The rhythm of love beats nonstop and it's such an awesome feeling to have those sweet feeling lurking in your heart along with the heartbeats...

It's love in the air, it's love in the breeze, it's love in the dreams, it's love in every sound you hear… it's love everywhere…. No one wants to come out of the mesmeric cocoon love weaves around you.

Soon they reached the destination.

The time passed so quickly, Mary thought. And Sam too thought like that…

They haven't actually talked anything… They want to tell many things, but couldn't, because when love is overflowing, words stop.

Souls need no words for communicating, and minds too.

Your feelings, sensations, everything becomes one common thing and you just float in that love bliss… such a magnificent thing love is!

Mary's parents were at home. For a surprise, Mary actually didn't inform them that she is coming there with Sam. It's a two-bedroom apartment and very spacious for a single family. Her parents were very happy to see them and welcomed the guest, Sam, with a smiling face.

"I was on night duty yesterday. So, have two days holidays- today, and tomorrow Sunday. And Papa has two days weekend-off these days, Mary's mom, Preetha said.

"Why to work so hard. We have only one naughty child, and here she is. Always busy with research… and no time for even marriage! By the way, hello Sam, where's your native place?" Mary's papa, Koshy Mathan asked.

Koshy is in his late 50's- a very fun loving and sincere husband. Everybody calls him ichayan, means elder brother in the vocabulary of Kottayam (Kottayam is also known as the language-capital of Kerala) Christians. And contrary to typical American Malayali husbands, he never cooks!

"I had been brought up in a Christian orphanage at Kakkanad, in Ernakulam dist of Kerala. Before joining U.S. defence service, I was a pilot in the Indian Air Force," Sam said.

"Shall we take dinner outside today? This is the first day our guest came, and do you want to bore them with your cooking experiments, Martha?" Koshy asked.

Preetha scolded him, "Don't make fun, ichaya. Today they'll take my homely food only. And I'm sure that Sam will give me full marks today for my cookery expertise. (to Mary), come molu, let's go to the kitchen now."

Koshy ichayan took Sam to the balcony sit-out. It was around 8pm then. Ichayan has a habit of taking two tots before dinner, and Preetha has no objections as it's within control. He persuaded Sam also to take a tot of Whisky.

Koshy ichayan took two tots extra that day because he enjoyed the company of Sam, his future son-in-law. After drinks, ichayan has a habit of talking little bit extra. He was in good mood that day.

Koshy is very proud to be a Kottayam Nasrani (local term for a Christian). Kottayam district is always in the forefront in literacy and education in Kerala.

Ichayan said to Sam, "We're from Kottayam and belong to a respected Christian family there. We have a large house there and 5 acres of property with rubber plantation. Now everything is looked after by a distant relative. We used to go home once in a while. My parents are already in the abode of heaven and I have no other siblings.

"So going to native place, Kerala is not a priority anymore. There are not many friends in Kerala other than two close friends as we have been in the U.S. for the last 20 years … And the local Malayalis there have not much liking for the NRIs."

"Why is it so," Sam asked.

"The local Malayali with typical cynicism and false pride, sees us American Malayalis as very rich and snob people. Actually they are jealous of us. So I don't care much about it. The same people who make critical comments on us secretly come and visit me when I go to Kerala. They're very fond of the foreign liquor I give them during casual talks… After consuming two or three large, they start talking about their poor financial situations, and bad fate etc., and simply take 100 or 200 bucks from me. They say it's taken on loan, and everybody knows it'll never be returned. And it's repeated every time I go to Kerala."

Sam laughed while sipping the whisky. "You're a very close observer, uncle," Sam said.

From the balcony they can see the streets and some distant hilly area decorated with pink and yellow lights, which looked like a star studded sky.

Koshy itchayan carried on,

"Malayalis are a special class, they are educated, and neat and clean. They have excellent managerial capabilities. But in their hometown in Kerala, they just sit idle, thinking about how to trap one another.

"Kakkanad is your hometown isn't it?"

"Yes, but I don't have a wider friends circle there."

"No, I was not asking that. I want to know the progress of the Kochi Smart City project there. It was inaugurated several years back as a joint venture with Dubai based TECOM Company specifically for IT/ITES/allied services, and still things have not much progressed above the discussion level, as far as I know. The project was expected to create over 90,000 direct jobs and both the LDF and UDF governments, who come to power alternatively, simply delayed or postponed various legs of the project."

"You said it. The govt is active in politics, but not that smart in implementing job oriented schemes," Sam agreed.

"Do you know that these Malayalis when outside Kerala act entirely different? They're very hardworking, helpful and efficient managers and have a reputed name the world over. They'll do any work outside Kerala, like salesmen in grocery shop, operators in petrol pump, gardener, and even daily wages labourer etc. But in Kerala their arrogance and false pride don't allow them to do such works, and everyone looks for government or white collar jobs or simply sits idle doing nothing."

Ichayan is in great mood today as he has somebody to listen to him with interest.

He talked further...

"And look at the government employees in Kerala. They show all their power, arrogance, and misuse the rules to harass the common people and delay their applications. If somebody submits a proposal to initiate a start-up company or industry, they'll deny permission or delay it endlessly if huge bribes are not paid."

While Koshy ichayan in full swing kept on talking about his native place and the situations there, Mary came and chided,

"Oh, papa, don't punish Sam like this! He won't come again to this place if you bore him so much."

"Don't worry, Mary. He's not boring, but quite interesting. He is telling very important points... and I fully agree with him," Sam supported ichayan.

Soon the dinner was served and everybody spent time together happily. After dinner they talked about many things, and even played cards till late night.

Next day Koshy ichayan and the whole family went to church, prayed peacefully and took part in the holy Qurbana.

After returning home, Mary said, "I need to take some blood samples of papa and mom. This is to add to my DNA sample collection."

"What is it for?" asked Koshy.

"As you know I'm collecting DNA samples of all species of creatures and people on Earth. That's a huge collection for experiments on cloning, and also for preservation," Mary explained.

Mary's eyes became wet as she went along,

"This is somewhat similar to the story of Noah's ark in the Bible. As Noah gathered a remnant of all the world's animals to be kept alive in the ark and saved from the deluge, I too do this collection with the will of God almighty. They will be preserved and will be used to recreate another Earth in case of something wrong happens to our mother Earth.

"If climate change or any other untoward incident destroys life on Earth, somebody can possibly take my collection away to a distant solar system and recreate a copy of our beloved mother Earth there.

"I hope God will guide me or somebody else to carry out this marvellous task, as he did with Noah. It's written in the scriptures that God gave Noah instructions for building the ark, and seven days before the deluge, told him to enter the ark with his household and the animals.

"So, I do this task with perseverance and dedication as per an intuition that life will continue forever in the Universe with the mercy of God. If human's wrong doings make Earth uninhabitable, let's hope that God will provide another option."

Mary took the blood samples as Papa, Mom and Sam looked on eagerly.

Before going, Sam told Papa and Mom, "We need your blessings. What Mary said about coming of the Noah's 2nd Ark may look like a hallucinatory verbiage in broad daylight. But when you meditate and concentrate your soul on the divine soul, then eternal things in the Universe will be revealed. We need not to see it or prove scientifically to believe it.

"What Mary started through the DNA collection could be a harbinger of future happenings yet to evolve. When the global warming induced climate change, a looming nuclear war and other issues threaten life on Earth, we have very limited time to do the preventive measures. What Mary intends to do here has great meaning. It could be a divine mission, and I'm happy to take the burden of it by being associated with Mary. We need the prayers and support of every living being on Earth to pursue this great mission. And we're sure that the Omnipotent, God almighty will preserve the life on Earth. Let's hope for the best."

Preetha then asked, "There was the command and signature of God for Noah's mission, but what about you?!"

Mary told her that they too need a heavenly interference to carry out their mission. It's not possible for them do it singlehandedly; the mission is that much complicated and complex. They too expect God's command at the proper time. Now they just follow their intuition, which also might be guided by the omniscient, almighty.

Koshy Ichayan gave his blessings to Mary and Sam, "Our prayers and well wishes will always be with you. Even though we didn't fully understand your mission, we hope that it'll be something great and helpful for the humanity. May God bless you in all your endeavours."

Sam and Mary left after lunch.

♣ ♣ ♣

9 ADVANCING THE PLOT

Once the spy incident was over, Mary was eagerly waiting for Franklin's mail. After returning from her parents' home, Mary checked the mails as soon as she reached her apartment.

There was no mail from Franklin in her Inbox. However, she got a mail from the CIA office next day morning in her official mailbox. It said the Iran spy's mobile phone was fully burnt and so no data could be segregated. The mail also cautioned them to be more vigilant next time and further advised to analyse all future correspondence with Franklin to ascertain whether he came to know about the American mission.

Mary and Sam were restless. Now their mission is in jeopardy. It'll be on hold till they get some news from Franklin. Two days went by but there was no mail from Franklin.

Mary visited Franklin's mom, Martha and spent few hours there to check if she knew something regarding the incident involving the Iran spy. It was clear that Martha didn't get any communication from Franklin. If Franklin has clues about Mary and Sam, and their CIA link, then he would have cautioned his mother through the agents. That means hope is still there. However, there is no guarantee that Franklin will definitely inform his mother about the spy incident.

Day 4 also gone without any info from Franklin...

Mary and Sam had discussed their future course of action in case CIA decides to abort the mission. Sam will go back to US Air Force and Mary will regain her work with NASA. There won't be any further communication with CIA and the Mission Milky Way. Even though the mission has great many risks, both Sam and Mary know they're not happy with aborting it. In fact they are disappointed with the turn of events because it's so thrilling for them to be part of a great scientific achievement – that's, to attain light speed.

Finally light seen at the end of the tunnel. After a long wait, good news came on the seventh day - Mary got Franklin's mail on that fine day.

Hi Mary,
Sorry for the delay. I was busy with conducting scheduled interviews with pilot cosmonauts and spacecraft designers. Because of the top confidentiality of the mission, we could contact only limited number of people. And sadly, people in our list were not capable of handling the sophisticated spacecraft project.

Then I introduced Sam to the Iranian authorities. I checked his credentials. He's ok. But there was the security procedure for our secret agencies to check Sam Ananthan's connection with US government. We had to wait for the security clearance before notifying you. That's why this delay occurred…

So, you can now inform Sam about our light-speed spacecraft project. And be prepared, you'll have to move to Iran at short notice. Things have to move faster now. Also reply today itself so that I can update the ministry officials accordingly.

Have a great time.

Regards,
F.

P.S.: Thank you for explaining your research on diabetes and other diseases in your last mail. I'm happy to know that my invention to cross the light speed limit has such great application in cloning and treating serious diseases.

Mary spoke to Sam and straightaway wrote a reply to Franklin:

Hi Franklin,

Thank you for the mail. Everything is ok here. I had a detailed discussion with Sam, and he's thrilled to take part in the project. Space travel, spacecraft designing and piloting etc. are his favourite subjects. And as he's an Indian, he's just like me as far as loyalty to America is concerned. He has no objection to come to Iran for this dream project.

Because Sam is at a time both a test pilot and a spacecraft designer, he'll be like a 2 in 1 addition to your project team. So the ball is in your court now- please advice next step.

Thanks and regards,
Mary.

Mary then informed Sam to get everything done so as to leave U.S. at any moment from then on. Mary and Sam sent mails individually to CIA Director via satellite communication about the new development in the Mission.

The CIA Director sent reply within an hour…

He said, "I'm very glad that you have smartly handled the mission so far, as per plan. You need not to come and meet us personally. Now follow Franklin's directives and go to Iran. All your family's needs and your personal affairs in the U.S. will be looked after

"The mission is now under your full control and you can take any decisions independently favouring the interests of the United States of America. Sam will be Commander-in-chief of the Mission Milky Way; however at critical situations when contact is not possible between both of you, independent decisions can be taken. If something goes wrong, try to take shelter in the embassy of a nearby friendly country like Saudi Arabia or Iraq. President of the United States also conveyed his best wishes to you for the mission."

There's not much time for Sam and Mary to get prepared for the journey to Iran. Nothing is concretely planned yet, Mary thought. After going to Iran, it's not clear when it would be possible to come back. This could also tragically end up like a one-way journey! But Mary felt no fear.

Why am I feeling that some invisible force is supporting me in this mission? - Mary wondered. It's an intuition, a strong feeling, which you can't easily define, but it's driving you ahead, and always supporting you from within.

Mary then called her parents and told them that she may go to Middle East sometime sooner. It's in connection with the DNA sample collection. Her parents were not convinced first, but were relieved when Mary told them that Sam will also be accompanying her on another mission for U.S. Air Force.

Then there were hectic activities…

Many things have to be done, and Mary ran hither thither to complete each and every task. More DNA samples are to be taken from few more insects that are key players in the food chain. It's not sure whether they will get another chance to do that considering their dangerous mission to Iran.

When collecting genetic material from each animal species, the thought of Noah's ark struck Mary's mind. Now almost all specimen copies of tissue, gametes, viable cells and DNA of all known species on Earth are collected except the ones on the Middle East deserts. All those stored DNA samples have been packed safely for easy transportation.

Mary now has the DNA footprints and also the technology to recreate all those species of animals and human beings as per the will of God.

Because it is a secret mission, Mary and Sam couldn't say goodbye to anybody. That's a really touching situation. There are many close friends, and it really hurts to depart without telling a word.

Sam also readied everything for moving to the new destination. Franklin's message could come any moment.

If the thought of Noah's Ark was reverberating in Mary's mind, the love scenes of Titanic movie were echoing in Sam's mind.

When thinking about the love theme from Titanic, lot many thoughts used to rush to Sam's mind. The earnest love and the objections to it from the tyrannical upper class society, the ice-cold waters of the sea, dangerous travel through the hidden huge icebergs, etc. etc. Then the titanic ship slowly turns into a spacecraft and the hero and heroine become Mary and Sam. And their spacecraft starts moving at the speed of light through the Milky Way galaxy, and beyond.

And at times, Sam doubted that his mind was going out of his control, and getting driven by a super conscious entity or something like that. Sometimes he felt he was travelling in a time machine to past and future events! Now and again the Titanic tragedy is visible to him in real life, and he is the captain of the ship that time.

The next moment the ship will turn into the spacecraft. He could see some tragic events happening below as he flies up. Everywhere there are fire and smoke - then the things become blurred and could not identify what's happening… Anyway, Sam felt that he's getting a vague message of impending tragedy in the near future… Then no dreams or visions will be there for a few days, and again the same horrible scenes repeated.

However, Sam also had the intuition that some positive power accompanies him always – he thought it's positive because it's supportive, not destructive.

Sam also checked with a psychiatrist to know if his illusions have anything to do with mental disorder. The psychiatrist had done all tests and found absolutely no problems with Sam. He assured that the intuitions would not affect his career as a pilot as he didn't have giddiness or eye-sight problems.

The psychiatrist also advised Sam not to react against the intuitions or try to suppress them because there could be problems if they are stamped down. Just follow the visions, nothing harm in that. The doctor also quoted some very rare cases where people get the power to see future happenings. So, he wished Sam all the best.

●●●●   ●●●●   ●●●●

There was a meeting going on at the conference hall in Franklin's underground office in Iran.

Envoy of Iranian President, representative from Ministry of Intelligence, executive secretary of Minister of Communications & IT, Space Agency Chief, Chief of SAVAK (secret police force & intelligence wing), and Defence rep from General Headquarters of Armed Forces are the participants.

This is the second such meeting of very important personalities in the Iran administration. The first one was held when Franklin arrived in Iran around six months back.

The meeting was conducted in a happy mood as everything is going on as per plan and their mission has achieved another milestone.

The Chief of SAVAK said, "Thanks Franklin, great achievement. We are very much impressed that you are able to enrol two Americans— that too highly qualified and capable of successfully completing our mission. We had conducted verifications of the two Americans through our agents in the USA, and everything is ok."

"Shukraan. What's next step? The Americans will have to be brought to Iran as fast as possible to complete our spacecraft project," said Franklin.

The Envoy of Iranian President instructed SAVAK Chief, "If the security clearance is over, then follow the procedures to bring the Americans, Sam and Mary to Iran. Coordinate with the Ministry of Intelligence to make it a foolproof operation. The American intelligence should not get any leaked information- a slight doubt can jeopardize our full plan."

The representative of Ministry of Intelligence then informed the team, "One of our agents is reported to be killed in the US. He was following the cloning researcher, Mary. We didn't get any report from him, so it's advisable to keep a constant watch on both the Americans after their arrival too. We shouldn't take any chances. Bring the Americans, Sam and Mary via Qatar. Our agents should meet them in Qatar, and bring the pair safely to Iran. Let Franklin do all the correspondence with them."

"Shukraan. It'll be managed. I'll now write to Sam and Mary to start their journey as soon as possible. Our agents should go to Qatar now," said Franklin.

After the meeting was over and the VIP's left, Franklin told his team about the arrival of U.S. spacecraft designer and a cloning scientist. All were happy that the project would now speed up momentum.

Franklin wrote to Mary without wasting any time.

Hi Mary,

There's good news. Everything is ok here and both of you can start the journey anytime from now. Send me your bio data and photographs. First come to Qatar. Our agents there will meet you and take you to Iran. And remember to transfer all money in your bank account to your relatives' accounts - sometimes the US government may freeze all your money if they come to know about your decision to cooperate with us! Resign from your current company or take long leave so that nobody should notice your absence… And keep it as a top secret; don't even tell anything to your relatives.

And I would like to add that in Iran too you'll get the same salary and perks that you are getting in America.

Also, life will be better here compared to USA. You're going to get a VIP treatment throughout the project. You'll come to know about the care and concern of Iranian people and how they respect the guests irrespective of religious believes.

All the propaganda that Iran is religiously intolerable and there is no personal freedom here has been made by the United States and its Western loyalists. You'll realize it after reaching Iran.

Inshalla.

Your friend,
Franklin.

BOOK – II

SPACECRAFT TESTED AMID GLOBAL WARMING THREATS

Building Up And Water Testing The Ark

God said to Noah, "...So make yourself an ark of cypress wood; make rooms in it and coat it with pitch inside and out. This is how you are to build it: The ark is to be three hundred cubits long, fifty cubits wide and thirty cubits high. Make a roof for it, leaving below the roof an opening one cubit high all around. Put a door in the side of the ark and make lower, middle and upper decks..." (Genesis 6:9-9:17)

1 GLOBAL WARMING AND WE

Sam reached Mary's apartment on a Tuesday evening with flight tickets to Qatar. He came with bag and baggage and is ready to move.

"So, tomorrow we're moving as I messaged you. Have you finished all preparations and packing?" Sam asked her while looking at Mary's packed bags.

"Thanks Sam. Everything is ready here… However, I'm facing a problem now. I earnestly want to see my papa and mamma, but can't go to them because I fear that once I see them I may disclose everything about the mission. And if they came to know the things, they'll never allow us to go to Iran."

"True, they won't in any case allow us to pursue the dangerous mission. Why don't we talk to them via Skype call? And you'll be able to hide some emotions when talking indirectly. I'll also participate in the call so as to manage the situation well." While they were discussing the pros and cons of visiting Mary's parents, suddenly the calling bell rang. Mary and Sam sprang into action. It could be another spying attempt.

They took all precautions and Mary went to the door and looked through the peephole. She loved it! It's her parents waiting outside. She quickly opened the door and hugged them like a kitten.

"What a surprise! Why didn't you tell me you're coming, Papa?"

"See my child; we had a strong desire to stay with you for a couple of days… Your mummy can't resist the feeling. And you know what'll happen if I don't agree to her demands…LoL :-) We took leave accordingly and here we are."

Preetha asked Sam, "And Sam, how do you do? When are you moving to Qatar?"

"We're moving tomorrow. Ticket got Okayed today only… We were about to call you on Skype, and you came here personally. Glad to again meet both of you," Sam replied.

They seated in the reception room.

Preetha patted Mary's hair back into place and smiled into her eyes. "Why are you going to Qatar now? For how many days will you be there?"

"I'll be there at least for six months, Mom. DNA samples are to be taken for not only the desert species, but for some rare marine algae varieties also."

Sam tried to explain his version, "I'm going for a global expedition program of NASA, currently to the Middle East region. It's related to global warming and climate change. The scientific tour may take around six months."

After listening to them, Koshy ichayan said, "We're happy that both of you are going…and Sam, are these global warming and climate change, a real threat?"

"Ichaya, it's very much there- a real thing. Global warming is happening now, and we have already started realizing its bad effects! The average global surface temperature on Earth has increased by 1.4 degrees Fahrenheit since 1880, much of this happened in the recent decades! We used to hear words such as flash floods, cloud burst, heat wave, sunstroke etc. more often these days."

Mary was impressed to hear Sam's knowledge on climate change. She said, "Oh, Does global warming interest you too, Sam?! It's my favourite subject. It's a pity that we humans are destroying Mother Nature as we overuse the resources on Earth and pollute the atmosphere. Our nature-abusing industrialization, urbanization, and overpopulation lead to global warming and climate change. Many people don't take it seriously, and I fear one day it'll cause some major catastrophe which will have the proportion to threaten life on Earth."

Sam agreed. "You are 100 percent correct, Mary. And what do you say about overuse and misuse of Pesticides?"

Mary replied gravely, "Pesticides have a very serious environmental impact. The overuse of chemical fertilizers and pesticides has become common practice these days. It badly affects the soil and the eco system, and poses serious health issues for human and other life forms.

Mary lectured while her papa and mamma also has shown interest in the subject.

"The misuse of pesticides has resulted in serious health implications to man and his environment. The world-wide deaths and chronic diseases caused by pesticide poisoning amount to millions in every year. One of the dreaded diseases human beings face today is CANCER, and a high percentage of its occurrence can be attributed to the pesticides entering our body through food and air."

Sam said, "True. I read somewhere that most of the (over 95% or more) sprayed insecticides and herbicides reach a destination other than their target species through air and water, potentially affecting other species and the environment."

"We'll have to shift completely to the organic farming method, which is an alternative agricultural system without the use of harmful pesticides," Mary explained..

Listening to Sam and Mary, Preetha said, "I'm glad that your interests and favourite subjects match, one complementing the other. Hope you'll continue to remain this way forever."

Koshy intervened, "I'm also very much interested to know about this climate change thing. So, let's enjoy the evening with two tots! Preetha has brought home food for dinner…"

Sam thanked Preetha. "Very nice. I like aunt's preparation. Last time it was superb."

Preetha took that compliment happily. She smiled at Sam. "Thanks, dear Sam. So let me and Mary go to kitchen to arrange everything…you people relax."

Koshy ichayan winked at Sam, "Yeah, Preetha these days frequently mentions that Sam very much liked her food items – I started doubting Sam's food tasting abilities; anyway that'll save Mary from lot of trouble. Ha..haaa.."

Everybody assembled at the reception room after bath. Not yet time for dinner. Koshy ichayan already had two tots of whisky.

Sam switched on his laptop and showed few PowerPoint slides depicting the serious consequences of global warming... He also talked about each slide, explaining the causes of climate change and the remedial measures the world should take. Everybody listened with a tensed mood.

And lastly Sam said, "The international community should come forward to do preventive measures on a war footing...Not only the governments, but each and every individual also should take part in this antipollution drive...It's the responsibility of one and all..."

A worried Koshy ichayan asked, "What'll happen to the world if this global warming is not controlled and kept under limit? Will climate change affect America too?!"

Sam explained, "There are different opinions among the scientists. Some say it's not that serious, but recent studies by NASA say things are in grave situation. The climate change and its consequences may not be fully visible to us in the initial stage...but it doesn't mean that it's not there; it's very well there, and progressing steadily, not much traceable because we don't have the means to measure it in the beginning... but after reaching a certain state, the climate change will increase exponentially, and we humans won't be able to arrest its further progress then."

Mary also believed in that way. She asked Sam, "When do you think this catastrophe will occur? - Do you have an approximate time period?"

"There will be clear-cut signs within the next 50 years or so. Situation will worsen from there on... calamities like floods, drought, Earth quakes, famine, and epidemics etc. will be regular events in all countries. In the next step, human and many other species of animals and plants will be annihilated from Earth"

Preetha couldn't control her emotions…she asked, "Oh, God! You mean the apocalypse, Sam?"

Sam ascertained, "Yeah, almost something like that. The Earth may explode, and the moon will escape its gravitational pull and fly away into empty space… let's hope it won't happen! NASA is conducting a top secret research on this matter to ascertain the facts. Their report will throw light to the actual situation. America will try to save its VVIP people first in case of an emergency…"

Sam has shown a popular blog post of his close friend, regarding global warming and climate change. "See this blog article, it's very interesting" :

"Global Warming & We
The Ganges will soon be reduced to a seasonal river…
Reports say the great river Ganges in India (Ganges to India is more or less like Nile to Egypt) is going to be reduced to a seasonal river because of the glacier melting effect on the Himalayas due to global warming. Doesn't it ring a bell somewhere?

That is just one of many expected consequences that Global warming may force on our climate and eco system. The scientific studies have predicted more epidemics, coastal flooding, droughts, forest fires, disappearances of several species of plants and animals etc. - just to enumerate a few.

The Nobel winner world body of Intergovernmental Panel on Climate Change (IPCC), at its 43rd Session (Nairobi, Kenya, 11 - 13 April 2016), decided to submit a Special Report in 2018 on the impacts of global warming of 1.5 °C above pre-industrial levels and related global greenhouse gas emission pathways. It's aimed at strengthening the global response to the threat of climate change, sustainable development and efforts to eradicate poverty, according to IPCC website.

IPCC's report: "Climate Change 2007: Impacts, Adaptation and Vulnerability," published in Brussels on 6 April 2007 summarised that a growing impact was happening to nature and the flora and fauna as Earth's temperature rose degree by degree.

The world's climate scientists have also reported unequivocally that the Earth's climate system is increasingly heating up. The high rate at which the Greenland ice cap (in the arctic region) is melting away triggering Earth quakes as pieces of ice several cubic kilometres in size break off is clear evidence (this is a first time happening in the history of Earth).

The heating effects are strongly visible in the melting of snow and ice, rising global mean sea level, widespread changes in precipitation amounts, ocean salinity and wind patterns. The overheating of Earth's atmosphere is also responsible for aspects of extreme weather including droughts, heat waves and the intensity of tropical cyclones.

The Scientists caution that the effects of climate change are rampant throughout the World. A massive change is on the go across the globe and in Earth's atmosphere, it is reported, that is affecting not nature alone, but the lives and homes of millions of people spread across different countries.

Devastating changes are noticed from the highest mountains to the world in the ocean bed and are steadily causing extinction for parts of Earth's rich biodiversity. As far as human beings are concerned, these alterations in climate are mostly hazardous to people who live near to sea shore and those who are already suffering from drought, flooding and poverty. Many of these effects had been known previously and the IPCC's comprehensive report gathered together and analyzed hundreds of published research papers on the subject.

According to IPCC reports, temperatures are sure to rise faster in the next decades than they did during the same time span in the last half of the 20th century and it will follow with catastrophic consequences.

The scientists and researchers are pinning the cause directly on pollution and human greenhouse gas emissions.

Is it too late to prevent these catastrophic effects on our future generations? If we show some real sense and willpower to take concrete steps, then we can reduce its impact on our lives...In fact, all the nations in the world has to consolidate their actions towards preventing global warming and preservation of our environment.

There are also individual contributions that everybody can do to reduce global warming, and thereby stop climate changes. Patrick Gonzalez, a Nature Conservancy climate scientist who worked for UN had remarked that climate change threatened natural communities and human well-being; each person could make a difference because one small positive act multiplied millions of times would produce immense benefits.

Patrick pointed out simple actions that all of us could take which collectively might greatly contribute for a better and greener Earth. His tips included: advocating teleconferences instead of flying, less use of automobiles, more usage of recycled and energy-saving products, planting more trees, using public transportation in and between cities etc.

Let's use cleaner (bio-fuel is an option), more efficient vehicles and reduce driving: one gallon of gas burned creates 20 pounds of CO_2. At all government levels, an efficient energy policy should be developed moving away from fossil fuels. We can replace light bulbs with low-voltage compact fluorescents and buy renewable energy, like wind and solar generated and also discipline ourselves with reduced use of air conditioners and room heaters.

....And start doing these things today itself!

If CO_2 emissions can be reduced to a great extent, the IPCC report estimated, the atmosphere could be stabilized at a much lower level of greenhouse effect than it was forecast then. But, the bad effects of global warming will remain here for a very long time, the IPCC said, because of the inertia of the atmosphere and oceans and the hundred or more years of persistence of the greenhouse gases.

So let us first start from our own courtyard…our simple and determined efforts will surely inspire many others and collectively we can save our good Earth and ourselves.

Please remember that it's a now-or-never type situation we are facing now.

So folks, wait not. Let's do our part, START DOING it this very moment…"

Sam concluded reading the article.

When taking dinner also everybody thought about that disturbing topic, the global warming and climate change. They were wondering if such a catastrophe would ever occur. Is Apocalypse on the doorstep?

Not able to believe it, but nobody could escape from the disturbing thoughts also.

Next day, that's on Wednesday, Sam, Mary and her family went for morning mass at the nearby church. Then they did a brief shopping and returned home after having lunch in a hotel. Their Doha flight is at 9.20 pm, and so need to reach NY Airport at around 6pm. Also there is two hours journey to NY.

After reaching Mary's apartment, they did all the luggage packing and other works. And it is time now to start the journey. Sam and Mary had transferred all their money in the bank accounts to Koshy ichayan's account as Franklin had directed. This was done to take Franklin and the Iranians into confidence. They know that all their movements are watched…

After locking the flat, Mary gave the key to her parents.

When bidding farewell, Preetha has noticed great sorrow in Mary's eyes, and it disturbed her deeply.

2 IN IRAN

Sam and Mary's flight reached Doha at 6pm on Thursday. The connection flight to Iran was around 12 at night same day. A lady wearing an 'abaya' (loose over-garment, essentially a robe-like dress) received them at the Doha airport. She took them to a hotel. Two separate single rooms were booked for Sam and Mary.

They took bath and relaxed for some time. After dinner, it was almost time to leave for airport. This time, a man came to take them to airport. He introduced himself as Abdalla. His walking style and body language betrayed his military grooming.

Abdalla told Mary that contrary to general belief, there are not much dress restrictions for Western women in Iran. Just use a scarf or a black cap. And you can wear jeans and shirt as you are wearing now. Please avoid wearing half pants and sleeveless top. That's all.

Soon they went to Doha international airport...

Abdalla also will be travelling with them to Iran.

The flight from Doha to Iran started at 00:45 after midnight. They reached Tehran Imam Khomeini International Airport at 3 A.M. Abdalla took them to a hotel. He said, "Please take a full day rest; I'll take you to the office on Sunday morning. Call me at any time, if you need any assistance."

Before leaving, Abdalla gave Sam and Mary new activated SIM

cards and also his mobile number for contacting.

Secret police agent, Saleh Hameed, and his assistant came next day afternoon to meet the Americans in their hotel room. However, they were not that intelligent as expected from police agents. Their foolishness was visible in their talks and deeds!

Saleh checked Sam and Mary's passport and other documents. They also asked few questions that were not relevant in the present situation. It showed that they have somehow adjusted their job with Iran government! Then quite unexpectedly they took Sam and Mary's passport and also collected their personal mobile SIM cards.

Even though Saleh took the passport, Mary and Sam had other diplomatic passport, which they kept it as a secret. They may require it in case of an emergency.

If they get access to Franklin's discovery prototype and the laptop containing all the theory papers, then the first option is to take it away and run to a nearby friendly country- Kuwait, Iraq or Saudi. That time they need those passports.

Weapons will be given to them at some convenient place by CIA moles in Iran. That was all they know now.

Because the police agents were dumb heads, it was easy for Sam and Mary to pretend that they are real scientists and not even distantly connected to CIA. They pretended that they hate America and are happy to run away from there and that they will be settling in Iran permanently.

But there was another hurdle. They were given several forms and data sheets to be filled in detail. It sought personal information, and other testing queries like loyalty test, personality test, and lie-detection testing etc., which were cleverly introduced by Iran intelligence to check Mary and Sam's real intention, trustworthiness and loyalty.

But the commando training in the US covered all these type of intelligence sharing and management, so it didn't pose any real challenge to Sam and Mary...

In fact, they used it to trap the Iranians showing disguised loyalty and sincerity.

When all is done, secret police agent, Saleh Hameed said, "We'll give your security report to the authority today, and once it's cleared, Abdalla will pick you up tomorrow to Franklin's office. Till that time, please stay in the hotel itself."

"By the bye, did you suspect Abdalla is a secret agent?" Saleh suspiciously asked Sam.

Sam played innocent, "No, not at all… Why? Anything wrong? We felt he's a normal messenger or driver."

Saleh too played innocent, "No, no… Nothing wrong… just asking."

Saleh then winked at his assistant, justifying his decision to utilize agent Abdalla as a driver to secretly spy on the Americans without arising any suspicion.

Saleh continued, "Abdalla will be looking after all your travelling and residential requirements while you're in Iran. You can talk to him in Arabic. He doesn't know much English. So you can also have private talks in English without Abdalla understanding anything…"

Sam and Mary were thinking about the foolishness of Saleh to conclude that they didn't suspect Abdalla! Sam knew that Abdalla is fluent in English and that he is a dangerous guy who can kill anybody in cold blood.

After Saleh and his assistant departed, Franklin's call came for Mary on the new SIM number provided by Abdalla.

"Hello Mary, How are you? Welcome to Iran!"

"I'm fine. Thank you, Professor. How are you? How's your project going?"

"Everything is on track. I'm eager to see both of you…Once Sam joins our team, everything will move fast. Congrats to you for bringing him too. Convey my regards to Sam also."

"Sure … when will we have a meeting?"

"Tomorrow morning the driver will pick you up from the hotel to our office. There will be an official meeting with dignitaries and our project technical staff. After that we'll be free to discuss everything in detail."

Next day, a conference was held at the date palm processing plant's underground warehouse office where Franklin and his team worked. The VIP meeting was held to introduce and welcome the two Americans.

While introducing Sam and Mary to the audience, Franklin explained how their arrival will boost the light speed space project. He also narrated latest developments in the project and assured everybody that soon the project will take wings!

Sam and Mary also discussed what they could do in helping to successfully complete the project and achieve the great milestone. They thanked everybody for the warm welcome and said that they didn't know Iran is such a hospitable country.

When all VIPs have gone, Franklin called Mary and Sam to his office.

After personal talks of well being, Franklin discussed about his spacecraft project.

"Any rocket can achieve a very high speed if it accelerates for a long time. A conventional rocket has a hard time doing this because a huge amount of fuel must be carried into space in order for this to happen. This may make the rocket too heavy to lift off. It requires 36,500 mph for Earth to solar escape compared to 17,000 mph for getting into space and attain Low Earth orbit.

"With increasing speed it becomes harder and harder to gain another mile per hour. This is because the amount of fuel one has to carry becomes really big, and it becomes difficult and expensive to lift that much fuel into space. Solar escape velocity is nearing the practical limit of how fast one can move with conventional rockets.

"You know the galaxies are flying away beyond the speed of light, so it's not impossible to attain speed faster than light. Consider the Faster Than Light (FTL) theory. A bright explosion emits an expanding spherical shell of light or other radiation. When this shell intersects a surface, it creates a circle of light which expands faster than light. A natural example of this has been observed when an electromagnetic pulse from a lightning flash hits an upper layer of the atmosphere."

The topic greatly interested Sam. He asked, "That means faster than light travel is possible, isn't it?"

Franklin nodded happily and continued. Sitting in Franklin's room they can watch the team members through CCTV.

"So, I thought FTL travel is possible for a machine run by human beings too. There is no proof that the speed of light is the universal speed limit. We simply have no access to other things that move faster than light, and we don't come close to possessing the technology to achieve building light speed spacecraft, but that doesn't mean light speed is the ultimate imitation of speed.

"However there were so many complicated issues to be solved to go ahead with my concept.

"I have thoroughly studied the warp drive concept to think about faster-than-light travel. The warp drive envisaged by Mexican physicist Miguel Alcubierre was found to be difficult to achieve as it requires prohibitive amounts of energy to move the device which was supposed to bend the space-time."

Mary inquired, "Isn't warp drive just a science fiction?"

Franklin's eyes shined to see Mary's interest in the topic. He answered, "It's not just fiction, Mary. Some physicists are seriously doing research on the subject. They argue that adjustments can be made to the proposed warp drive that would enable it to run on significantly less energy.

"But one thing distracted me from this theory: it's the viewpoint of the physicists advocating wormholes, warp drive etc. that those devices allow travelling at many times faster than the speed of light.

"I concentrated on the idea to first achieve the light speed travel, and the rest will follow suit. A device travelling at the speed of light will be easier to manipulate than those travel at 10 or more times faster than light.

"That was a right decision, Professor," Sam said.

"Thank you," Franklin nodded and recounted:

"So, I left all time travel and bending the space-time theories and focussed on conventional rocket propulsion we used for space travel.

"Fuel is one major factor that restricts the speed of the spacecraft. So that was the first obstacle in my problem's ladder. I decided to depend on atomic energy that gives infinite energy to our Sun and other stars - so, research was carried out on atomic fuel and its conventional drawbacks."

By that time coffee and snacks arrived. Mary was surprised to see there are only lady attendants in the entire office set up. She noticed it while watching the CCTV screens.

After the break, Franklin said, "I have to attend a ministerial level meeting today, so I'm leaving now. The technical head, Mr. Hatoum Mustafa will explain the spacecraft details to Sam. He'll show your desks and introduce you to the team."

Franklin lifted the intercom, "Mr. Hatoum, please come."

Hatoum came. He's in his late fifties. Fully grey haired and sleepy eyes. "These are the Americans, Sam and Mary. Sam is an astronaut and spacecraft design engineer, and Mary is a cloning scientist. Please show them their office desk and introduce them to the team," Franklin told Hatoum and left for his meeting.

"Glad to meet you. I'm from the Iran Space Agency, currently on deputation to Franklin's research lab," Hatoum introduced to Sam and Mary. He took them to the other team members and shown them their cubicles.

Hatoum then welcomed them to his office. "See. I'll explain Prof. Franklin's landmark invention on my laptop. Mary can go to your system if you want to concentrate on your cloning research."

"No, I'm very much interested in the spacecraft design. I need to conduct the cloning research in space too."

"Ok, nice. Our Professor Franklin is a genius. He singlehandedly invented this foolproof theory to cross the light speed barrier, " Hatoum said and showed the spacecraft dummy designs on the screen.

"Initially Ionic propulsion will be used to fly the spacecraft into space. From there, we give a controlled atomic explosion to increase the speed exponentially. For this, the spacecraft uses nuclear fusion and pulse drive, which is based on fusion-antimatter catalyzed nuclear pulse propulsion technology.

"You can see here, we also use thrusters to get augmented speed for the spacecraft. For that an advanced technology, the nanoparticle field extraction thrusters (nanoFET) propulsion method, is utilised."

Using a pointer, Hatoum has explained the flow chart and prototype of the spacecraft.

"With the fusion antimatter pulse drive on the main spacecraft Power Unit and the additional hyper power boost of the nanoFET thrusters, we aim to achieve around 10 Lakhs Kilometres per Hour or more in void space."

Sam was curious. He exclaimed, "Yes, I heard that latest spacecraft designs by NASA and European Union tested the same."

Hatoum gestured in agreement.

"Yeah, that's true. Prof. Franklin's turning point starts from there. When our spacecraft flies at that super-fast hyper speed, it gets extraordinary lift or thrust by virtue of its special disc shape. Its speed then dramatically multiplies by thousands and millions times and finally attains the speed of light, that is, 1.08 billion km/hour.

"Compare it with the phenomenon of an aircraft that moves on the runway at high speed eventually attains lift due its aerofoil shape. The case of spacecraft can be said to be at a 4D world when its spiral shape takes it into the realm of light speed from the 3D level of outer space.

"The design and shape of the spacecraft have done the magic. Prof. Franklin says he conducted more studies on quantum theory and wave theory to finally evolve a formula whereby a spiral shaped spacecraft can cross the light-speed barrier. The final formula and its detail are in his laptop, which haven't been revealed to the team so far."

Sam and Mary secretly exchanged a glance, while Hatoum continued.

"Attaining light speed was not the end, there was the question of how to travel safe in a spacecraft that moves at light speed. The professor has cleverly overcome this difficult situation by making the spacecraft into two capsules.

"Inside the disc shaped spacecraft there will be a spherical shaped capsule in which the pilot and space travellers can be accommodated.

"Once the disc shaped spacecraft attains the speed of light, the spherical capsule will get lifted from its pivot point and rotate like a spinning top. So the people sitting inside will have relatively no speed at all. So they don't experience any bodily changes that may come with light speed travel.

"One great advantage here is that once the disc-shaped spacecraft attains the speed of light, there is no energy needed to go on like that. No fuel needed as long as we can retain the speed of light because it then faces zero friction and will move on by its inertia quality.

"Another plus point is that we can tap innumerable energy from the main capsule for all the energy and electricity requirements inside the spherical capsule."

"Again there will be more and more wonders yet to be revealed as we attain the speed of light and dash through the interstellar space. Prof. Franklin's project thus becomes a treasure trove of hidden secrets! Hope we'll succeed to catch hold of it. Inshallah-God Willing."

Sam and Mary were very much impressed to learn about the theory to break light speed barrier.

Mary thought: "The world will be surprised to hear about this great invention. Lot many scientists are engaged in researches to achieve the speed of light. And here, Prof. Franklin has discovered it, but he likes to stay away from the limelight - For the sake of his country? For the sake of his religion? Or just because he hates America?!

However, the world desperately wants this achievement."

When Hatoumn concluded, Mary and Sam stood up and gave him warm shake hand. They then went to their respective cubicles.

When Franklin returned in the evening, Sam said, "Wonderful achievement, Professor! You deserve a Nobel Prize for this."
Mary added, "This is a big leap for the mankind. And your name is going to be honoured forever."

Listening to their enthusiasm, Franklin shook his head in disagreement.

"I don't need the Nobel Prize or any other honours from the U.S. or its allies. If we give this discovery to America, they'll endorse their superiority in the space too. They will colonise other inhabitable planets in our galaxy. They'll resort to bombing and destroying Allah's creations there also. Here in the Middle East region, it's no one but America is creating all the bloodshed and violence... What do you say, Mr. Sam?"
"I agree with you. The U.S. foreign policy has its drawbacks. It

favours only those close allies and ignores the third world countries…. I don't support the U.S. administration's partiality in this regard."

"I'm happy to know that both of you understood the hypocrisy of America. Now Sam, I desperately need your help to complete this mission. You should give me a smart spacecraft design as I have explained. We can't even trust long-term ally Russia also because anybody will try to take away this discovery. That's why you have been brought this way, and I trust you."

"I'm fully prepared and eager to start the spacecraft design work. With your smart team here, I hope to complete the mission very soon."

"You'll get all the technical help and latest technology available in Iran."

Franklin then told Mary that he will make arrangements for her to get all the facilities needed for her research too.

Mary thanked him. "Great to know Prof. Franklin. I'm happy to hear it. I want to conduct research and experiments on the effect of super speed travel on human body and the DNA samples.

"If we want to take life from Earth to another solar system, this study is a must because we'll have to travel through space at least four years continuously to reach even the nearest star next to Sun."

"Let's see if we can reduce that time period. Once we achieve light speed travel, it may not take much time to reach new milestones in speed," Franklin said.

Mary showed much enthusiasm, "Thank you Franklin. I look forward to it. I have more experiments to be conducted at the speed of light with respect to space cloning and its possibilities, but I need to complete some homework first. I hope to catch up with you as your technical design and other things progress."

Franklin assured her, "Give the list of items you need for your experiments and we'll provide everything. This underground research institute has all the facilities of a university."

Mary continued. "Nice to know that, but I fear time is a critical factor here. Global warming and climate change have advanced further. Several years passed after the initial signs. Now we have no idea how fast the climate change and the destructive forces are escalating. A catastrophe can happen any time."

Franklin's eyes widened. He looked at Mary unbelievably. "Oh, is it so?! Actually I didn't give climate change that much importance. Now, if you're correct, we'll have to finish our spacecraft project pretty fast. What's your say, Sam?"

"I support Mary's views. Global warming will finally catch upon us. Astrophysicist Dr. Robert Smith of University of Sussex said that the aging Sun would eventually accelerate global warming to a point where all of Earth's water will simply evaporate. He added that in a billion years the Earth would be a very hot, dry and uninhabitable ball."

Mary further clarified Sam's point, "But the sayings of Stephen Hawking, I think, are more applicable in our present world. When the normal process of destruction of life on Earth would take around a billion years, Hawking says human related exploitation of Earth's resources will lead to life's destruction in just under thousand years."

When Mary concluded her speech, both Franklin and Sam fully agreed with her views and appreciated her knowledge in that area.

Franklin then talked to Sam, "So, Sam, now the ball is in your court. We hope you'll come out with a brilliant spacecraft design to give wings to our plan!"

Franklin then looked at both Sam and Mary, "Look, your work cabins are readied on both sides of my cabin. While working we can also see one another with the see-through window. Here the internet and all other external communications are controlled by a local server. The world has no access to our data and the same way we also don't have access to the external world. This is necessary to safeguard our discovery from Western hackers.

"Nice meeting both of you. Now let's move to business. Please proceed to your cabins. Your computer systems are connected to everybody's desktop in the team. So you can access all data about our research and findings. The network administrator will help you whenever needed. So continue guys…"

After the discussion, Sam and Mary went to their respective cabins. They didn't show any intimacy as they have no idea how Franklin will react. They know that there are surveillance cameras all around, so no foul play or other planning for the Mission Milky Way at the moment.

Now what is needed is just to concentrate on the research and be active contributors to the experiments. So both of them have decided not to discuss anything personally; they will act when the right time comes.

Rather than running off with the discovery, which is not possible at the present situation, Sam has started concentrating on the design of a spacecraft as per Franklin's theory.

Sam had carried some spacecraft designs from NASA in a pen drive, but the security staff in the underground research centre had withheld it. With Franklin's approval Sam got the pen drive back and now he has access to some latest spacecraft designs. Sam started working on it….

But Sam soon realized that he has to think and act differently because Franklin's spacecraft idea is entirely different from all the known designs in the world.

And those special features are the ones that are going to give humans the power to travel with the speed of light. If it was in the United States of America, then the task would have been taken over by a big company itself which might have created a high level team of expert spacecraft designers.

This is going to be a Himalayan challenge, Sam calculated. Iran's space technology is not on par with the modern world, so it's not easy to get specialized spacecraft designers here. However, he has an intuition that the victory will be in their side without much delay because their mission has the signature of God almighty!

Sam thanked God for giving him the opportunity to be a part of this historical mission.

Soon he realized the presence of a cosmic energy influencing him in his work. It thrilled him with joy. Oh, this could end up like Noah's Ark in the Biblical Great flood era, and the mass destruction thereafter!

If unchecked, the global warming and its consequences can create a climate catastrophe leading to destruction of flora and fauna similar to Noah's time. In such case, our spacecraft could end up like Noah's ark – quite unbelievable at this time. But who knows what's in store for us!

Large scale melting of ice in the poles, glaciers, Greenland and West Antarctica causes continuous sea level rise. Sam read in an article that many islands are on the verge of disappearance. Almost 75% of islands of Maldives also had gone under water.

And eventually, it'll mix up with other natural calamities which could lead to the end of the world. In that case, Mary's DNA samples will preserve Earth's current species safe inside the spacecraft, just like Noah had taken two of every kind of animals into the ark, and preserved them.

Sam wondered why and how these amazing thoughts are passing through his mind…The goodwill of Mother Nature might be influencing his mind!

The one who created this beautiful Earth and the amazingly diversified life here must be a great thinker. He has such aesthetic capabilities and wonderful imagination- incredible and awesome beyond the scope of our thoughts. He will not simply destroy everything he created. There will be an escape route...

Thinking positively, Sam dedicated all his energy and time for the spacecraft design without any tensions because he knows that it's God's will is happening...

3 BEGINNING OF THE DEVASTATION

One fine morning, a very sad breaking-news took the world by storm. North Korea had dropped a powerful nuclear bomb on Seoul in South Korea!

South Korea also retaliated with nuclear bombs and within a few hours both the countries emptied their nuclear arsenal on each other. The result was terrifying! Both the countries had become a nuclear wasteland- the complete population had been wiped out! A massive Earthquake also occurred at the region. There was utter chaos everywhere... Red Cross and other Humanitarian organizations couldn't go anywhere near the Koreas as there were very dangerous levels of nuclear radiation in the countries.

China's border areas were also highly affected by the spread of atomic radiation. In fact the nuclear war had affected the whole world. It has accelerated the rate of global warming. The atmosphere was filled with dust and debris caused by the massive explosions.

Red Cross has no idea how many people were alive and need medication. Hospitals and the complete government administration had stopped functioning.

All countries had to stop flights to Korea. The Korean region was completely isolated. No one could go there and no one could come out from there... It was a complete nuclear wasteland with human and animal body parts strewn everywhere!

When the dangerous radiation level around the Korean region has improved, the international community has shown interest to help both the countries.

On one side the USA and European Union and on the other China and Russia took this opportunity to study the aftermath of a nuclear war. They offered donations to clean up the nuclear mess and free help to rebuild the Korean countries.

The research teams sent by both the parties conducted elaborate studies and collected data about the destructive powers of nuclear bombs and how it can paralyse a modern-day society. They were collecting those details to form war strategy and efficient defence systems to tackle any future untoward incidents happening in their respective countries.

Due to widespread destructions caused by climate change, the world slowly receded into hopelessness and chaos. The mood of pessimism prevailed everywhere.

Nobody has any serious thoughts about the future as they felt that the world is doomed. Now the immediate feeling is how to survive on Earth which is gradually becoming hostile for life.

Heat wave casualties during summer have increased many times that of the deaths due to cold wave conditions in winter. Polar bears became extinct and shipping industry worldwide faced dangers due to the high presence of floating icebergs coming from polar melting.

The rapid growth of CO_2 emissions in the atmosphere also drastically varied the sea water chemical combinations and balance causing it to become more acidic.

Oceanic food-chain has been disrupted due to increased ocean acidification. This potentially harmful phenomenon has threatened food chains of whales and other marine life connected with ocean ecosystem.

Ocean acidification has been called the "other CO_2 problem" or the "evil twin of global warming" because it's caused by the same human induced CO_2 emission that causes global warming and climate change.

In such worse conditions of natural disaster, an important meeting was conducted at the CIA office. The Secretary of Defence, White House Chief of Staff, Joint Chiefs of Staff of U.S. Department of Defence, NASA Administrator, and the CIA

Director were the participants. It was a tight security secret meeting.

The discussion was started by White House Chief of Staff.

"Our scientific and reconstruction team to the Korea has given their report. We'll have to make some key changes accordingly to our defence systems to minimise the damage in case of a nuclear attack."

"Already the planning and discussion are ongoing in the defence establishment. But I fear, we won't be able to do much if a 3rd World War takes place. Just remembering Albert Einstein's words in this pitiful situation; it assumed more meaning now. Einstein had said that he didn't know what lethal weapons man would be using in 3rd World War; but he was sure that humans would be using stones and sticks in the fourth World War," explained the Joint Chiefs of Staff of U.S. Department of Defence.

NASA Administrator talked about the consequences of climate change around the world and particularly, the devastating effects in America.

"Temperatures have soared in the Gulf countries and the region has turned unfavourable for life. The oil production has drastically reduced due to less demand as people around the world stopped tours and travels. Rich Arabs had migrated into safe places in our country, the Australia and Europe.

"At many hilly regions across the globe, climate turned unfriendly and dangerous due to record snowfall and other climatic abnormalities.

"Drought, flooding, cloudbursts, land sliding, massive Earthquakes etc. have become routine events everywhere. Millions died and as many displaced due to the outbursts of epidemics. The world order is changing now."

Everybody had a grave and thoughtful expression. They asked the NASA administrator to further explain the depth of global warming.

He continued, "Earth's rock systems have undergone irreversible changes due to ruining factors of a man-made era. This included huge quantities of ashes emanated from fossil fuel burning, sea-level rise due to global warming, increase in erosion and sedimentation, reaction of radioactive waste materials etc.

"The Intergovernmental Panel on Climate Change (IPCC), which has over 1,300 scientists from the United States and rest of the world, had given warning that Earth's average temperature will rise between 2.5 to 10 degrees Fahrenheit over the next century.

The National Oceanic and Atmospheric Association (NOAA) also warned that climate change is happening in real time as the global surface temperature and sea surface temperatures, and global sea level were the highest on record at the moment."

The Secretary of Defence added, "In spite of our warnings, countries around the world didn't do much to reduce the greenhouse gas emissions. Many people had thought that global warming and climate change are something that'll happen to the future generations only.

Now we'll have to face the wrath of Nature for spoiling its chemical and eco balance. Instances of more heat waves, droughts, severe hurricanes, flooding, and epidemics etc. happening in front of us were predicted well in advance- but the world as a whole failed to stop global warming and climate change."

International news clippings were continuously shown on Plasma TV displays, in addition to weather forecasts.

The White House Chief of Staff then asked the CIA Director, "What about our Milky Way Mission? It's going to be almost nine months since our commandos left for Iran. What is the latest news about Prof. Franklin's discovery? Anytime the need may arise for us to evacuate from Earth. The situation is getting worse day by day. If we want to escape into other solar systems, we must have spacecrafts travelling with the speed of light, not the current hypersonic ones. We have a long list of heads of state, and billionaires seeking America's help to escape from Earth in case of a catastrophe. They have offered billions of US Dollars for that.

"And now US President has asked a quick summary report about the ongoing Iran operation to hijack the scientist who ran away from the United States. Please explain the progress of the Mission Milky Way."

CIA Director replied, "People offered Dollars?! Will our Dollars have any value once we leave Earth and go to another Solar system? Even in Mars, the rules will be different. China and India are better equipped and more populated than our Martian settlements.

"Now coming back to the Iran mission, sorry to say that we still don't have much information about the agents, Ananthan and Mary. Their parents are also observed all the time. Their work with Franklin's discovery might be progressing well.

"We're expecting good news anytime. We have info that they are alive because the microchips implanted in their organs which work on body heat are still active. Our Arabic agent in Iran could detect the signals sent by the chips which are traceable within 3kms distance.

"The signals are static, that means they are not moving to any other location; may be staying at the work place itself. If they come out from the current location, our agent will help them to run away from Iran…"

The Secretary of Defence then asked, "Why can't we plan a rescue mission? If we can save the agents and get the scientific discovery papers, then other things like consequences in international relations etc. can be managed later."

CIA Director negated that idea-

"No, we can't do it now. If the mission fails, we may lose the great discovery that's the only hope now to escape from this dying planet. We'll closely watch the situation there from our Iran spy who is in the locality.

"Anyway, we'll prepare a contingency plan with Secretary of Defence for a rescue mission in the near future! Our Iran agent knows approximate location of the commandos.

So we can easily plan an evacuation operation from our Saudi Arabian base using two helicopters and a fighter aircraft. Let's wait for one or two months at least."

Just then CIA Director received a call from his assistant. After attending the call, he again addressed the meeting.

"We have good news. Our Iran spy has sent a message. He states that the U.S. commandos have moved from the date processing plant. They are now somewhere inside the security zone of Iran Space Agency."

NASA Administrator said in a thrilled voice, "That's great news. They are moving into the space agency means they might be in the construction or testing phase of a missile or spacecraft. One thing we can make sure that Iran has completed the initial processing and feasibility of Prof. Franklin's theory on crossing the light speed barrier. That's great development. We'll closely watch Iran Space Agency now."

The fresh news from Iran has altered the mood of the discussion.

White House Chief of Staff added, "I'll inform this new development to the President. It's not sure whether the commandos will be able to break the tight security system of Iran and bring back the blue print of the light speed spacecraft. Anyway, sending them to Iran has yielded good result as they are in the centre of activities pertaining to Prof. Franklin's invention. Guys, be prepared, the President will take a decision soon."

Then the Joint Chiefs of Staff of U.S. Department of Defence said,

"I can assure you that we're always ready for the Iran evacuation program. Another thing I would like to remind you that our nuclear arsenals, just like the case with other countries in the world, are vulnerable to the unexpected and huge natural calamities happening these days.

We'll have to sit in another meeting, for which I have already given notice, regarding dismantling of some of the nuclear stockpiles at geographically weak areas."

The CIA Director thanked everybody for attending the conference and, sharing information and presenting valuable opinions.

Arrangements were also made to inform the high commissioners of Saudi Arabia and Kuwait to look for two American commandos sending messages or entering their countries from Iran. The meeting was then dispersed.

4 LIGHT-SPEED SPACECRAFT & LOVE TRIANGLE

For the last six months, Sam was fully engaged in spacecraft designing and research. He studied all the available data on spacecraft models and utilized them for developing Franklin's prototype spacecraft. At last he was successful in coming out with an excellent spacecraft design that suits Franklin's theory of crossing the speed of light.

The main body of the spacecraft has been made disc-shaped while the human capsule (inner capsule) inside is in the shape of oblate spheroid. The human capsule is strapped onto a dish antenna type stand fixed at the centre of the main capsule. Those straps can be hooked or released through attached levers while sitting inside the human capsule. Once the main capsule achieves the speed of light, astronauts inside the human capsule will release the straps and the inner capsule will just lift up and continue to rotate.

The spacecraft model has water vapour detector and microbe life monitoring systems which can discover life on a planet well in advance while travelling at light speed by the side of a solar system. These sensors used laser pulses which can travel at several times faster than the speed of light. So the astronauts could come to know if there are inhabitable planets in a solar system well before entering into the gravitational pull of that star (or Sun).

Travelling through the space on that spacecraft would be like venturing out into the sea in a motorised canoe. You'll have to face so many dangers at sea like monster waves, squalls, Bermuda triangles etc. Likewise in space, there are hazardous zones such as black holes, star flares, comets and asteroids etc. A close confrontation with any of these could be fatal. The only hope is that the speed of light will save the spacecraft from several threats. Once it moves as energy, as it happens while travelling in light speed, it won't get affected by bombarding with foreign objects in space.

Black holes are real dangers. They can swallow even stars in their vicinity. Nothing can escape them, even light! So there are adequate alarm/warning measures included in the spacecraft design to detect and keep black holes at safe distance.

Gigantic explosions in space such as a supernova star explosion and other such incidents, and the immense energy released through shock waves and hot particles having millions of degree temperature are other possible dangers the space traveller would have to face in the open space. So, certain warning systems were also designed in the spacecraft to escape these hazardous zones.

If at all there come some encounters with aliens as we see in space wars, provisions are made in the spacecraft model to manage it. The spacecraft is also armed with light missile launchers, mini-guns for aerial gunshot etc.

Brilliant brainstorming sessions were conducted and further changes made accordingly before the final prototype design was submitted for verification. Franklin was happy with Sam's spacecraft design features. It has also got the final approval of Supreme Council of Space Research (chaired by Iran's President). Iranian Space Agency soon took up the project and its manufacturing unit has started making the spacecraft.

Mary was also very busy during those six months. When all attentions were on Sam and his spacecraft model, Mary had enough time to complete her research works on space cloning theories. She also collected DNA footprints of many species in Iran which differs from the already collected samples.

It's clear to her that climate change is a reality, no more a myth as some people still like to think. They are like ostrich which digs its head in the sand when danger appears, foolishly thinking that the enemy won't see it and thus it can escape!

The actual fact about global warming and climate change is that life won't be possible on Earth after the next 50 years or so. The danger can come even in this decade also. So the DNA collection assumes more importance now. It's the only way to transport life as existed on Earth to a distant planet somewhere in the Milky Way galaxy or beyond.

Mary has asked for including some additional features in the spacecraft design by which she can carry her DNA collections safely and effortlessly. Sam readily incorporated them in the prototype and sent to the manufacturer.

Mary has already developed the technology to develop human and animal clones from the DNA samples. Also new organ cells or the entire organs can be developed from those DNA samples, and these cells or organs can be injected or transplanted into human body to control the aging process.

Mary was conducting the experiments and planning everything all alone. There was nobody else to consult, but she was overjoyed to see the positive results.

By replacing the aging vital organs of the body with young ones periodically, a person can stay alive for 500 or even 1000 years while travelling through space. To reach distant stars in the galaxy it'll require hundreds of years even if one travel with the speed of light, and so prolonging the travellers' lives is a necessary requirement to reach an inhabitable planet alive, Mary thought.

Also there is huge possibility of wonderful things to evolve while travelling with the speed of light.

If a cloned baby made in the human capsule can be transferred to the main capsule through a valve or vacuum space, then there is chance for a miracle. The baby may remain alive in a cocoon stage without body growth for so many years because travelling at the speed of light means the child will be converted into energy. But Mary has so far didn't disclose these eventualities to anybody as she is not sure about the result. It has to be proved by practical testing and experience only.

"So, let it wait. And if God almighty also wants it that way, then what else can stop humans venturing out to distant stars?" Mary whispered to herself.

"So everything is almost ready now for the Milky Way voyage, Inshallah," Franklin thought.

For the last six months, Mary and Sam's love also continued in a subtle manner along with the research. Love is such a feeling which when suppressed coils back in double strength. When it's not openly expressed, it flows through subconscious mind and then attains supernatural powers which can convey your thoughts without the need for any physical medium.

The lovers' minds then become transcendent and can understand the feelings and intense thought processes of each other.

A sort of telepathic powers worked between Sam and Mary. They both wondered how each one can easily read and understand the other person's feelings and thoughts.

They could exchange hundreds of love messages with a single look through their eyes. And the interesting thing is that they can share the inner feelings of love even without seeing each other.

It's true that love needs no eyes, no ears - it'll make you simply flow like a stream of water through the jungles or it'll make you fly like a pappus (feathery seed) across the lands, through the breeze etc. It'll carry you to hitherto unknown valleys where sweet golden fruits are hanging from every branch of trees!

The tough research which kept everybody fully engaged for almost 10 to 15 hours per day however couldn't rein in the love feelings of Sam and Mary. But one thing has affected it little bit!

Franklin has a special affinity towards Mary. He has expressed it indirectly. Mary could not accept it or deny it altogether because she has no idea how Franklin will react if she denies his love.

The mission was too important and it was not advisable to displease Franklin. So, Mary followed the delaying tactics.

Franklin used to advise Mary about religious topics. Mary considered it as a desire to convert her to Islam, but Franklin never compelled. Then she thought Franklin is becoming more and more religious, and affected by religious sentiments.

Though he is a pious man, Franklin's desire was not preaching Islam to Mary; actually he was trying to offer his heart to her.

The problem with intellectuals is that most of them don't know how to express love- they often fail to nurture love because love needs lot of labour (illogic) and patience. And these intellectuals lack the time and intelligence needed for the silly labour which is required to grow romance!

Franklin's case was no different. He loved Mary pretty much, and wants to talk to her very often, but he ends up discussing about Quran…The main difficulty was that Franklin doesn't have much time to spare as the research takes away much of his time. And so Mary was never put to real test such as answering a Yes or No to Franklin's love.

Once the spacecraft design had been submitted to Iran space agency's manufacturing unit, Sam, Mary and Franklin got some spare time.

On Fridays they started going out for picnicking, evening walk etc. Security people will be following them everywhere, but more freedom is given to roam around.

Nothing wrong has happened after the arrival of Sam and Mary, contrary to the suspicion of Iran's intelligence and secret agencies.

Mary and Sam's absence has not created any issues in the US. They had come to Iran for a crucial mission, but both were not working in any security related or defence organisations that's why US govt. has not come to know about it, Iran intelligence agents thought. So they have lifted all security tracking on the two Americans. However, phone calls and open internet facilities were still not permitted for them.

One day Mary went to a remote beach area along with security guards for some DNA collection. An hour after Mary's departure, Franklin got a call from the guards stating that Mary had a quarrel with some local people. Franklin quickly went there for Mary's rescue.

Franklin reached the spot and talked to the local people and shown his high profile identity card. Some youngsters had created a scene by seeing Mary's western style dressing. When Mary had reacted sharply to their sexy comments, they gathered the locals and didn't allow Mary and the guards to go.

Franklin had warned the people of serious consequences if any such incidents occurred in the future, and took Mary and the guards away.

Franklin then went for a walk with Mary along the beachfront. Mary was upset and angry. They sat on the sand bed for a while.

"There is no benefit in having a great religion- hooligans & eve teasers are the same everywhere, and won't be reformed," Mary aired her anger.

She lamented as Franklin listened to her sympathetically. "I'm frustrated today...let me at least send an SMS to my mother now."

Franklin has no option other than agreeing to her because Mary's temper was not good. He gave his mobile phone to her.

Security guards were standing far away. So, Mary typed the message without them noticing it.

"Dear Papa & Mom,
Here everything is fine. My work is going smooth; it'll take a few more months to complete the job. Seeing Sam every other day... All well. Not in a position to talk to you now as I'm in a remote area where there is no mobile coverage. This message is sent from the phone of my friend who is in the city. See you soon take care.

Bye.
Mary."

Once the message has gone, Mary felt very happy. She smiled at Franklin and said, "Thank you so much for this favour. I'm indebted to you..."

Franklin also felt cheerful to see Mary in a happy mood. He found this as a nice moment to express his love.

He whispered to her, "Mary, I want to tell you an important thing. Don't know how to say it, but I'm deeply in love with you...the feeling was conceived in my mind long back... I considered and pondered the idea so many times... I can't suppress it anymore. Tell me, don't you also feel the same, don't you love me too?"

Mary was embarrassed to hear that – she knew that she'll hear it someday, but it came in an unexpected moment like this...

She doesn't know what to say. Somehow she regained her composure and decided to open up her mind.

"I like you very much, Franklin, and trust you too, that's why I left everything in the U.S. and came to your side. But my feeling towards you is not love, it's a feeling of deep respect towards a great scientist - it's kind of worship, not love that I feel…"

"But Mary, in my mind, you are still a lover… I can't get your beautiful smile and eyes out of my head. Couldn't you rethink? Can't you be mine, sweetheart?"

"I could have loved you… but Professor, let me tell you the truth now. I'm already engaged- Engaged to Sam Ananthan. I wanted to talk about this matter with you, but couldn't find the appropriate time. We were all busy with the research… and as this delicate subject needs proper time and mood to discuss, I couldn't disclose it to you. We were also not sure how you'll react…I feel sorry for that, forgive us."

Franklin was really shocked to hear that! He was taken aback by Mary's denial of his love. He never expected it; his mind became completely blank. He couldn't speak anything further.

Mary was also upset and had no idea how to handle the situation. Luckily for both, the guards came and hinted to go back because it was not advisable to stay there for long.

5 LAUNCHING OF THE ARK- THE SPACECRAFT

Another secret meeting of Iran government officials is being held at the date processing plant where Franklin's office worked. As usual, the attendees are President's envoy, Ministry of Intelligence representatives, Minister of Communications & IT, Space Agency Chief, Chief of SAVAK, and Defence rep from General Headquarters of Armed Forces.

Space Agency Chief said, "The manufacturing of the spacecraft is getting completed at the prototype production line. We can expect the final product this month-end itself if everything turns out to be as per the specified standards at the satellite test house. Our Satellite launchers have the capability to carry the spacecraft to Earth's orbit. So Prof. Franklin, are you okay with our satellite launch vehicle taking your spacecraft to the outer space for conducting your experiments?"

Franklin answered, "If we carry out the experiments near the Earth orbit, the whole world will see it and come to know about our discovery. America and their allies could also hijack or destroy the mission because they have complete control over there near to Earth space. So we'll have to take our spacecraft to at least the Martian orbit to safely apply my theory to test the spacecraft for light speed travel."

"But, how could we take the spacecraft up to Mars? Iran has so far not gained the technology to venture out into the interplanetary space," Space Agency Chief grumbled.

"Actually I forgot to inform you about this requirement in advance. Yes, we'll have to get external help to carry our spacecraft into Martian orbit. China, Russia and India seem to be possible options."

Tension was written all over Space Agency Chief's face. "We already have space mission cooperation with China and Russia, but both the countries can't be trusted for this mission as they may try to take away the great discovery from us. Also this can affect our cordial relationship with Russia for not sharing the information about the light speed theory. We don't want any such things happening at this critical moment.

"And so it seems we have left with the only option of India; and what about India? Can we trust them?"

Then the representative from the Ministry of Intelligence said, "India has been our good friend from ancient times. They never backbite. With its huge population, India always needs more money, so if you give them a space mission project paying huge fees, they'll happily take it without much queries. The advantage is that they normally won't spy on us. So our project will remain secret and safe."

Franklin was happy to hear that- "That's great idea! If you're going to select India to launch our spaceship, then we have the added advantage of two Indians being members of our research team here. What do you say, Sam and Mary?"

Sam and Mary readily agreed to the idea. They said India could be the best option as far as spying and hijacking the mission is a possibility with other countries. Not only that, India is now the topmost performer in satellite launching to Mars and beyond, so we have the advantage of getting the best service also.

Till date, their ISRO space agency had safely launched over 200 satellites on Earth orbits belonging to major countries in the world such as Germany, France, Japan, Canada, U.K. and the U.S. They also successfully completed Mars and Jupiter missions.

India also has mastered the space technology to send humans into deep space and they have acquired the capabilities to land on Mars surface. They don't have any space mission failures to Mars or elsewhere, Mary and Sam emphasized.

Okaying Sam and Mary's points, the representative of Ministry of Intelligence further said, "So, we can almost finalise India, pending approval from the supreme authority of Iran… Now, you space scientists do prepare all the technical things and other requirements regarding the launch of our satellite by India. Our Ministry and the External Affairs Ministry will sort out all the diplomatic and other business formalities with the Indian authority. Our high commissioner to India will accordingly be briefed today itself."

Once the supreme authority of Iran has approved the collaboration with India, the official level discussions between Iran and India have started.

Even though UN sanctions against Iran were lifted, the talks about the satellite launch were held very secretly as per Iran's request.

India didn't doubt Iran's intentions and their demand for confidentiality because India knows that the US and its allies are not in good relation with Iran. They may unnecessarily create some objections for the spacecraft launch.

Franklin and his technical team, especially Sam and Mary, had discussions with ISRO officials through video conferencing. Franklin's invention and the objective of testing the spacecraft for light-speed travel were not revealed to India's ISRO.

They just discussed the technical data and formalities for launching and releasing the Iran satellite into Mars orbit.

After putting the spacecraft in a specified Mars orbit, India's reusable launch rocket will come back to Earth. Full control of the spacecraft will then be transferred to Iranian team; no queries or questions will be asked further…

Once they get the satellite into Mars orbit, Franklin and his team can safely and secretly conduct all the trial run of their satellite for light speed travel.

In a Mars orbit, they will be comfortably away from the sharp eyes of US spy satellites.

However, another issue came up as they discussed things further.

Because they are going to launch the spacecraft from another country, they'll have to make major additions to the spacecraft design.

If somebody detected the peculiar disc shape of Franklin's spacecraft, that'll be sufficient to suspect Iran's real intention. If Indian scientists see the disc shaped spacecraft, the information may be leaked to U.S. or they themselves may spy on the mission. So, hiding it smartly was the foremost thing to be looked into.

Sam had to work more hours and study additional satellite building and design parameters to create a mother ship for the disc shaped spacecraft. Time restriction is there but no compromise can be made on the levels of quality and technology that are essential for spacecraft designs.

It took around two weeks to make the technical design changes on the disc shaped spacecraft so that it'll comfortably fit inside the mother ship spacecraft. This time the Iran Space Agency's production engineers also helped Sam as they are experienced in conventional satellite making. The disc-shaped spacecraft is on production stage and so it's not difficult to carry out the additional modifications and system fitments. The disc shaped spacecraft has to go smoothly into the mother ship and stay there during the entire launch mission to Mars. The spacecraft also has to be ejected safely from the mother ship after India hands over all the controls to Iran.

ISRO will guide the mother-ship spacecraft through outer space and into Mars orbit by burning the inbuilt rocket motor. Their work will be over then, and all the controls will be taken over by Iran space agency.

The new design allows the disc shaped spacecraft to be successfully injected out of the mother ship spacecraft into interplanetary trajectory away from the Mars orbit. The disc-spacecraft can then be tested for light speed travel while the mother-ship will be rotating around Mars. The disc-spacecraft can also land back into the mother ship during the trial and error testing process.

If they achieve the landmark target of crossing the light speed barrier, then the disc-spacecraft can directly come back to Earth also while the mother ship remain orbiting Mars. Provisions and design facilities have also been made for the disc-spacecraft to safely land on Earth.

Finally the spacecraft and mother ship production have been completed. It was made in record time. There was special order from the President to do so. All govt. machineries worked in unison and the result was amazing. Iran space agency could make the first phase of Franklin's dream project a reality. Sam and the technical team had thoroughly checked the satellite combo for design perfection. All okayed and the mission is now ready for takeoff.

The satellite was packed and preserved for transportation to India. It was decided that Sam, Mary, two other scientists and the security people will go to India to witness the launching procedures.

Sam and Mary got their passport back. They took it with a sigh of relief. This is the proof that Iran officials have now full confidence in them. That means their Milky Way Mission is super success till date. Without any bloodshed, they could handle everything through clever planning and safe execution of the plan. Only problem is that they couldn't communicate the progress of the mission to CIA Director. But there is hope now as they are moving to India.

Once they land in India, they can somehow manage to message or call their contact person in America. However, the priority for them at the moment is to successfully test fly the spacecraft and to ensure that Franklin's theory is correct.

Franklin has called Mary to his cabin one day prior to her departure to India. Mary was in tension and was eager to know what's in Franklin's mind after his love was denied.

When Mary reached his cabin, Franklin signalled her to sit down. "Hello, Mary. How are you? All set to go to India?"

"I'm fine, Professor. Everything is ready for departure tomorrow. Hope you're okay."

Franklin tried to hide a dry smile. "I'm okay. That day on the beach when you said 'No' to my love, I was totally upset. It disturbed me a lot. But when I contemplated the whole episode, I understood that you were never at fault. I should have disclosed the matter to you earlier, sometime after you met my mother in America. So the fault is mine, not yours.

And I appreciate your sincerity in telling me the truth. You're a courageous lady. I could have troubled you here because nobody would stand in favour of you in this country if I talked against you. But you have shown the guts to openly tell your mind. I could have donned the role of a villain here as usually happens with love affairs."

Mary looked at him passionately. "I know it, Franklin. You're not only a great scientist but a good human being too. I just adore you..."

Franklin sighed in relief as he saw no anger in Mary's expressions. "I still love you, Mary! And I feel sorry to sacrifice it... but we plan something and God decides something else, so can't help it. This is the first time I felt love, didn't have any infatuation till these 35 years in my life. And let me now think that no such feelings (towards you) ever happened in my mind."

Franklin now lowered his voice and said, "Anyway, go to India and come back after successfully completing the mission. The security commandos accompanying you will be closely watching everything

."If ever you do something to jeopardize the mission or try to leak information, they'll not spare you – they have orders to kill in case of treason. They'll use the Polonium radioactive food poisoning method to kill you that won't leave any traces of evidence. It's a slow killer with no cure! So, if ever you get any issues with the security people, don't take any food they offer you... I shouldn't have disclosed this, but I can't resist revealing it to you!"

Mary was so emotional to hear that... She wondered how great Franklin is! Still loving her knowing that she won't return the love, and still doesn't want to see any harm done to her.

Mary said with wet eyes, "How should I thank you for this, Prof. Franklin? My heart weeps and kneels down in front of you... and I give you my word that your love will not go in vain....I'll walk like a magician into the mesmeric world of cloning; I'll churn out the seven seas to bring a gift to fulfil your love…your love's labour will never be lost…

"You need not to wait for long, Professor. God willing, you'll get a surprise gift from my cloning lab which will have the romantic touch of a Keats' poem. Till that time, keep calm and be happy, for the king of romantic poetry, Keats, said that pain of love is beautiful. So be content that you're passing through that beautiful stage now!"

Franklin couldn't fully understand Mary's thoughts because she was uttering it in a prophetic tone…. But he knew that something good will happen in the future, and bid good bye to her.

"Ok, nice to hear that. So, I wish all the best for your journey tomorrow. See you soon."

"Bye, see you," Mary shook hands before leaving.

Even after Mary has gone from his room, Franklin's mind was yearning for her presence…he continued to think about her. He wondered how charming is Mary and how she elevates his mind and mood. She is provokingly beautiful, intelligent and very smart too. Franklin has a strange feeling that Mary loves him too the same way as she loves Sam. She is already engaged to Sam; she can't love both of them – Is it the pain of love? And Keats said the pain of love is beautiful? He might not have thought about the love triangle then...

Franklin assured himself that Mary has some surprise for him. He's ready to wait for that. He has no longing for any other woman. He, however, can't fully explain his love for Mary. He had read some Hindu scriptures that say love sometimes follows you from previous births! Franklin now started thinking that way, yes that can clearly give some reasoning to his passion for Mary.

Franklin thought he'll time-travel back to hundreds of years to check when his soul was linked to Mary. Mary also might be facing similar thought process that is why she said, "Your love's labour will never be lost."

Franklin slowly slipped into a visionary dream as he sat in his office cabin thinking about Mary... He is now travelling by his light speed spacecraft into the emptiness of deep space. His eyes are half closed and he utters strange sounds that nobody could understand...

"Autopilot engaged." "Autopilot engaged." Announcements heard from autopilot system.

"Oh, I feel that have become super conscious... I can see past and future events. Is it called time-travelling? YES, I can now travel back in historical time and also travel forward into the future happenings in a precise manner. Wonderful. That means Einstein's Universe in four dimensions (the three dimensions of space, including up-down, left-right and backward-forward, and the one of time) is being displayed in real time in front of me now. How amazing!

"Errr....hey, that means the fourth dimension of the Universe is nothing but one's MIND, achieving SUPER CONSCIOUSNESS when the physical body travels at the speed of light, or when you have powerful visions or intuitions. And it allows me to time travel to the past as well as to the future, and see the happenings there.

"But I just don't want to go and watch the future now as it'll spoil all the suspense in life...rather I'll go back; I'll travel back in time. What's that, isn't it Mary's pretty face? Yeah, I'm going back to know the origin of my love towards Mary. Once I know it, I can convince her.

"Ok, lemme now move back 2000 years in history and then slowly move forward to see whether I had a connection with my beloved Mary in the past. It's amazing, I'm now seeing everything that happened 2000 years back.

"Oh, my! Jesus Christ might have lived on Earth somewhere during this period and let me see If I can find out glimpses of the messiah. I'm now travelling towards Israel, and lo, there is the aerial view of the old City of Jerusalem with the Noble Sanctuary or the Temple Mount displayed vividly..."

The telephone rang abruptly. Franklin's sleep was broken!

Franklin was shaken by the overwhelming revelation. Like a bolt from the blue, he realised it - it dawned to him that he got the clue to one of the greatest unanswered questions in cosmology that used to keep Physicists awake at night, that is, the time travel paradox. This is more than the invention of the light speed spacecraft itself.

Franklin thought that the Einstein-Rosen Bridges (Wormholes), thus allow the human mind to travel through time. It also helps the human mind to travel into vast expanses of extragalactic space, many light-years from Earth, in only a fraction of the amount of time that it would take it with conventional space travel methods. This all happens when you travel with the speed of light, and your mind achieves sort of omniscience, travelling along the sphere of time-the fourth dimension of the Universe- into the space-time curvature.

When your mind travels along the sphere of time, it can lift your spacecraft from one galaxy to the other or to the edge of the Universe as you wish, Franklin guessed. Your mind then becomes a dummy God that can see the Universe in its entirety in a four dimensional view watching from the axis of time.

But that doesn't mean that you become more or less equal to the God – your super consciousness depends on the weight of your spacecraft gliding through the edge of galaxies and the curvature of space-time...you wouldn't be able to act upon or influence anything you see on your way because you have no physical presence there; things are just reflected to your mind as you move along the line of Time.

And Time is an illusion, as described by Einstein. You get all these visions about past and future events by virtue of your light speed travel, which gives you the capacity to perch on the fourth dimension of this Universe and watch things in their three dimensional entirety.

"So where does God stand compared to the time traveller?" Franklin asked himself.

While time travelling on your light-speed spacecraft, you are just a traveller and spectator of the abundance of this Universe, whereas God, the almighty, is the creator superpower of the universe who can control and influence everything (omnipotence) because of his mass, which is equal to the mass of the universe in toto- that's the difference!

6 IN INDIA

Iran's technical team for the spacecraft launch reached India. The launching was planned at the Satish Dhawan Space Centre (SDSC) or Sriharikota High Altitude Range (SHAR) of Indian Space Research Organisation (ISRO) and situated at Sriharikota in Andhra Pradesh. The Iranian team and Indian officials have discussed all technical requirements and completed the required formalities. Everything has been done as per the rule book and the Countdown started.

The total countdown will take about 56 hours. One day prior to the spacecraft launch, Sam and Mary went to the nearby Church. The security personnel accompanied them, and they waited outside the church as Mary and Sam went in for prayer.

They knelt down in front of the crucifix and prayed. It was weekday and Morning Prayer was over. Nobody was there inside the church. Mary quickly told Sam about Franklin's love request and the things happened there after. Sam also thanked Franklin's great mind.

Then Mary whispered something for which Sam was eagerly waiting.

"Sam, I have a wish. I want it fulfilled now - not sure if we get another suitable moment for the same. I just fear that the end of the world may come at any moment. The climate change is dragging us towards the Apocalypse, may be…"

"You're right, Mary. We're already witnessing the aftermath of climate change. Mother Earth is becoming very hostile for mankind. There would come some disastrous events in the near future itself… Ok, now come to the point, what was the wish you were talking about?"

Mary took out something from her purse. "I brought this gold thali chain while coming from the States. Please tie this nuptial knot around my neck with the holy crucifix witnessing it… every woman needs this, it's our right, please don't say no."

Mary's lips were trembling, and her eye were filled with tears. Sam was seeing Mary so passionate for the first time. He felt that Mary was looking awesome in that situation.

Sam readily took the gold chain, prayed and tied the nuptial knot; then he slowly kissed her neck- it was so soft and warm.

Sam whispered, "Don't worry, dear. Even if this Earth burst out, and the nuclear fumes gnawed the last traces of life on Earth, I'll be there to protect you… I'll stand strong to take you away from dangers, and carry you to safety… To the unknown worlds of twinkling stars and shining moons. I'll lead your way and look after you like a precious pearl… because you are special, and very dear to me."

Mary spoke sweetly, "While wandering through those crazy dreamy lands, I'll give my love to you. I'll give my love to you and our generations will spread in the entire universe…I'll also nurture and enliven all the flora and fauna of Mother Earth there too, so they grow in abundance and praise the God – Amen."

So they are now married… newly married, young couples. God only witnessed that rare nuptial ceremony- it really happened in heaven in front of God.

Mary took a Selfie picture on her tablet with Sam touching her nuptial knot in the backdrop of the Crucifix. Now both Mary and Sam are happy and contented because lovers always have a hidden fear in their minds about fulfilment of their love. Now they are a married couple, not just lovers – so, that element of fear is no more.

It's time to go back now. As Sam and Mary came out of the church, the security guards noticed a vibrant smile on their face. The loving pair also didn't bother to hide their joy, come what may!

The countdown for Iranian satellite has progressed to the final stage…Sam, Mary and the Iran scientists are seated at the ISRO mission control room watching the final launch proceedings. Just one hour left before the takeoff. High level ISRO officials, including Mission Director and Spacecraft Operation Manager, are watching last minute proceedings.

Suddenly there came an urgent call for the Mission Director from the Prime Minister's office (PMO). The Director came back to the control room after the talk with PMO. He looked very concerned and serious. He called the Iranian team for an emergency meeting.

Addressing the Iranian team, the ISRO Mission Director said, "We got a routine but urgent warning message from the United States of America, stating that Iran might have hijacked a great scientific discovery by a US scientist (who's missing now), and so everyone has to keep a watch on Iran conducting any new scientific missile testing which will have far reaching consequences on all Nations in the world. So, PMO has asked us to make sure that this has nothing to do with the ongoing satellite launching programme."

The Director went on, "I need an assurance from your end that this satellite mission is not related to the so called U.S. warning."

Upset with this unexpected turn of events, Sam spoke with a stern voice, "See Mr. Director, this mission is going on as per the agreement between Iran and India governments. I hope U.S. has no role in it. And I assure you that our Mars mission is not aimed at harming any countries. Our vision is to help the humanity, not to destroy anybody."

Mission Director clarified, "That's true, we know it, but we need some assurance from some senior govt official in Iran. May be Iran's ambassador in Delhi should be contacted. But you'll have to hurry now; we have only one hour time left with."

Sam straightaway contacted Franklin on hotline mobile. "Hello Franklin, we have a serious problem here. India govt had received some routine warning from the US govt that Iran had hijacked their scientific discovery, and so there should be an assurance from the Iranian authority that this satellite mission has nothing to do with the US concern.

Please do something urgently, Professor – we have only 50 minutes time left! If we had to abort the launching now, then it may be delayed for months for getting another suitable launch time. Also if a UN mission gets the nod to check our launch program, then the world will come to know about our discovery and the US will somehow seize it."

Sam's message came as a shock wave in Iran. Franklin was really taken aback at this last minute obstacle, but he didn't show it.

"Sam, don't worry. I'll do my best to solve the deadlock. Please be standby," Franklin assured Sam.

It was a very pressurized situation at ISRO's Mission Control Centre. Tensed moments elapsed, and now only 20 minutes left before the launch to be called off. On one side the counting down for the satellite launching is on where as on the other side the counting down for the message from Iran govt is ongoing!

Now just 10 minutes left after that the launch will be aborted...Sam and the team are in a real pressure cooker situation...

Unexpectedly there came a call for the Mission Director from PMO. Thank God. It was the All Clear message.

It was such a relief to everybody. Nobody bothered to ask how the problem was solved. All are now tuned to the final moments of the historic launching of that special satellite which could change the fate of humankind.

Launch data analysis and other announcements are heard from each computer desk in the control centre. The Mission Director has given final launch authorization order. The last phase final countdown started... 10 seconds...9, 8, 7, 6, 5, 4, 3, 2, 1, 0 +1, 2, 3, 4... And there came the success call: "Rocket Lift off Normal."

Message received after 44 minutes that the RLV launch vehicle carrying Iran satellite has reached the predetermined Earth orbit. It will wait for another day before starting its journey towards Mars by operating the Liquid Apogee Motor to get the required boost and thrust. There will be a space journey of around 2 months to reach Mars. During initial Mars expeditions, it took around 8 months to reach Mars. Technological advancements have reduced that time to around 3 months now.

India has the full control and responsibility of the mission till the satellite is successfully put into the Mars orbit. The satellite controls will them be handed over to Iran.

The satellite launch is over and now there is a wait for 2 months for it to reach Mars and for Iran to take over the control. The Iran team can now go back.

Mary then asked Sam to stay a little while more in India. She has to collect a few DNA samples and also want to go to her native place in Kerala state.

Sam asked Franklin to extend their stay in India for at least one week. Franklin said he'll call back and cut the phone abruptly. Sam and Mary feared that Franklin did not like the idea for leaving them in India.

Sam and the Iranian team had completed all the agreement signing and other formalities of the satellite launching with ISRO, and returned to their hotel rooms. Everybody packed their bag and baggage…

Sam and Mary also packed their belongings as they were not sure whether Franklin will agree for their extended stay in India. Just as everyone was ready to leave for the airport, Franklin's call came. Mary and Sam can stay for two weeks in India. However, the security guards will follow them wherever they go and no international telephone calls as usual.

Mary and Sam said good bye to the rest of the team and left for their India tour. They rented a Land Cruiser vehicle and visited all the tourist destinations in North India. As Franklin had directed Mary, they also visited Taj Mahal, the amazing monument of love.

They also went to the Himalayas to collect the DNA samples of some rare species of plants and animals.

It was also a honeymoon trip of sorts and the couple enjoyed every bit of it notwithstanding the glare of the security hawk eyes. Wherever they went, the car stereo music system used to play their favourite romantic songs of latest Hindi movies.

Time went flying away as it happens with all honeymoon adventures. Soon one week was finished. Sam and Mary also secretly discussed about passing the information to CIA office in America.

"Why can't we plan an operation to escape to the US or at least inform them about the progress of our Mission Milky Way?" Sam asked one day.

But Mary cautioned him. "Now we're in the middle of the mission- not sure about the result. If some changes are needed in the spacecraft design to achieve the final goal, only Franklin can do it. So, suppose if we inform CIA, they'll surely interfere and force India either to abort the Mission or to hand over it to the UN organization. Either way there are high chances that the experiment won't be completed successfully... And the most important thing in this critical situation of climate change and impending catastrophe is that we should develop a spacecraft that can travel with the speed of light. It's of utmost importance to transport and preserve the life in case of the end of Earthly world."

Sam was impressed to see Mary's foresightedness. "You're right, Mary. In such a position, our responsibility to CIA and America may lose its significance. The more important thing now is to get the experiment completed successfully and then we will decide as per the situation pertaining to climate change and the destruction of life on Earth."

"Not only that. Actually, I don't feel like cheating Franklin and take away his discovery. He was so sincere to us, and if we betray him, God won't forgive us..."

"Yeah, he could have harmed us when you didn't reciprocate his love. He forgave us without revenging for his lost love, which ended one-sidedly. That shows his greatness as a human being."

Sam and Mary thus concluded that they will wait for the outcome of the satellite speed test before taking a final decision on leaking or hijacking the discovery. If at all they take the discovery to the US, they will also take Franklin into confidence and convince him to go to America and continue his research.

Soon Sam, Mary and the three security guards started their journey from North India towards the South side. They visited many places in Goa and Karnataka. While travelling through a remote village in Karnataka, one day they got stuck on the way as their tyre burst. It was a deserted area and they took the route as a shortcut to avoid hectic traffic and to save over 100kms.

They could not use the Stepney tyre because it has been used to replace another punctured tyre a few kilometres back. This is the second time troubled by a tyre.

They found a small teashop and cycle repair shop nearby. Sam went inside the teashop and saw a very old man there. He'll be in his 80's or even 90's, but still looked very active and dressed well.

Sam introduced him to the old man.

The old man smiled and said, "Ok, Sam, I'm Chakrapani. What do you want, tea, or cool drinks?"

Sam was happy to see the old man speaking nice English. He told Chakrapani that they are on a road trip to see the soul of India and now on the way to Tamil Nadu. Sam asked if he can do something to help them make their vehicle alright.

"Here we have a cycle repair shop where they could have done the sealing of your punctured tyres. But the person is sick and admitted in hospital. His son is there who can carry your tyres to the town in a bicycle. But it'll take around one hour or more," Chakrapani said.

Sam gave money to the boy who took the tyres and went to the town.

Chakrapani welcomed Sam and Mary inside the teashop and gave them tea and snacks. Lunchtime was over and so nobody was there in the hotel.

Chakrapani started a warm conversation with Sam. "As you told you want to see the soul of India, you should also have travelled by the train..."

"I was a pilot in the Indian Air Force and used to travel from North to South India by train."

"Oh, great to hear that. I had also served the India Air Force as an aircraft technician in the 1980's. Train travelling in India those days was sort of a soul searching...

"Yatrigan kripya dhyan dijiye (Passengers, your kind attention, please),"

"How can we forget those announcements at the railway stations hearing it repeatedly with the innumerable journeys we ventured with Indian Railways while serving in Indian Air Force?!

"Getting leave itself was the first hurdle- then running for reservations, waiting list, travelling by military compartment and sometimes by the side of the toilets etc. etc...and for South Indians, it' was almost a minimum of four days horrendous journey...A soldier should be given special awards for all those hurdles we suffered with Indian railways :-)

Mary looked around. The hotel and premises are very neat and clean. Pictures of Ganhiji and President are hanging on the walls.

Mary liked the sincerity and openness of the Veteran. There is a special charm in the way he narrates his experience.

"Uncle, please talk more about those journeys. We never heard about it, and no more chance to listen it from somebody else," Mary cheered the aged, but stout airman.

The old Chakrapani carried on,
"Some of those journeys still haunt us...
"Did you know it used to take almost five days from Jammu & Kashmir to reach our home in South India? As you are a Keralite, I'll tell you my senior lot Malayalis used to say that they had to spend even seven days or more to reach Air Force Units in Chabua, Tezpur, Jorhat etc in upper Assam region from their native hometown in Kerala. These long journeys before and after leave was part and parcel of their service life. No direct trains were available.....They had to travel through three broad-gauge trains- from Kerala to Madras, Madras to Howrah, and Howrah to New Bongaigaon...then change to meter-gauge train from New Bongaigaon to Chabua and other places in Assam. And no seat reservations because of these train changes along the journey...

"Even from New Delhi to Kerala, there was no direct train those days. First travel from Delhi to Madras and after waiting for a whole day, you get train from Madras to Kerala in the evening. For going to Eastern Uttar Pradesh or Bihar Air Force bases, first travel from Kerala to Madras, then change train to reach Itarsi or Jhansi; then again change train to Barauni, cross a ferry there and catch another train to the final destination. Also there was nothing like pantry car those days except in very few premium trains."

Sam listened with interest. "Thank you for mentioning those good old stories...I never knew old Veterans like you had to face that much hardship while serving in the Air Force."

Chakrapani was happy to narrate his experience as he has two good listeners. "Here is another account of the train journey from the Eastern area to South India as told by a senior Airman: "I still remember my first posting at Air Force Station, Laitkor Peak, Shillong. We used to get 12days travelling time, but normally it takes 5 to 6 days to reach home - first by bus from Shillong to Guwahati, then by Kamrup Express meter gauge change to broad gauge to reach Calcutta. Next leg of the journey was by Coromandal Express from Calcutta to Madras – and from Madras to Madurai by either Vaigai Express or Pandian Express. Then to reach home town, travel by bus from Madurai to Periyar Project near Thekkady, which used to take around four hours. I reach home somewhere around 2a.m. and the whole family used to wait for me till that late night."

Chakrapani further said, "And for me, I recall my journey from Dibrugarh to Hubballi in Karnataka those days when I was posted in Assam. There was only one train called Assam Mail from Dibrugarh to Barauni with a running time of over 50 hours. In its history, the train was never on time. Containing haulage of about 42 bogies, and occupied more than 80 percent of it by defence personnel, the Assam Mail that time looked like a moving Army convoy!

"But people were of very helping nature those golden days of my past. Because of those train journeys only we had the great experience of knowing the pulse and soul of India. People used to trust one another and nobody hesitated to help others in trouble...Even if you lost your purse in the middle of the journey, you won't be starved- that was for sure."

Sam remarked, "That's a wonderful experience you shared. We can't even believe travelling was that difficult during your defence service tenure. Yes you are correct, in today's world, we lack trust. Nobody is bothered about helping others. People have restricted their social life to mobile phones and social media. There are very less personal interactions even among family members...yes things have changed a lot from your time- for good or bad."

"However, side by side with difficulties, we also enjoyed those journeys by easily mingling with fellow-travellers, and sharing stories and experiences of a lifetime. Card playing, drinking a tot of rum, which we used to carry in our bags, going for sightseeing in the nearby villages when trains were halted indefinitely etc. were the other pastimes," the Veteran added.

It took almost two hours for the boy to return with the tyres repaired. But the charismatic figure of Chakrapani and his life experiences when told in an interesting and simple style took Mary and Sam to a different world than theirs. They never felt boring. In fact, they wanted to stay there for some more time and listen to the old Veteran, but they had to rush as reaching a city before nightfall was a priority.

While the security guards were fitting the tyres, Sam and Mary bid good bye to Chakrapani. Sam gave him a 500 rupees note, but Chakarapani didn't take it, saying they were like his grand children, and moreover they have a common link- the Indian Air Force! Chakrapani said he'll take a gift when they come next time, even though both the parties know that they will never meet again.

Soon they resumed the journey.... After Karnataka, it was a long journey through Tamil Nadu. They stayed one day in Ooty, the famous honeymoon destination in South India. With its pleasant climate and exotic topography, Ooty is said to be a romantic abode amidst the Nilgiri Hills.

Next day morning they started the journey from Ooty to Palghat in Kerala·via Coimbatore in Tamil Nadu - Reached Palghat at 12.30 pm. And around 5pm, they reached Ernakulam, Kerala and rented a hotel. Rest of the day was spent sightseeing in Ernakulam.

Next, they went to Kakkanad in Ernakulam district to see Sam's orphanage. They called in on the vicar of the church who manages the orphanage, gave presents to the children and made a good amount of donation to the orphanage. The children were very happy to hear that Sam was once a member of the orphanage. So, the children dreamt that one day they will also become a successful person like Sam.

From the orphanage, Sam and Mary went to see Fr. John, who is suffering from Alzheimer's disease and now on bed rest. Sam sat by the side of the father and enquired about his health. Sam felt very sorry to see the predicament of the Father as he could not recollect his memories about Sam even though he knows that Sam is dear to him.

Sam told Fr. John about their relationship starting from his childhood and how the Father helped him to become successful in life etc. Sam also told Fr. John that from then onwards he'll contribute a handsome amount for research foundations for Alzheimer's disease. In this pitiful ailment, human beings are reduced to such a pathetic condition without even knowing who they are!

Mary then said cloning and Nano technology would soon come out with a suitable medical solution for the dreaded disease.

Father John prayed for Sam and Mary and blessed them. Mary talked to the doctor who treats the Father and it's been revealed that Fr. John is in the final stage of the disease and may not live for more than six months.

Sam talked to the Bishop and offered to donate for the last rites and other requirements of Fr. John.

The Bishop said everything will be taken care of by the parish authorities, and no funds are accepted for that purpose. He added that as such they were very happy with Sam's annual contribution to the orphanage.

Next they went to Kottayam to see Mary's relatives. They were all happy to witness this surprise visit. Some uncles and aunties didn't even recognize them. It was such a warm experience for Mary. Sam came to know the love and affection of close relatives.

They stayed at Koshy ichayan's house for two days. It was a big house Mary's papa constructed in his parental property, thinking that one day he'll leave America and return to his native place.

A male servant now looks after the building and its premises. Koshy ichayan's two close friends, Monayi and Avarachan, with whom he used to have liquor parties when visiting Kerala, came there to meet Sam and Mary. They talked about their wonderful experience with Mary's papa. They were such happy go people and talked about many things that Sam and Mary came to know about the rural life of Kerala.

Next day, when bidding farewell to those close kinfolks, Mary felt sorry thinking that it could be her last visit to Kerala – no idea whether she may get another chance to return to that beautiful place. She has more responsibilities to look into and coming back to Kerala may not be a priority.

The whole world needs her service. It's her mild hands that have been bestowed upon the task of regenerating Earth's life in some other distant planet if this world fails to survive a climate related disaster.

Two weeks quickly passed… Sam and Mary returned to ISRO's office in Sriharikota. They viewed the latest position of the RSLV launch vehicle carrying the Iran satellite; thanked all Indian officials and scientists and returned to Iran.

7 BREAKING THE UNBREAKABLE

The day has come!

It's the day when two months have been completed after the launching of Iran satellite from India – that means today India's RSLV launch vehicle will put Franklin's spacecraft and the mother ship into Mars orbit.

It's going to be the beginning of a historical event for the mankind. It'll decide whether human can get into the club of light-speed travellers. Hitherto it's possible only for the heavenly bodies, angels and other celestial beings.

Franklin's office had been shifted from the date palm processing area into a new underground location, an annexure to Iran Space Agency Centre. The full team has been assembled there and they are in touch with ISRO officials regarding the latest satellite position. There is a live hot line communication link between ISRO and Franklin's office.

Everything is working fine and the commands have been given from ISRO centre for operating the inbuilt rocket motor on the mother-ship spacecraft to inject itself into the Mars orbit from India's rocket launcher.

Ten minutes are required for the signals to reach Mars from Earth – During the initial Mars exploration era, it took almost 10 days for the signals to reach Mars. The mother-ship spacecraft is being tracked by the 32m and 18m diameter antennas of Indian Deep Space Network (IDSN- communication facilities that supports the interplanetary spacecraft missions), that are established at the IDSN campus, Byalalu, Bangalore.

Before reaching the Mars orbit, the speed of the mother-ship spacecraft has to be considerably reduced as per required specifications. If a slight error occurred in its speed, the mother-ship may either fall into Mars atmosphere or escape from Mars orbit and move away into deep outer space beyond our control – in both these situations, we'll lose the mother-ship and along with it Franklin's precious light-speed spacecraft.

The Mars project is passing through critical moments - tension can be seen in the eyes of both the officials at ISRO and the Iran Space Centre.

Everybody is glued to the computer screen. Half an hour passed after the inbuilt rocket motor (named LAM) on the mother-ship spacecraft was operated to insert it into the Mars orbit.

Then, to ease all worries, there came the happy signal that everything is fine and the mother-ship spacecraft has been successfully injected into the Mars orbit.

The news was welcomed with great applause in Iran. The Iran Space agency and concerned government officials congratulated and thanked all the ISRO scientists.

After completing all formalities, Iran govt took over the full control of the mother-ship spacecraft.

The transfer was smooth as there is cordial relation between India and Iran.

After one week, the ISRO Mission Director formally closed all Indian access to the spacecraft as per the contract agreement and informed Iran space agency accordingly.

Now everything is fully under Iran's control. Their monster DSN antennas will control the space probe without the world knowing anything about it.

Franklin, Sam, Mary and the scientists in the team have prepared everything to get ready for the historical moment of testing their spacecraft for light speed travel. Now it is left with just getting the formal go ahead from the Director of Iran Space Agency.

One week elapsed. The team has now all the permissions to conduct the speed test. On a fine day when the position of the mother-ship spacecraft was best accessible from Earth position, Sam gave the signal to eject the disc-shaped spacecraft into outer space away from the Mars orbit.

It'll take 10 minutes for the signal to reach Mars.

That 10 minutes, however seemed like 10 hours while waiting eagerly for the result at the satellite control room.

At last, message has been received confirming that the mother-ship has pushed the disc-shaped spacecraft out of the orbit of Mars and into the deep outer space.

Everybody applauded to hear that the first step is smoothly carried out. Without wasting a minute, Sam gave command to operate the atomic booster motors fitted on the light-speed spacecraft to increase its speed. He then changed the direction and trajectory of the spacecraft towards Earth. This is done to avoid the spacecraft going beyond the reach of Earth antennas after attaining the speed of light.

Now it's again 10 minutes wait to see the result.

Franklin's recorded message was played through speakers in the hall.

"When the atomic booster motors are operated, the disc-shaped spacecraft in outer space will get higher speeds of up to 80 to 90 times the speed of Sound (over 30kms/second). If the spacecraft in the vacuum space achieves that much speed, it'll soon gallop up to the maximum speed possible for an object (that is, the speed of light- 3Lakhs Kms/Second) by virtue of its disc shape and special design excellence – according to Franklin's theory.

"And we're going to witness it today.

"The spacecraft will then fly like a magnetic wave through the curvature of space-time four-dimensional continuum, as per Einstein's theory of relativity. It'll be gliding through the waves of galaxies in the universe, and may tread the royal paths of the gods and angels. Also as the space-time stretches from past to future in a world-line, it could be possible to travel to the past or to the future after you attain the speed of light. These are myths and assumptions. We'll have to attain the capability of light speed travel to authenticate whether time travel is possible or not.

"In 1906, about the same time Albert Einstein announced his special theory of relativity, his former mathematics teacher, Hermann Minkowski, realized that space and time are really part of the same reality, a single geometric object. In a now famous speech Hermann announced that, "The views of space and time which I wish to lay before you have sprung from the soil of experimental physics, and therein lies their strength. They are radical. Henceforth, space by itself, and time by itself, are doomed to fade away into mere shadows, and only a kind of union of the two will preserve an independent reality."

"The relation between space and time will be better understood if you could get up to the speed of light.

"It's now within a matter of time to know whether human can cross the speed of light. If we can achieve that milestone, then it could be possible to travel to another solar system within the time frame of a human life period.

"With the current conventional speed of our spacecrafts, it'll take many thousands of years to reach other planetary systems – which will prevent any such missions to be fruitful due to the reality that an astronomers life is limited to a mere 100 years!

"There may also come some other interesting capabilities when you travel with the speed of light. Once you move with the speed of light, your body will be transformed into energy and won't be affected by aging process, so it's one step closer to immortality-wow!"

While everybody was listening to the amazing facts about travelling at the speed of light. Somebody then said 10 minutes are over, but no signals!

All eyes are at the computer screens searching for the signals from the spacecraft– the signals that'll confirm whether the disc-shaped spacecraft has entered the realm of light speed travel or not.

But alas! No signals came. The spacecraft's position was not behind Mars (the occult period); in such case the signals could be blocked. So, why didn't they receive the signals?

10 minutes, 12 minutes… the time slowly elapsed… The

spacecraft's trajectory could not be tracked so far.

Franklin was very upset; he started walking here and there like a maniac. Did that historic moment just slip away from his hands?!

Signals are sent and received by Deep Space Network antennas fixed at the rooftop of satellite control centre. Among the X-band and Ka-band channels they are using the powerful Ka-band. Also the channel is set to signals amplified mode, so there are no chances of missing the signals coming towards it, if any.

As the full team was utterly confused, something flashed in Sam's mind.

He suggested, "Prof. Franklin, why don't we try changing the bandwidth of the Space Antenna's signal receiver to get light-speed signals?"

There was a sudden unexpected gesture from Franklin. He yelped, "What?!", and grappled Sam's throat viciously.

Franklin was behaving like a lunatic. Sam was taken aback by the sudden reaction from Franklin.

As everybody rushed to the spot, Franklin was actually appreciating Sam by patting on his shoulder.

"You said it, Sam. Oh. God, why didn't I think about it earlier?! Yes, when the spacecraft moves with the speed of light, then we should have kept our antennas in low reception range because signals from spacecraft will be coming at very high speed that time."

He ordered the technical staff to shift to X-band on the space antenna receiver, and then to change the amplified mode to normal mode. But still the signals from the spacecraft evaded them.

Then the team has decided to check the trajectory of the disc-shaped spacecraft through spectroscope test. The most powerful and huge telescope of Iran Space Agency was put into service.

Through the telescope they analyzed all the rays of light coming from Mars towards Earth and also the light rays going back into space from Earth along the supposed trajectory of the spacecraft.

Eureka!

The spectroscope analyzer spotted the spacecraft travelling with the speed of light. It has actually touched down on Earth and reflected back to Mars by that time.

Jitters turned into cheers. Franklin was all smiles and thanked the team members. They all exchanged happiness, and praised God.

Next step was to check the actual speed of the spacecraft through spectroscopy test.

Yes the result confirmed it- the spacecraft is travelling at a speed of 3lakhs Km/second - Exactly the light speed.

So mankind has ACHIEVED it!

Sam soon tried to take control of the spacecraft. He tried to reduce the thrust of the atomic booster motors- (AbM), but there was no effect on the spacecraft's speed. With clever thinking, Sam then switched the AbM motors to the reverse direction. Yes, this time it worked. The spacecraft speed slowly reduced from light-speed and it regained the physical shape from the light beam shape.

So that's it. Human race has cracked the biggest question in astrophysics- achieving light-speed for a spacecraft and then taking it back to physical form by controlled speed reduction.
Franklin's name will be remembered forever for this invention. All the team members praised him for this brilliant achievement.

The door to the interstellar space, the pathway to other solar systems in our galaxy and beyond, has been opened for Homo-Sapiens.

While manoeuvring the spacecraft from light beam to physical form, something struck Sam's mind.
In the Bible and Hindu scriptures, there are several instances of gods or angels come to meet the humans. They come as a sharp light and then transform into a half light and half physical shape form.

That means the 'devas' (gods) might be travelling with the speed of light, and for most part remain in energy form, making them immortals – the great secret of the gods, goddesses and many other divine and semi-divine figures have thus been revealed!

Sam has practiced transforming the spacecraft into light beam and then back into physical shape. When it attains solid shape, the Ka-band channel of the Space Antenna started receiving signals. He kept the spacecraft orbiting around Mars, but away from its gravitational pull.

All amazing things are happening around. All are in a dream land of the Utopian World. It was a marathon experiment trial for everybody…

Almost seven hours has gone since they started the spacecraft test at morning six o'clock. Nobody took food, just had snacks and drinks brought inside the satellite control centre by security guards.

As Sam has gained considerable control in the piloting of the spacecraft, next thought was whether it's possible to bring back the spacecraft to Earth and to Iran. When the spacecraft travels at light speed there is no requirement to make changes to its speed for atmospheric entry into Mars or Earth. That's great advantage because we can save lot of fuel as there is no need to burn extra fuel to further accelerate the spacecraft when it's already in light speed. Also, the spacecraft consumes very less or nil fuel when travelling with the speed of light due to the characteristic of inertia.

Mary asked Sam, "So, if you're bringing the spacecraft to Earth, how much time will it take to reach us?"

Sam replied while concentrating on the control panel, "It'll take 12.5 light minutes, that is, if the spacecraft starts from Mars and travels with the speed of light, it'll reach Earth after 12.5 minutes.

"Once it reaches near our satellite control centre, we'll have to reduce and adjust its speed using AbM motors in such a way that it'll remain in a semi-transparent state or half-physical shape inside a halo of light. What do you say, Prof. Franklin?"

Franklin said in a happy mood, "Inshallah. Let's do the same thing to see what will be the result… Use your piloting ability fully, Sam, to create history."

Mary intervened, "Excuse me, may I add something? If we can bring the spacecraft here and keep it in a semi-static position as Sam said, then can we send a military dog to space and do some experiments?"

Franklin was impressed to hear that. He thanked Mary for her intelligent and imaginative thinking, "What a brilliant idea, Mary!

"We can also send some of your tissue samples of animals to the space. You can watch the biological changes happening to the DNA footprint of those species."

"Exactly, Prof Franklin. I'll prepare some test tubes with the gene pool of animal species. Meanwhile can you please make orders for preparing the military dog for the space travel?"

"It'll be taken care of, Mary. You can now proceed with your work."

"Ok. Prof. Franklin, let me now ask one thing- As you have achieved the speed of light, will it open up more doors towards space-time travel and attaining higher speeds than light and such things?" Mary asked.

"Yeah, exactly…crossing the light speed barrier is the beginning. Now there are more spheres to explore in this timeless universe. We have heard about "warp-drives," "hyperspace," "subspace," etc. in science fiction stories…"

"In Isaac Asimov's Foundation series of science fiction books, the epic tale of the decline and fall of the Galactic Empire, he narrates about an Empire comprising 25 million planets, knit together by sleek spaceships hurtling through the galaxy.

These spaceships are said to cross the vast gulf between the stars by jumping through hyperspace."

Franklin then read a paragraph from the book, *Foundation (Foundation #1)(5):*

"...He (Gaal) had steeled himself just a little for the Jump through hyper-space, a phenomenon one did not experience in simple interplanetary trips. The Jump remained, and would probably remain forever, the only practical method of travelling between the stars. Travel through ordinary space could proceed at no rate more rapid than that of ordinary light (a bit of scientific knowledge that belonged among the items known since the forgotten dawn of human history), and that would have meant years of travel between even the nearest of inhabited systems. Through hyper-space, that unimaginable region that was neither space nor time, matter nor energy, something nor nothing, one could traverse the length of the Galaxy in the interval between two neighboring instants of time....

Gaal had waited for the first of those Jumps with a little dread curled gently in his stomach, and it ended in nothing more than a trifling jar, a little internal kick which ceased an instant before he could be sure he had felt it. That was all...."

After reading that interesting story about hyper-space jump, Franklin further said, "So we'll have to make a bridge between reality and fiction. Let's hope that getting into the club of light speed travel will help us to explore further into travelling at many times faster than the speed of light, and more."

There are 10 minutes left for the spacecraft to reach Earth. After listening to Franklin, Sam observed, "There are rumours that NASA might be in the process of shaping up a spacecraft that will travel faster than the speed of light with the help of Warp Drive or Wormhole concepts..."

"We cannot rule out that possibility. With top class facilities and talented scientists and designers available at hand, NASA could do it. It's just a matter of time. But the Americans would become more oppressive after achieving that milestone," Franklin agreed.

Mary then suggested one important point, "Prof. Franklin, now that you have a wonderful invention at hand, why don't you bargain with America to be nice with Muslim countries. If America is ready to change their policy, you can work with them once again and avail all the facilities at NASA to greatly improve your achievement. Am I wrong?"

"No Mary, you aren't wrong...I appreciate your optimism...But considering the treacherous nature of CIA, we have to be extra cautious while dealing with them...If America can change their policy towards Iran & the Muslim brethren, we can keep that possibility open.

"But at the moment, we have to concentrate and do the spacecraft tests ourselves...God has led us up to this stage, so let's hope that he won't test us anymore...Once we have full control over the spacecraft, we can think of making dialogues with America," Franklin opened his mind.

Sam and Mary were happy to know Franklin's thoughts and his honest nature. Franklin then dispersed the team for some time and Mary went for collecting the DNA samples to be sent on the spacecraft.

BOOK – III

APOCALYPSE IS HERE NOW, BUT NOT BY GOD OR DEVIL

Final Chaos And The Ark Sets Sails For One-Way Journey

"Now the flood was on the Earth forty days. The waters increased and lifted up the ark, and it rose high above the Earth... And all flesh died that moved on the earth: birds and cattle and beasts and every creeping thing that creeps on the earth, and every man."
Genesis 7.17-21

1 IS CLIMATE-CHANGE THE HARBINGER OF APOCALYPSE?

Delegates consisting of scientists, scholars, engineers, sociologists and other experts from all countries have assembled at the UN headquarters to discuss global warming.

The main theme is to discuss ways to save Earth and mankind from an impending disaster in view of the rapid climate change escalation. A climate cell has been opened in the UN office and they used to conduct daily meetings of representatives from world nations. And once in a week the world leaders also addressed the climate conference.

The UN representative has started the dialogue.

"Global warming and climate change have severely affected life on Earth. The vast system of ocean currents has become irregular and affected the Global monsoon periods on all the continents. Global warming has virtually shut down the thermohaline circulation in the North Atlantic Ocean causing irreversible climatic damages in Eastern North America and Western Europe.

Over 60% of world's coral reefs have already been destroyed beyond recovery, and many species of fish have been lost forever.

Glaciers and polar ice have melted in alarming proportions. Arctic sea ice has melted rapidly, further accelerating the climate change. On the West Antarctic Peninsula, massive ice shelves had crumbled into the ocean and the process continues in an alarming scale now.

Deadliest hailstorms, severe droughts, huge Earthquakes, bigger and worst volcano eruptions, famine, flooding, epidemics of huge proportion, large forest fires and such extreme natural calamities have destroyed over 30% of human and animal population in the world. And day by day the situation is becoming worse and worse. Almost half of Earth's surface has become uninhabitable for human and animals - and additional quarter has swallowed by rising oceans. The Korea and its border areas had already become hostile land for living things.

That means Earth is on her deathbed now and she can't sustain the growth of flora and fauna in general. We couldn't avoid the much talked about environmental catastrophe.

This had been predicted by several scientists and writers, in addition to the international scientific and political communities, through various climate forecasts."

The delegates were taking notes and discussing things pointing to news items and reports in their laptops. Everyone looked very anxious.

The delegate from Australia added,
"The Copenhagen Diagnosis, a report authored by 26 leading climate scientists led by the University of New South Wales Climate Research Centre, Australia, had elaborately discussed the devastating effect of climate change induced by CO_2 emission and rise in global temperature. According to the scientists in the Copenhagen Diagnosis, some tipping points will be crossed before they are recognized if we continue to wait for higher levels of scientific certainty on global warming and climate change. The objective of these climate scientists was to update the world on findings since the publication of the UN's Intercontinental Panel on Climate Change Assessment Report.

"The Copenhagen Diagnosis proved correct as we didn't recognise the crossing of a few socio-ecological tipping points in the climate system that created huge instability in our environment.

This has led to the present outbreak of severe climate change and its devastating consequences.

"In a Reuters article published in 2015, engineer and science writer David Auerbach had elaborately written about catastrophic climate change, taking inspiration from a doom prediction made by the Australian microbiologist Frank Fenner that declining food and water and worsening climate change mean the human race's days are numbered once we reach 2100."

Most of the participants affirmed the Australian delegate's points regarding the nonrecognition of the climate tipping points.

A senior professor from Pennsylvania State University got up to discuss the issue further. The conference went on like a roundtable meeting. Anybody can start a discussion and people can intervene to ask questions or to air their objection.

The Professor said, "Climate researcher David Archer, who used to write for the Nature magazine, had warned us about the serious issue of C02 emissions from fossil fuels. He was of the opinion that only about 75% of the C02 emitted from burning a single tonne of coal or oil today would be absorbed over a few centuries by the oceans and vegetation, and around 25% of it would still be lingering in the atmosphere in 1,000 years, and 10% still remaining and impacting the climate in 100,000 years time. That means several thousands of years needed for fully absorbing this harmful CO2 emission through the natural climate cycle.

"A research paper about unstoppable ice collapse in West Antarctic Ice Sheet (WAIS), co-authored by Rob DeConto, of the University of Massachusetts at Amherst, and David Pollard, of Pennsylvania State University had been published in 2016, in the journal Nature. The two scientists, in the paper, warned that if we didn't take remedial measures, the unabated greenhouse gas emissions for a few more decades could result in sea-level rise of over 3 feet from WAIS by the end of 21st century. Massive chunks of ice would also melt from Greenland and mountain glaciers, and considering this with continuous melt from Antarctica, things would go beyond any human control which would result in sea levels rise of over 50 feet!

"But nobody took those warnings seriously, or better say, no one wanted to compromise their modern-day luxurious life styles.

As individuals, nobody bothered about the solutions given by scientists for the question, what is the one best thing everyone could do to slow down climate change? And as Nations, no country took substantive remedial measures as suggested by environmentalists related to the question, what is the best politically realistic approach to slowing climate change?

Global warming is created by our own wrong doings and resource mismanagement, and now we'll have to bear the brunt of the venom it spits through the climate change."

Next, the Chinese delegate initiated a debate.

"The disastrous impact of climate change has psychologically affected the human species as a whole. Civilization, culture, social behaviour etc. have been redefined in societies due to these new developments in the eco system and human life cycle imposed by catastrophic climate change... International law and treaties between nations have become ineffective. A breakdown is visible in the global economic systems. Things have gone similar to the situation in primitive human era. The powerful and mighty started taking over control.

"There was huge money deposited in the United States and European countries by our Chinese establishments and Middle East nations, which has become the bone of contention now.

"The US and their allies say they won't return the cash as they suffer from large scale national calamities. But we can't agree to that as we also suffer from huge losses incurred by climate change. We'll have to take stringent measures if the Americans and the Europeans do not follow international laws."

A US representative objected to the Chinese remarks. It has resulted in hot talks and threatening by both the parties.

The Marshals quickly interfered and asked the delegates to keep quiet. There were tight security arrangements made in the conference hall as the organisers know that tensions can arise at any moment between contending nations.

As the crisis loomed, some feared a third world war could erupt at any time.

The Indian delegate was the next to talk.

"In view of the climate threat, thousands of people have already moved to Mars through space shuttle services provided by America, Russia, China and India for their Mars colonization projects. They had signed for one-way journey – that means those people are ready to face the fact that they will never return to Earth. My appeal is to request all concerned to keep decorum and observe nonviolence in Mars colonies.

"We're watching that borders of the countries have almost become obsolete. Global political instability has risen to its highest level these days. People have fled from hostile areas and started living in open areas by erecting tents as used by the gypsies. Everybody expected that the apocalypse may come and the world is about to end- it can happen at any moment.

"One group of scientists predicts huge changes to Earth's equilibrium and lean in its axis as the arctic ice is melting in huge volumes. When vast chunks of ice cubes from the poles begin melting and move into oceans, the existing ratio of land and sea will drastically change and this will destabilize the tectonic plates. The outcome will be unpredictable- there can be massive disasters.

"Earthquakes, tsunamis, avalanches and volcanic eruptions occur as the geology is altered and it started shaking the Earth from its very own foundation."

While things were becoming gloomy as each day progressed, there was a secret meeting planned at the CIA office. The agenda was to discuss about the Milky Way Mission, and the commandos, Sam and Mary currently in Iran. VVIPs were present in the meeting as usual.

The Secretary of Defence, White House Chief of Staff, Joint Chiefs of Staff of U.S. Department of Defence, NASA Administrator, and the CIA Director were the participants.

The Secretary of Defence first asked, " What's the latest news about Mission Milky-Way (MMW) and the commandos in Iran? The President wants to know if there is any hope at all."

CIA Director promptly replied, "We have to assume that Prof. Franklin's discovery related experiments have not found result yet. Commando Mary managed to send one SMS to her parents a couple of weeks ago.

"It said that her research is still ongoing and it'll take some more time to complete. We can interpret it as an indirect message to us, as she can't directly send any message to us from Iran due to security reasons."

"That means if we conduct an aerial attack on Iran as planned earlier, it may not help much as the research is still in progress," said Joint Chiefs of Staff of U.S. Department of Defence.

NASA Administrator and CIA Director also agreed to that point. If breakthrough is achieved in their experiments, then the commandos will somehow inform us or they'll plan an operation to hijack the discovery with a do or die attempt as per the orders given to them. A premature attack from the part of US Military could spoil the great discovery also.

Again, as climate change has clipped the wings of humankind and made life almost impossible on Earth, it's not sure if they can carry out such advanced tests now to achieve the speed of light! They may not get sufficient time also for that.

These were the common feelings and thought process expressed by everybody in the meeting. Nobody had recommended a negotiation with Iran as there was never any progress in diplomatic relations with them – otherwise United States and Iran could have collaborated with the spacecraft project.

NASA Administrator then highlighted the plight of humans as natural animals.

He said, "Not only Iran, almost all world countries are now looking at one another with suspicious eyes and hatred. Seeing all the horrific natural calamities, all are worried about how to save themselves, so no time to worry about others!

"Morality, social cause, humanity, world piece and such words have become just ornamental things- nobody cared really. So, when the final destruction of the world is nearing, humans will also act just like animals – they simply become a part of the food chain as far as survival instinct is concerned. So that's all about our humanitarian thinking, kindness, virtues etc. – all meaningless words when you see death in front of you!

When the discussions were over, the Secretary of Defence concluded,

"Ok, I'll report the matter to the US President. And also let's wait for any messages from the commandos in Iran to move further. However, there are chances that the President may order an aerial commando attack and recovery mission anytime in Iran. If we can get hold of Franklin and his thesis and bring him here, then there could be some hope – some of President's advisers think so! That means, be prepared for some sudden orders accordingly from the top."

2 WILL THE ARK FLOAT SAFELY?

At the Satellite Control Centre in Iran, Sam checked the controls and signals to manoeuvre the spacecraft on Mar's orbit so as to bring it all the way down to Earth, the way Franklin has desired.

Sam was utilizing his full piloting abilities to experiment on the disc-shaped spacecraft. Once the spacecraft attains the speed of light, it received the signals from the control centre within seconds as compared to the time of 10 minutes or above as required for normal satellites orbiting around Mars.

Sam changed the direction of the spacecraft and turned it towards Earth.

As it was moving with the speed of light, the spacecraft would reach the concrete terrace above their satellite control centre within 12.5 minutes.

All arrangements were made on the terrace to receive the spacecraft, and all are now waiting with great interest and anxiousness at the control centre.

There's a very high compound wall around the space centre, so no outsiders will be able to watch the spacecraft coming. Moreover, there's no residential area near to that place so it remained almost a deserted spot.

Mary and Franklin went to the terrace to watch the spacecraft while Sam and other team members controlled the spacecraft from inside the space centre. Mary talked to Sam via intercom from the terrace. She had a box of DNA samples and the military dog ready for sending to space.

Around 7 minutes passed after Sam started the spacecraft from Mars and that means now around 6 minutes left for it to reach Earth.

Suddenly Mary thought about getting affected by radiation from the spacecraft as it used atomic energy and was coming directly from outer space with the speed of light.

Mary and Franklin ran fast and went into the space centre via the lift. They quickly wore the space suit and helmet, and came back to the terrace.

Now only 2 minutes are there for the spacecraft to arrive if everything goes as per the book.

Sam slowly reduced the speed of the spacecraft by adjusting the power of the AbM motors.

Mary and Franklin could hear Sam's countdown calls via the intercom. 50 seconds, 40, 30, 20, 10 seconds.... They saw some vague light ball coming from the sky.

Wow, it has now reached above their head.

As Sam reversed the thrusters and slowly reduced the speed of AbM motors, the spacecraft gradually assumed its disc shape and stood just above them within a light halo! How amazing!

As per Franklin's voice messages and directions via the intercom, Sam brought the spacecraft very near to them and opened its doors. Mary climbed a ladder, and put the DNA box and the military dog inside the human capsule of the spacecraft. She came back to Franklin's side and gave the all OK signal to Sam.

Sam has a difficult job ahead. Now the spacecraft's speed has to be increased rapidly to attain the speed of light and move ahead.

That's a critical situation as the spacecraft can explode or any other damages could occur while suddenly changing the speed into maximum.

Sam asked Franklin and Mary to come back from the terrace to be at safe distance.

Sam prayed to God and began increasing the speed of AbM motors from idling to max speed. The thrusters are accelerated to max speed and simultaneously the grid fins/speed breakers are adjusted for drag reduction. And then, like a fighter pilot crossing transonic speed, Sam tuned the AbM motors into maximum power and behold, the spacecraft lifted straight upwards, attained light speed and disappeared.

Everyone stood up and cheered, and looked towards the sky to say prayers to God almighty - without His consent nothing would have been possible.

And going to Mars again, this time with a solid purpose...

The most important thing at that time was the fact that the military dog and DNA samples are inside the spacecraft. Within 11 minutes, the spacecraft reached Mars. After moving around Mars for three times, Sam directed the spacecraft towards Jupiter, the gas giant in the solar system.

The dust and other foreign particles present in the deep space don't put considerable drag on the spacecraft as it travels with the speed of light. The spacecraft will continue to move through space at light speed without using its motor power due to the factor of inertia. So fuel usage is not any botheration.

That's the most unexpected trump card they got from the trial runs. What a critical bonus point! A grave concern of carrying massive quantities of fuel for journeys involving thousands of years along the golden valleys of Milky Way galaxy in search of inhabitable planets is thus solved.

Jupiter was close to Mars in its trajectory that time. So the spacecraft reached its vicinity within 15 minutes. A normal spacecraft with conventional speed of 50 mach would have taken a whopping 5-years' voyage over 2.8 billion-kilometres to reach Jupiter from Earth.

Getting a light-speed spacecraft to mankind today is like getting a bullet train to the Stone Age man that would have tremendously changed the scope of their lives.

Humans can now gallop and advance their civilization so fast into the Star Age.

The spacecraft orbited Jupiter for three times. While the spacecraft was moving towards Jupiter through deep space under Sun's gravitational pull, Sam practised few steps and trials to perfectly handle the spacecraft. All the flight data and other info are being recorded at the space control centre in Iran for further studies and research.

Their plan was to keep the military dog and DNA box at the speed of light for over one hour in the deep vacuum of interplanetary space. This way they can check whether any physical changes would happen to the dog and the DNA samples.

There are provisions for continuous Oxygen supply and temperature controls inside the human capsule where the DNA samples and the military dog are kept.

The team also checked through spectroscope light analysis, and found that the space dog is in safe condition.

Soon the spacecraft returned from Jupiter.

While taking the spacecraft back, it suddenly struck their mind that many people from different countries had gone to Mars for permanent settlement. So they thought it would be better to land on Mars and directly see the people and the settlements there. It will also be a vital landing practice for the spacecraft.

By virtue of its light speed travel, there are not much complications or speed adjustments needed for the spacecraft to enter the atmosphere of Mars and land on its surface.

However, the team decided not to land on Mars at that time because if somebody notices the spacecraft in physical form, the news could reach America.

The U.S. will then try to attack Iran and hijack the discovery. As they are in the initial stage of testing the spacecraft, it's better to avoid a confrontation with the U.S. government.

After entering Mars atmosphere, the spacecraft moved towards the area where the human settlements are seen. It travelled and roamed over the location in light speed. The cameras fitted on the spacecraft took images of the first Martian village. People were staying in radiation-proof tents.

The Mars villages looked like a colony or refugee camp. The settlers are adventurous and brave people, some of them were rich in their motherland. They paid huge amounts of money to settle on Mars. As hundreds of people are daily dying on Earth due to natural calamities, they thought it's better to escape into Mars. But their life fully depended on the supplies of food, medicines and other essential commodities coming from Earth.

The organizations handling their contract had agreed to provide food and other supplies. It'll continue till some steps are taken to cure the Martian land and do agriculture there to make the colonies self sufficient in food procurement.

After observing the colonies for a while, the spacecraft was redirected to Earth. Sam has become an expert in remotely controlling the spacecraft. He's doing all spacecraft manoeuvring with ease and in full control.

Only thing then left for Sam is to get inside the spacecraft and pilot it. That would be another turning point and very dangerous phase of the mission. But before that they have to check the bodily changes to the military dog sent on the spacecraft. If it is satisfactory, then only Sam could try.

The spacecraft is being returned to space control centre in Iran, and Franklin and Mary went to the terrace to receive it. They are wearing space suit and helmet which could reduce the light intensity of the spacecraft splashing the eyes when kept in semitransparent form.

As they waited on the terrace, Sam spoke through intercom that the spacecraft is approaching to land. Soon a light ball appeared above them with bright red light. After reaching close to the terrace surface, it transformed into semi-transparent form inside a bright halo.

When Franklin gave clearance, Sam opened the front door of the spacecraft. Mary looked inside the human capsule for the military dog and the DNA box. She got astonished not to see the dog anywhere inside the human capsule. She called Franklin and they both checked thoroughly inside and took out the DNA box. They informed Sam and the team about the missing dog, which is going to be another puzzle to solve.

Sam guided the spacecraft to light speed and gave commands for it to orbit the Earth. He put the spacecraft in autopilot and joined others who have gathered in the conference room to discuss the latest developments. The disappearance of the military dog really took everybody by surprise. They argued every possibility for a viable explanation. Time is very limited for them to complete the spacecraft project- any obstacles on the way could hinder the timely completion of the mission.

The consequences of climate change happening on Earth can affect their mission any time by damaging the installations or inflicting casualties.

Any issues have to be sorted out at the earliest. The Earth could explode or turn into a barren land like Venus in the aftermath of extreme climate change. And that's not something which will happen only in the distant future.

If they couldn't complete the experiments and make the project ready for manned space voyage very fast, then all their efforts so far could go in vain. It's a do-or-die mission- a last resort to escape from Earth before the apocalypse or the end of the world comes. But they put everything in their belief on God almighty with whose willingness only they could to reach up to this stage...

So He will allow them to complete the rest of the project too...

The love of God towards the living beings on Earth is well known. The great flooding and His hand in helping Noah to make the ark and save life on Earth is the specimen example for that...

Now as climate change has become an irreversible destructive force, only the light speed spacecraft can transport life from Earth into another inhabitable planet deep inside the Milky Way galaxy.

Franklin and team have discussed all possibilities leading to the disappearance of the military dog.

Franklin said, "The dog might have moved from the human capsule into the main capsule of the spacecraft while travelling at the speed of light. And it might have been converted into energy form due to light speed travel."

Sam supported the point. "Yes, it's possible. There is an emergency passage from human capsule to the main capsule for escape in case of fire or other emergencies. It might have opened due to some false alarm or the dog might have applied pressure on the handle and the fire exit might have opened by itself."

So, they checked the spacecraft thoroughly through the spectroscope. After analyzing the light emissions from the spacecraft they could conclude that there is the presence of military dog inside the main capsule. But they could not guess its present condition, whether it's alive or not because everything inside main capsule is in ionised form.

To change the physical state of the dog, they will have to bring the spacecraft down to Earth and land on the terrace. When spacecraft attains full physical state, the dog will also be converted into physical form. But the team is not sure about the result of landing the spacecraft on Earth. So far they have kept the spacecraft above the ground in semi-transparent state only.

Then Mary suggested one thing. "Can we ask the dog trainer to get inside the spacecraft and open its emergency exit from human capsule so that the dog may come out?"

Franklin liked the idea. He said, "That's very smart thinking, Mary. We will have to do something to break this deadlock. We're not sure if the trainer will agree but we will ask him. There are no other solutions coming to mind this time.

"The first option of landing the spacecraft can be more troublesome. If we land it here, there is a chance that it may lose its ability to transform into light speed again. We'll have to prove it by conducting a landing practice on Mars. Otherwise the outcome could be disastrous. If we land it here and suppose the spacecraft failed to lift up vertically and attain the speed of light. That could be the end of our mission.

"We'll have to start everything from the beginning in such a disastrous takeoff failure situation. We need to again make a mother-ship spacecraft to carry our disc-shaped spacecraft, and probably need the help of India again to launch it into Mar's orbit. Can't think of the situation again. And probably the time factor also may not favour us."

So they contacted the dog trainer and told him about the matter. He is a thorough military man and was ready to do anything for his country when he came to know that the project is directly under the orders of the President of the Islamic Republic of Iran. Moreover, he also loved his dog very much, and is ready to try all possibilities to save it.

All the controls, switches and gauges inside the human capsule are also available in the satellite control room. They have shown everything in the control panel to the dog trainer so he will have a feel of it. They also showed him the fire exit door and its handle on the computer screen where live view of the spacecraft is available. The pilot's seat inside has a hook where a cable has to be tied and the other end of the cable to be attached to the dog trainer's body before attempting to open the exit door to main capsule.

That was a precautionary measure not to be sucked into the main capsule and convert into energy form when the exit door is opened.

That time an idea sparked in Franklin's mind. The dog trainer is ready to take risk and all are planning for any eventuality, so why not try to further explore the things by taking the dog trainer for one or two rotations around Earth. It'll be a matter of an additional few minutes, but a great trial for the mission.

Everybody agreed to Franklin's suggestion and thought it's a fantastic plan. Human testing of the spacecraft mission thus has come in an unexpected way, and much earlier; even before the team has sorted out a plan for the matter.

Sam didn't hide his happiness. He yelped, "That's brilliant. By sending the dog trainer inside the spacecraft for a few minutes of trial run, we can also check the functionality of the controls and levers inside the human capsule. This will also be a serviceability check for the operation of emergency exit door."

As everybody agreed to the critical experiment, Sam gave a little bit of training to the dog trainer who came from Iran police. Sam showed him how to operate the speed control switch and lever for AbM motors at the control panel placed in the satellite control room. Same switch and lever will be there inside the human capsule of the spacecraft.

While travelling in the spacecraft, dog trainer should operate the switch and lever when a green light blinks on the front control panel, and a message appears on the screen saying, "Controls Transferred to Spacecraft from Ground Station."

That time he should move the AbM switch on the front panel to upward direction (for ON) and move the lever 1cm forward from centre mark, then count up to 10 and bring it back to the centre mark.

Next step is to move the lever 1cm backwards, count up to 10, and bring it back to the centre position. Sam made the dog trainer practise it two-three times at the control room. Sam also wrote the procedure on a piece of paper and gave it to the dog trainer.

Then Franklin and Mary took the dog trainer to the terrace. All three were wearing the space suit and helmet. Sam brought back the spacecraft above the head level and it assumed semi-transparent shape as usual.

Mary briefed the dog trainer what to do if he feels suffocation or tiredness while flying in the spacecraft. She also gave him some capsules to reduce BP and for other symptoms of tension.

Mary then helped the dog trainer to get inside the spacecraft by mounting on the ladder. After he tightened the seat belt, Franklin gave ok message to Sam. The spacecraft then lifted up vertically and after reaching around 10 feet high, it transformed into a ray of light and disappeared.

3 THE FLOOD BEGAN AMID A LIGHT-RAY OF HOPE

Earth's temperature has risen around three degree Celsius and the sea level has been affected with a rise of over five meters.

Many islands and cities have gone under seawater. The world witnessed an unprecedented flow of refugees across the globe.

This forced displacement of societies has created emotional trauma and struggles in the affected countries. As major portion of the coral reefs have disappeared, many fish species also vanished.

Tempests, huge hurricanes and tsunamis have become regular events at seashores.

When the Himalayan glaciers started melting dangerously, there occurred heavy casualties due to natural disasters in the Indian Subcontinent. Many dams and water reservoirs have collapsed, resulting in huge flooding and loss of lives and property.

Some geologists suspected that the massive Earthquakes, flash floods and landslides in unison with polar ice melting might have affected the spontaneous rotation of Earth in its axis.

A UN summit was organized in Ney York to discuss this grave situation.

Even though all the Nations in the world started forming separate alliances to adjust to the new world order, everybody agreed to stay united in the efforts to save Earth.

All have signed to drastically reduce man-made greenhouse gas emissions, and resort to renewable energy though the result at this stage is uncertain. We have crossed a few critical tipping points resulting in irreversible damages to the climate system.

Electricity power production has cut short due to heavy damages. Travelling by air, sea and land has largely limited to emergencies and goods transportation… Operation of thermal power plants and use of electrical devices in homes and commercial buildings, such as air conditioners, heaters and domestic appliances have been minimized. Deforestation has stopped.

All these factors have contributed to the large scale reduction of CO2 emission. But nobody is sure whether this will help reduce global warming and its destructive effects. Many scientists think that a climate-change related chain reaction has already started and it can't be stopped now. Earth looked like a ship slowly sinking in the Milky Way galactic Ocean.

Heads of state of their respective countries used to conduct aerial surveys to fathom the devastation caused by climate change. Natural disasters have its heavy toll on humans and animals. You can find carcasses of animals heaped at many places…hospitals and government machinery are not functioning properly due to lack of infrastructure and other facilities.

Road transportation is not possible at several places as roads were washed away due to floods and landslides. Many cities were deserted and every place now looks like war torn areas. Media don't report anything due to censoring. It's like emergency rule in almost all countries around the world.

The USA, Russia, China, India and European Union conducted space shuttle services to carry people who want to go to Mars. Enormous sums were levied as fee, but many people still signed the agreement. They sold all their properties and everything else to go to Mars, knowing very well that it's a one-way ticket, and they will never return to their homeland.

An unexpected thing that happened during this chaotic situation was the rise of suicide squads in every country. People who can't witness the end of the World join hands to form groups consisting of thousands of members. The doctor members in the group help the individuals to die peacefully. Hundreds are dying daily in this way as governments have no control over these suicide groups.

That was the general doomsday mood prevailing everywhere...

People are ready to go to Mars seeing such a hostile scenario on Earth. Only rich people could afford to go to Mars...and even their lives were not without risk.

The breakthrough in extracting water from the rock formations in Mars was a decisive factor in colonizing the red planet. There were efforts to increase the atmospheric temperature so that the polar ice will melt and give rise to the shaping of lakes and rivers.

If it's successful, Mars will have plenty of water for the human colonies of all countries. Atomic reactors will be deployed to create chemical factories which will pump out different types of gases including CO2 into the atmosphere aimed at eventually increasing the surface temperature.

Without water, living in Mars for those many people would not have been possible. Still there will be several obstacles for the Martians and nobody knows if the concept of permanently living in Mars will be successful.

Experiments were conducted on war footing to grow vegetables in Mars. Once they have water there, it could be possible to plant vegetable gardens.

The U.S. and its allies and also important world leaders such as Russia, India and China had funded for making Mars an Earth like friendly planet. Martian soil at that time was not good for plant growth. It's affected by Sun's radiation and the soil was not fertile. They'll have to process the soil to make it healthy.

The plan to release huge quantities of Oxygen from Iron oxide in the mineral stones is ongoing. The oxygen will support bacteria growth in the soil and make it fertile. If huge quantities of oxygen could be freed into the atmosphere, it would help to create an artificial Ozone layer. Once the Ozone layer assumes significant size, it'll stop harmful radiation from the Sun.

Even though elaborate plans are being made, the Martian colonies at the moment are fully dependent on supplies from Earth for all food items.

People are living in special tents constructed to live safely on Mars. Some are living in natural caves inside the rocks. There is a high risk of getting affected by radiation as Mars doesn't have a strong atmosphere. You won't be able to go outside without space suit.

Some key decisions were made in the UN meet conducted in New York. A secret contingency plot was made for the safety of the heads of all countries assembled there, including America, Britain, Australia and Europe. In case of a massive disaster happening here, all those leaders will escape into Mars!

As China has warned the US and European states to face consequences if their huge investment in those countries are not returned, a secret meeting of the leaders of US, Europe and Australia was also held in the sidelines of the UN submit.

They all agreed to annihilate China with a massive multipronged nuclear attack. Nobody in the world will have the power to object to it at this critical juncture of world disaster.

There was also another reason for them to take this aggressive step towards China.

In the colonization of Mars, China stands well ahead of all the other countries. They already captured most suitable and key areas on Mars and exported most number of their citizens and equipment there. They are building a red army there with huge weapons stockpile.

It was clear to America and other world leaders that China will be the super cop and unchallenged power centre in Mars.

The US and Europeans however praised India which is one step ahead of China in Mars exploration, but remained peaceful with all the nations of the world.

Indians are not aggressive like China and not a threat to America and its allies, but China is dangerous. They won't hesitate to attack the U.S. as threatened.

So everybody in that secret meeting agreed to send missiles and remove China from the world map at a suitable time in the near future!

With the latest developments, the U.S. President has also decided to conduct an aerial attack on Iran to capture the runaway scientist and his discoveries, if any. They don't have the time to wait for the commandos to do the operation. A high level team was set up to plan and manage attacks on China and Iran.

As things were looking quite gloomy on Earth, there was a light ray of hope building up in Iran. Franklin's spacecraft was getting air tested very secretly. If they succeed in flying the spacecraft with light-speed fully under control, it could at least carry the precious life from Earth into some distant planet.

One day, Franklin and his spacecraft team were discussing future plans.

Franklin started a dialogue, "Counting on the innumerable number of Sun-like stars in the Milky Way galaxy, scientists believe that there could be several planets similar to Earth. Some of those planets would have fully developed atmosphere and plenty of water resources, and even plants and trees! They will be just waiting for some advanced species like humans to land there."

"Just think about those stars we see on a clear night sky. All of them have planets, so we can just hope that at least a handful of them will be suitable to take the DNA footprints of different forms of life on Earth and evolving them into various species of flora and fauna on their soil, " Mar said.

Whenever they get free time they used to discuss matters related to religious faith, astrophysics, cloning etc. The entire team are fans of black tea, and they find it encouraging to discuss things while sipping hot tea.

The technical head Hatoum Mustafa expressed his view about the Universe. "Considering that this Universe is created and run by the omnipotent and omniscient God, we can assume that Earth won't be the only planet where life exists.

As you know our Sun is an average star in the Milky Way galaxy. There are countless stars in our galaxy alone... and think, there are countless galaxies also.

In this situation it's quite reasonable to ask: if god created life only on Earth, what for he made those innumerable stars like our sun in this vast universe?

The omniscient and omnipotent God knows everything and can do anything. If he just wanted life forms on Earth, then it would have been sufficient to just make our solar system only, not a universe of this enormous size."

"So, what are you aiming for?" Franklin asked.

"I just want to affirm that, this way, logically we can say that God has created the universe in its present state for some purpose," Hatoum revealed his thoughts.

The other team members rarely expressed their opinions. They find the discussions as a University lecture, and were happy to get informed.

Sam narrated his impressions, "There will be more activities going on in other parts of our galaxy and the rest of the universe, which is beyond our scope to imagine; only the omnipresent God knows.

"Being a super intelligent person, God will just get bored with managing the flora and fauna of a little planet like Earth. He will need thousands, if not millions, of Earths and heavens with complex life verities to govern, utilising his infinite mental resourcefulness and limitless creativity.

"Due to this reasoning, we can say that all is not lost even if our world would go to pieces tomorrow. We can always search and find another suitable place to live in this universe. However, we need to conquer the light barrier to know all those things."

Mary initiated another point, "Everything depends on Franklin's light-ray machine which could carry the genes of all the important life forms on Earth to far away shores of Milky Way. If a world-ending catastrophe occurs on Earth, Franklin's spacecraft will be the only hope for transplanting life forms from Earth to the rest of the world.

"Through the story of Noah's ark, God had once shown his kindness for preserving Earth's creatures even though they were mired in sin. God still loves his creation and let's hope that he'll order somebody to create another ark to save life when the doomsday dawns in our modern day world.

"When the most important species on Earth, the human beings, polluted it beyond regeneration, we can expect a massive demolition in the offing as happened during Noah's days."

Franklin further elaborated Mary's points. "In Noah's time, the destruction was through a gigantic flood, and in our modern day, it'll be something else more devastating as man can survive floods and famine etc. in this scientifically advanced age. So if there occurs some misfortune leading to the apocalyptical destruction, God has several homes in those faraway star worlds where he can accommodate specimen samples of gene pools carried from Earth.

"The voyage to another Earth through years of space travel will not be achieved like a cakewalk. It's going to be a hazardous journey, but human beings are very adventurous and can withstand hardships."

"Even though we do wrongs and mistakes that may lead us to this predicament, we'll get a chance to make amendments. There are plenty of resources available in the Universe which we would utilise to grow great many civilisations and generations of human and other species on new destinations," Mary remarked optimistically.

"Even if it's a hope, at least let's hope so." Everybody said in a chorus.

4 MARS LANDER

After sending the dog trainer for air test on the spacecraft, Franklin and his team at the satellite control room counted the seconds in tense silence, waiting for the spacecraft to return. When the spacecraft has gone around the Earth twice, Sam transferred the controls to the spacecraft dashboard (instrument panel) for the dog trainer to handle it as instructed.

Sam found out that dog trainer has responded rightly. He did everything as guided – increased and decreased the speed once and then transferred back the control to the satellite control centre in Iran. The spacecraft operation was normal while the dog trainer was handling it. All data and the operation of AbM motors were perfect. Control transfer was smooth. Everybody was happy to know about the fruitful outcome.

After the spacecraft has rotated Earth four times, Franklin decided to bring it back. Sam has operated the controls and directed the spacecraft towards their satellite control centre. Franklin and Mary waited at the terrace. Spacecraft came and halted just above the ground. Mary opened the door and saw the dog trainer sitting happily there. As Mary and Franklin directed, he tied one end of a cable to the seat and the other end on to his waist belt. As everybody looked eagerly, the dog trainer slowly opened the Emergency Exit Door to the main capsule. The exit path was like a corridor separating human capsule and main capsule with non-return valves on both ends.

When the exit door opened, there emerged a fireball from the main capsule. The dog trainer quickly closed the door and turned towards the ball of red light. As it entered the human capsule, lo, it transformed into the missing military dog.

The team wondered what was happening. Soon the dog trainer, his dog and the DNA box were taken to the medical lab at the satellite control centre.

And the team assembled in the conference hall to discuss the new developments.

"What happened to the military dog?" Mary asked Franklin. But he didn't even hear that question. As everybody curiously looks at Franklin, he is searching something on his laptop video footage – looks like he's contemplating seriously on the air test, so nobody wanted to disturb him…

After sometime, Franklin, looking at his computer screen, clapped in a hysterical mood.

He said in a very excited tone, "After a great discovery, we have now stumbled upon another equally important turning point in science. Just like a lifeless object, a living thing also gets transformed into energy while travelling with the speed of light. However, the living being doesn't lose its life while turning into a state of energy form, and also they can come back to the physical form without any possible difficulties.

"We can explain this energy transformation through Albert Einstein's Theory of Relativity which says that Mass, Energy and Time are inter related. Energy can neither be created nor destroyed. It can transform from one form into another form, and can return back to the original form without any loss. So, that's what happened to the military dog in our space experiment.

"Now let's wait for the medical report of the military dog- I think it may bring one more surprise piece of information."

"What's that," all of them asked at a time.

"Let the medical report come, and we'll come to know," Franklin didn't break the suspense.

Sam then demanded everybody's attention to the matter of landing the spacecraft on ground. If they made it to land on the terrace there, it could be a very risky affair. At the moment the spacecraft is hovering in the air by reducing its velocity little bit to come down from light speed travel and then maintaining a steady balance in semi-transparent form. If we land it on the ground, it'll come into full physical form and may lose its capacity to accelerate again into the sphere of light speed.

So, they have decided to try the landing on Mars. In Mars, the advantage is that even if the spacecraft failed to take off after landing, they can utilise the service of the mother ship spacecraft orbiting around Mars. In an emergency situation, the mother ship can land on Mars and lift up the disc-shaped spacecraft into the space and eject it into outer space. The spacecraft can then accelerate into light-speed travel with the help of AbM motors. However, we'll have a problem then to find out why the spacecraft can't rise straight up into the air after landing on ground and transform to light speed travel from there.

As per the plan, Sam took the spacecraft to Mars controlling remotely from the satellite control centre. There is plenty of fuel left with the spacecraft.

Very less quantity of fuel had been consumed because the spacecraft was travelling with the speed of light all the time. However, orders have been given to the Iran Space Agency for the production of two liquid fuel tanks and motors, additional thrusters, one more AbM motor and a few solar chargers to be fitted on the spacecraft. With these additional fuel sources and the solar power unit, the spacecraft will be able to travel thousands of years into deep space without fuel replenishment.

After 15 minutes of travel, the disc-shaped spacecraft reached Mars and orbited it once. It then established electronic communication and signals connection with the mother ship spacecraft already there on Mars orbit.

Next, Sam took the spacecraft down to Mars' atmosphere and into its surface. A spot was selected away from the colonies of Mars residents for the spacecraft to land on the Martian surface. First the spacecraft was brought to the standstill semi-transparent form 15 ft above the ground level. Then three thrusters (motors) were operated in reverse direction to allow the spacecraft to slowly and steadily move downwards. It's a very difficult operation and a risky one too. If something goes wrong, the spacecraft may fall down sharply and break its sensitive instruments.

Next step was to lower the landing gear with wheels. Everything went smoothly. Sam slowly allowed the spacecraft to drop height...but before it could touch down, suddenly some misfortune happened from an unexpected corner.

A tempest came like a bolt from the blue. The dust storm was so quick to arise, and the cameras could not pick it up early. Dust started rising and it won't take much time before the whole area will be submerged in dust, that's the case with Martian storms.

Something has to be done urgently. Signals are not reaching the spacecraft effectively due to the dust cloud. The spacecraft was tilting and started moving here and there due the wind power. Everybody in the satellite control room was crying and shouting, "Do something. Oh, God, Do Something..."

Sam acted very fast. He withdrew the landing gear by moving the lever from Down to Up and Off position. Then the thrusters, which were working in the reverse direction, were turned to the forward direction. Now the spacecraft is not fully visible in the computer screen. Dust particles are seen everywhere. There is only a few seconds left before the storm will engulf the spacecraft and then no signals will reach it.

Without losing hope and not wasting a second, Sam accelerated the AbM motors to full power. Next second the spacecraft was not at all visible on the computer screen and there was only the sandstorm. Was there occurred a slight delay for the AbM motors to boost up into full power? If so, it could be tragedy for the mission. If the sand storm came after landing, then they would have surely lost the spacecraft because once it's changed into full physical form, it'll take 10 minutes for the signals to reach it.

About 2 minutes passed without getting any signals from the spacecraft. Nail biting moments passed by - everybody felt too anxious during those most overwhelming period.

Did the dust storm spoil their dreams and cut their wings to stop them flying to the galaxies?!

And the spacecraft appeared on the screen all of a sudden. Ah, everybody breathed a sigh of relief! They prayed and thanked God almighty.

The spacecraft had flown several kilometres away from Mars because there was no time to turn its direction after the AbM motors were operated and the signals faded. But there was no issue as it was within their signal reach area. Sam straightaway changed the spacecraft's direction towards Mars. Once again it took an orbit around Mars.

Sam checked the serviceability of the thrusters, AbM motors and all controls– thank god, the spacecraft is safe. So they decided to do another attempt to land on Mars. This time they have selected a place not very far from the colonies. The residential place was selected because there are fewer chances of dust storms. The place is surrounded by large hills and rock formation.

Sam has aligned the light speed spacecraft with mother ship spacecraft in direct communication line. The spacecraft was then taken down to land on the selected spot on Mars. Same steps were repeated from a height of 15 ft as done in the first attempt to land.

The thrusters were operating in reverse direction to avoid freefall. Sam lowered the landing gear with wheels and the spacecraft slowly touched down like a helicopter making vertical landing.

Sam's piloting experience was fully utilized to do this historical event. The spacecraft just taxied for a few feet and halted.

Sam then switched off the engines of the spacecraft. Now they want to wait for 5 minutes to remove all effects of electromagnetic effect while it travelled in light speed. The experiment is to check whether the spacecraft can take off and attain the speed of light from static ground conditions.

Four minutes passed and Sam was preparing for starting up the spacecraft. Suddenly the Iran team noticed somebody, may be from the colony, slowly moving towards the spacecraft. That person is around 200 meters away. If he or other colony people happened to see the spacecraft and the crew, the news will reach America and they will suspect that it's related to Franklin's discovery. He might have been staying in some nearby caves and that's why he was not spotted earlier by Sam and the team.

When observed closely they saw the approaching person carrying a rifle. He must be a security guard who can harm the spacecraft. Sam thanked the decision to install weapons on the spacecraft for possible confrontation with aliens. He fired a few shots aiming 10 ft in front of the guard and also sent a warning missile to the air. The gun shots created a dust cloud in front of the guard and he looked puzzled and turned away.

Sam quickly switched on the AbM motors. They are facing a critical time now. If the spacecraft failed to takeoff and attain light speed, the mother ship will have to be brought down to give it lift. By that time the colony members and guards may return to see what's happening. They could also take pictures and send them to the US, and thus the secret of the light speed spacecraft will be revealed to the world.

Sam accelerated the AbM motors and adjusted the direction of the thrusters to balance the spacecraft. Yes, the spacecraft is getting vertical lift like a helicopter. After reaching 15ft from ground, Sam moved the undercarriage and wheels upward and to the Off position. He checked all the flight data and gauge readings in the instrument panel. Everything is fine up to this stage.

Sam then moved the levers of AbM motors to full power. And behold, it WORKED! The spacecraft straightaway augmented to light speed and disappeared! It was such a relief and great news for Franklin and his team that everybody stood up and applauded heartily.

Sam made the spacecraft to orbit Mars twice. Now they have acquired another capability. The spacecraft can land anywhere on the ground and take off to light speed on its own. So, putting the spacecraft in semi-transparent state is not a must now- if they are in a hurry, it can be done, and otherwise they can land it and later take off into space without the help of a rocket launcher. Great achievement!

Franklin has asked Sam to take the spacecraft back to Iran.

The tech team in Iran detailed for the spacecraft maintenance has been intimated to report at the Satellite Control Centre.

This time Sam landed the spacecraft not on the terrace, but at the technical area of Iran Space agency. It has been taken to a secret place in the aircraft maintenance hangar. Sam also went to the technical area to overlook the spacecraft checks and servicing. The technical crew inspected the spacecraft for possible damages inflicted by the sandstorm in Mars. Luckily there was not much damage. A few thermal tiles on the airframe structure have been slightly damaged. They were replaced then and there.

A thorough servicing was carried out on the spacecraft. A few modifications also incorporated. Sand filters and protectors were installed at sensitive parts of AbM motors, thrusters and other important areas. In fact, the accident on Mars was a boon; due to that only they were able to make those additional modifications. If it happened during their voyage to another star system, then there could have been trouble because there are no known workshops in other parts of the Milky Way galaxy!

There are also other works to be done on the spacecraft like fitting additional thrusters, more solar power units and one more AbM motor. The maintenance engineers have asked two days' time for those modifications to be carried out on the spacecraft.

While the spacecraft servicing and modifications were going on, Franklin has given two days off to the full research team. All the team members were very happy and went out for a picnic to tourist spots in Iran. They have achieved amazing things but were going through the trauma of it — the tensions and hard work have affected their health.

A break was unavoidable.

During a memorable desert safari trip, the team came to know that Franklin is a very talented singer. Sam and Mary performed a duet dance while Franklin sang a sweet song. Other team members also performed their favourite items and enjoyed the vacation to the last drop.

Mary was very happy to know that Franklin had no grievances against her and Sam, even though she had turned down his love proposal. But whenever Franklin looked at her, she saw a glimpse of sadness in his eyes. Franklin's love used to haunt her, and Mary used to become very upset whenever she thought about it…

Mary could collect some rare species of plants during that desert safari trip. One was a little plant seen only near oasis. That plant resembled an algae type small plant she had developed in the lab, which she named Manna. Manna will float in the air and sometimes stick to the ground. They don't have roots. Manna needs only CO_2 and sunlight to grow. They can withstand heat wave and snowfall. What makes it special is the fact that human can survive several days by simply eating it in small quantity. It is a rich source of protein and can be consumed raw.

Mary has developed manna for an important purpose. It's named after "Manna" the food from the sky, which was fed to Israelites by God when they were travelling through desert. Mary intends to grow Manna in Mars and check whether it'll supply food to the Martians. It'll grow easily in Mars as its botanical structure is suitable for Martian atmosphere.

Mary was thrilled and eagerly wanted to test the Martian survival capacity of Manna and the new algae species she got from the desert safari tour.

When the team returned to their office in the Satellite Control

Centre after the holiday trip, there were three good news items waiting for them.

First thing was that Mary's DNA samples were fully safe after the space travel. Second news was about the space dog, which survived a long journey in the main capsule of the spacecraft in energy form. The dog was in perfect shape without any signs of radiation or other illness. And the stunning fact as Franklin hinted was that there was no aging process happened while the dog travelled with the speed of light and was converted into energy particles.

That means if somebody travels in the main capsule at light speed, he won't become old! He or she can live up to thousands of years without aging by continuously travelling with the speed of light. Further studies are required to collect more data regarding this matter and the military dog will have to be sent again to space at least for a week to conduct further experiments.

The third news item was related to the dog trainer. He has some strange and interesting narration about his space journey. He felt extra energetic and was very happy and thrilled throughout the journey. The initial confusion and fear was replaced by a feeling of unknown joy. He added that it was like consuming two pegs of Johnny Walker. The effect was really stunning.

Even though the description of the dog trainer can't be fully believed, Franklin and the team members thought that the light speed spacecraft is surrounded by lot of mysteries beyond their imagination. It's a world hitherto unknown to mankind… The world will never be the same again.

The spacecraft was ready after servicing and modifications at the repair bay in Iran Space Agency hangar and presented to the Franklin's satellite control centre. It was brought to the terrace of the control centre via a corridor from the servicing section.

The complete collection of Mary's DNA library have been transferred to the spacecraft in special, temperature controlled medical-kits. The spacecraft can be taken to a few hours of daily flying in light speed and so the DNA collection will be better preserved inside the spacecraft than in the laboratory. Some additional layers and compartments were made in the human capsule to accommodate the DNA boxes. In case of an Earthquake or other natural disaster, the spacecraft is the safest place on Earth to preserve the DNA collection.

Now left with just test flying the spacecraft after implementing the modifications…

Taking into account the description of the dog trainer, there are no risks involved for Sam to go and pilot the spacecraft into deep space on a manned mission.

It's not advisable for two members of the team to go for the test flying because if something bad happens, they'll lose two members. But Mary wanted to go as things have to be done as early as possible.

Climate change or a world war, both are capable of inflicting unrecoverable damage to Earth. She has to test her Manna plants on Mars to check the possibility of large scale cultivation. Also, the DNA samples are to be subjected to more tests in the human capsule and also in the main capsule during light speed travel.

As the team was preparing for the manned spaceflight, there came an important message for the Director of Iran Space Agency from the Iran government.

The message was soon conveyed to the team at the satellite control centre. The highest civilian award of the Islamic Republic of Iran, Medal of Merit award, will be bestowed upon Franklin. All other team members will get next best awards from the President of Iran. It was such a happy moment for all of them. Their hard work is recognized and rewarded in the most befitting manner.

Soon the team also received an order to make a colony in Mars for the Iranians, as done by super power countries. Now as they have the light speed spacecraft, it won't be a difficult task. Iran Space Agency has given orders to its technical departments to arrange tents, equipment and other infrastructure materials required for constructing a colony in Mars.

First the manned spaceflight to Mars has to be conducted and verified before going for the tent construction. Everything was quickly arranged for the first spaceflight test. Mary and Sam will be going together.

On the stipulated day to go to Mars, Franklin called Mary to his office. "There were objections from the security department against sending both yourself and Sam together on the spacecraft without someone to watch over. But I have cleared you on my own risk," Franklin said while his fingers gripped on the paperweight.

" Thank you Franklin. I know your faith in us. We're indebted to you."

Franklin avoided looking at Mary's eyes. "During the initial days of my research in America and the discovery of breaking the light speed, religious thoughts had overwhelmed my mind. I was influenced by religious scholars in Iran and elsewhere. Now, after the spacecraft has been developed, all my dreams are spinning around it.

"You can hijack the spacecraft and my dreams while you're going for the test flying. Nothing can hinder you. The Americans and their allies will give you Nobel Prize also, but remember one thing; the spacecraft is my dream project and lifeblood.

"More experiments are yet to be conducted with this spacecraft. More discoveries are to be made and so many researches to be pursued- about gravitational waves, space time continuum, Intergalactic travel, black hole formation etc. If you take the spacecraft away to the US, then building up another one may not be feasible because of the catastrophic incidents happening on Earth. The time factor is crucial."

Mary assured Franklin, "We understand your concern, Professor. And you have all reasoning to think it so because America and NATO, and the erstwhile USSR had done such things during the cold war period.

"But things have changed now. Moreover, we also want that your research should continue and further discoveries made for the benefit of the whole world.

You can trust us, we're sure to come back, even though it's tempting to do otherwise."

5 LOVE IN JUPITER AND JUMP DRIVE TO ALPHA CENTAURI

Time has come for Sam and Mary to take the historical manned flight for space travelling at light speed… They are going to mark a major milestone in space exploration. Everything is ready. All eyes are on the spacecraft. First Flight Servicing of the spacecraft has been carried out by the ground crew.

Just before leaving, Sam said to Franklin, "See you soon, Professor Franklin. As we'll be handling the spacecraft controls from within, the satellite control centre won't have much role in the test flying. However, in case of any emergency, we'll hand over the controls to you, so keep a team member with piloting abilities standby."

"Sure, Sam. Somebody will be manning the control room always," Franklin affirmed.

"If everything goes well in the test flight, we'll complete several things before coming back. First one is to check all parameters of the spacecraft while flying at light speed. Then a proper place is to be marked for Iran's colony in Mars. And also Mary's DNA experiments, and her algae plant's cultivation trials on Mars soil also will be conducted before we return. It'll thus take a few hours to complete these tasks. We'll be sending messages to the satellite control centre every 15 or 30 minutes, so you can come to know we're safe."

"Ok, see you Sam. Wish you safe return. Take care."

"OK, see you, Professor," Mary and Sam said, after shaking hands with Franklin. The complete team members came to the terrace to see them off. Mary and Sam waved at everybody and boarded the spacecraft.

The light-speed spacecraft slowly lifted up 15 feet. The wheels went in and behold, it blazed into the sky with a splash of light. Sam was thrilled to fly the spacecraft. It was so easy compared to the controlling from satellite control centre. And as the dog trainer narrated they felt like a special energy flowing through their body and mind while flying at light speed. They thought their teenage has comeback when you're filled with power bombs to to travel around the world and conquer everything.

After a few minutes, Mary and Sam knew they were in high spirits as if got drunk on wine! Mary's heart was beating to the tune of their favourite love theme song from the Titanic movie..

But there was not enough time to dwell on the love theme.

Important works are to be completed. Mary prepared a set of boxes with the DNA samples and the manna plants. They have to be passed on to the main capsule for testing any changes happening to them while travelling with the speed of light.

Sam was fully engaged in manoeuvring the spacecraft. There are no flying manual or guide books; everything has to be learnt through trial and error method.

There are dangers lurking beneath their every move while operating the controls. A slight operational error can cause the spacecraft to move thousands of kilometres away before recognizing the mistake. But Sam was happy to take the challenge. Flying through space at light speed- it was such a fantastic experience. And for a born pilot like Sam, it's like his dream come true type situation.

Within 11 minutes, they reached Mars. Moving close to the surface and rotating around the planet, Sam searched a suitable place for the colony construction. It shouldn't be too far from other countries' colonies. Should be near to them but hidden at the moment from direct view. After moving around Mars for several times, they found an ideal place, a spacious cave surrounded by hills and situated in a comparatively higher place than the other colonies. It would have been a lake when there was plenty of surface water in Mars.

The sandstorm won't affect the area because of the hilly terrain surrounding it. The security guards of the other colonies won't be able to climb the steep hills to find out Iran's colony. They offloaded all the tent construction materials and other equipments brought in the spacecraft. All the items were hidden inside the cave.

They also hoisted Iran's flag there, and nailed a notice: "Sovereign Property of the Islamic Republic of Iran. Trespassers will be prosecuted."

Mary has sprinkled the manna plants in the cave and its adjoining areas. Their growth and reproduction are to be checked during subsequent visits. If the cultivation of manna becomes a practical reality, then the Martians can attain self sufficiency in food production to a certain extent.

Sam and Mary then decided to go to the outer planets, Jupiter, Saturn, Uranus and Neptune, the huge gas giants of the solar system. While travelling through the asteroid belt, the ride was a bit bumpy, but that gave Sam some spacecraft controlling experience.

Within 15 minutes they reached the massive Jupiter. Sam wanted to explore Jupiter and its 50 moons. He also wanted to check out those wide and narrow colourful bands made of whirling clouds. But after seeing the faint rings of Jupiter and the 50 moons, Mary thought about the blazing and spectacular rings of Saturn.

Mary said to Sam, "As time is not a restraint, why don't we go to Saturn?"

"Why do you wish so, my wife?" Sam looked at her passionately.

Mary smiled at Sam to hear him calling her "wife" even though they didn't have much experience as husband and wife after tying the nuptial note at a church in India.

Mary came to know that travelling at light speed is refreshing her body and mind...

She cooed, "I wanna glide through the beautiful rings of Saturn, dear."

Sam was also feeling love in the air...

"At your service, Your Grace." Sam added and sang from The Royal Concept's 'On Our Way':

"To your place, place, place... We're on our way, way, way... We're on our way, way, way..."

Mary too sang, "We're on our way, way, way... We're on our way somehow!"

"Hold me close, close, close... We're losing time, time, time... We're losing time, time, time!" Sam extended his arms for Mary.

Mary got up from her chair and slowly moved towards Sam. She passionately wound her hand around his neck and kissed on his cheek. Sam pulled her towards him and bit her lower lips. She sat in his lap and kissed him deep with sweet love.

By that time the lovely rings of Saturn appeared in front of them. They cuddled and Sam put the spacecraft on autopilot!

They moved around Saturn, gliding through the spectacular coloured rings which glittered with the seven colours of a rainbow.

As they were smiling and kissing, they saw a wonderful sight through the window – it was the tiny moonlet of Saturn, the 'Pan' close at hand... Sunrays were reflecting from the cute Pan's shiny surface and it's scintillating - wow what a fantastic sight.

And the pretty Pan stood there watching them and glittering like a diamond.

It was the perfect natural setting to enjoy love...

And Sam wanted it fast...and Mary too! His hands slowly unbuttoned her spacesuit...Mary wanted to caution him, but she couldn't.

Cuddled together, they lie on the floor of the spacecraft's human capsule. Sam kissed all over her body; her seductive smell intoxicating him further and persuading him to go deep into her softness.

Mary enjoyed his strong body weight on her. She lay there,

embracing him and offering herself to his thrusts, urging him to take her deeper and stronger. Sam kissed her deeply until she couldn't breathe and she was mesmerised on his scent ...

Travelling at light speed, there was heavy rush of energy flowing in their veins, and love made it more intense. Mary turned over and Sam pulled her on top of him. She pinned Sam to the floor, comfortable laying on him and being in his arms.

She kissed him lightly, softly again, and again. Sam thrust against her slowly, but she wanted it fast, and it went on.

Time was ticking away...

When the intoxication of love slowly melted away, Sam and Mary just relaxed and it took another 10 minutes for them to come to realities.

"Oh my gosh! Where are we now?" Mary wondered.
No idea.

They just peeped through the spacecraft window.
They are not anywhere near Jupiter - Not even near the solar system.
They stopped orbiting Jupiter and deviated from their trajectory at least one hour before! They are now moving at light speed deep into the Milky Way galaxy well ahead of the gravitational influence of the Sun.
Sam tried to locate their position relative to Sun and Earth, but he couldn't get a trace of the solar system.
Sam then tried to contact their Iran satellite control centre by sending signals to the Earth antennas - no way! No signals received back.
Finally they realised that they are millions and millions of kilometres away from the solar system. There is no way to check their current position with respect to Sun.
They tried to locate some Neutron stars or pulsars for their Galactic or Interstellar Positioning System and it's revealed that they are over a billion kilometres from Sun and now moving towards Sun's nearest star system, the Alpha Centauri.
Sam said, "Our GPS has to be modified to locate Sun and Earth from anywhere in the interstellar space. It's not giving exact

figures as we have not given much research into that area..."

"Sam, I think we almost lost our way...so why not try those jumping drive through hyperspace as described in science fictions?"

Sam looked out through the window glass and tried to locate some stars. "Good idea, darling. Let's try it. It seems we are not in the influence of any warping associated with star system and its gravity now."

Sam increased the power of the thrusters and accelerated the main rocket nuclear fusion unit to see whether they get any jumps. But alas, they didn't get any increase in the speed of the spacecraft...

They are just travelling at light speed only, nothing more nothing less, that's it. Increasing the engine power has no effect on the speed of the spacecraft travelling at light speed.

Sam and Mary discussed various possibilities and made some rough measurement of distance through astronomical units such as parsec (a parsec is equal to about 3.26 light-years - 31 trillion kilometres in length).

Returning to the solar system and Earth is not that easy without exact location specifications. Slight error in calculation could end up in losing their way and plunging into dangers.

Sam finally said, "Increasing the power of the motors has no effect on the speed of the spacecraft. So, let us try decreasing the power."

"Good idea...Let's try all options," Mary ascertained.

Sam then tried to reduce the speed of the spacecraft. He switched off the thrusters and reduced the speed of the main nuclear fusion engines.

The spacecraft has slowly come down from light speed and transformed into the semitransparent state.

Then Sam and Mary experienced something fantabulous.

They could see the Milky Way galaxy as a whole in front of them...All stars appeared as shining bright spots around them...They are seeing the four dimensional view of the stellar medium much compressed and zoomed in.

So far they had transformed the spacecraft into semitransparent form inside the solar system only where warping associated with gravity is present. That's why they didn't go through this 4-D effect which happens only in the interstellar space!

Sam then thought about an innovative idea.

When they moved from light speed travel to the semi-transparent form in the galactic space, they might have actually made a jump through the space! He then just tried to jump from the current position to another bright spot star visible nearby...

Sam had great experience in amazing road racing motorcycle jumps. He used to hit bigger drops and jumps on his sports model motorbike. Sam decided to just try it with his spacecraft too.

He simply accelerated the spacecraft into light speed travel aiming at the nearby star and then suddenly changed it into the semi transparent form, and again quickly into light speed. And wow, they got a thrilling interstellar hyperspace jump!

It was such a super-duper experience. Initially they didn't know what was happening actually. It was something strange...

Sam felt as if being lifted up and then his mind was travelling into the nearby bright star spot, which he aimed for the jump. His mind and body was lifting the spacecraft up and carrying it!

While going through the interstellar jump drive, Mary felt as if looking into the space with bright stars zooming out around her in quick succession, and she knew that she was in a pole vaulting mode in space, and might be travelling many times more than the speed of light.

Just after finishing the hyperspace jump, Sam felt relieved and normal. Slowly everything came under control once again. Sam checked all parameters of the spacecraft.

All ok, and they are now moving with the normal speed of light.

Then they felt like they are under the gravitational pull of the Sun.

Oh, does that mean they returned back to the solar system with that awesome hyperspace jump drive?

Sam just checked the properties of the Sun in their vicinity with the radio magnetic scanner.

Sam exclaimed, "Oh, God, it's not our Sun; it's Alpha Centauri star system!"

Good Heavens! They have reached the Alpha Centauri with a 5 minutes interstellar jump. In normal light speed travel it would have taken over 4 years. Aha! That is the fantastic jump drive through space-time.

It was such a marvellous experience for Sam and Mary- jumping through the interstellar space and landing at star systems within a few minutes.

That means without any warp drive propulsion systems or imaginary powers, they can do the hyperspace jumps between two stars with their down-to-earth spacecraft that never defies the theories of relativity and the universal speed limit- except during the jump drive.

Now scientists will have to come out with another cosmic theory to expand the theory of relativity and the laws of physics into the realm of interstellar jumps!

Mary was fully thrilled to experience the fictional stories of Star Trek and other hyperspace games in real time.

She said, "Sam, let's now jump back to our Sun and the solar system."

"Just wait, dear. Let's now have a close look at the planets of Alpha Centauri - for searching them, our scientists are planning several space programmes such as the Nanocraft of Starshot Space Engineering project, and the launching of a satellite just for closely observing Alpha Centauri."

Sam went through the possible interplanetary space surrounding Alpha Centauri A and the other two stars (Alpha Centauri B and Proxima Centauri) in the same star system.

After travelling the whole area around the stars, it's been revealed that there is not a single planet that's fully developed and containing water and a healthy atmosphere and habitable like our Earth.

Maybe because the complete dense concentrations of interstellar gas and dust (molecular clouds) had been fully utilised in the making of the three stars in the single system and nothing was left for life supporting planet formations.

That means Sam and Mary will never be coming towards Alpha

Centauri star systems again for search of Earth-like planets.

They then decided to go back to Sun and Earth, and left Alpha Centauri to reach the interstellar space where there was no warping related to gravitational pull of stars. Hyperspace jumping can't be done where warp pulling is active.

Like an ace bike jumper, Sam readied for another hyperspace jump drive. He aimed at the distant Sun, and Mary took a deep breath. Through the acceleration and deceleration processes, Sam magnificently carried the spacecraft into Jump Drive mode.

Mary could feel the zoom out and zoom in movement of the galactic space and distant stars sliding at hyper-light-speeds around them. She looked at Sam.

Sam is seen as if covered by a halo! He's almost in a semi-transparent form. Mary tried to touch him, but she could not feel it like touching a human being. You can't touch a light beam, can you?

Perhaps, Sam has been moved to the state of fourth dimension of space, that is, the Time factor, and moving the spacecraft from that sublime state of space-time curvature - may be.

Another 5 minutes through the jump drive and they reached the Sun's gravitational zone. Things are becoming so much wonderful and so easy now. Jumping in between star systems in the Milky Way galaxy takes very less time.

After the jump drive, Sam and Mary travelled up to planet Neptune and tried to contact the Iran satellite control centre. Yes, they got connected with Franklin. The complete Iran team was anxious to know what happened to Sam and Mary. Everybody was worried thinking some accident occurred and they lost the spacecraft.

Sam told Franklin everything happened during the last few hours, their straying in interstellar space and spot jumping to Alpha Centauri and back to Solar system.

Franklin was excited to hear that great news. So, jump drive is real. What he saw previously in a dream about hyperspace travel and jump drive happened to be the actual thing, not just an illusion. Sam and Mary have practically gone through that situation and it's now a scientific truth.

Franklin was proud that his spacecraft can safely take the star plunge and that his discovery is going to be a big leap for the mankind to scale the Universe in its entirety.

Franklin told Sam to try a few more jumps to the nearby star systems and collect the flight data and operational parameters. They'll have to confirm and make sure that interstellar jump is safe and a reality and it can be undertaken by their light-speed spacecraft at any time.

Sam and Mary are happy to know that Franklin is also thrilled to hear about the jump drive to stars. Sam then moved out of the Sun's gravitational pull and readily jumped the spacecraft into another star system. He jumped to and fro to Sirius, and Procyon stars from Sun's proximity. They also jumped to nine other star systems which are located in the Local Bubble, a region within the Orion–Cygnus Arm of the Milky Way. They tried the interstellar jumps to those distant stars and in between jumped back to the Sun also.

They felt it a very exhilarating experience. They also found it well and good and never experienced any tiredness or fatigue during those hyper jumps. One important thing they noticed is that the fuel consumption during the interstellar journeys was very less. The fuel efficiency of the spacecraft is so high that they can travel to the whole universe and comeback with the available fuel capacity. Also, the solar power batteries can be charged whenever they enter a star system.

It's time now for them to return from the world of stars. After successfully completing those historic jump drives to all the nearby star systems, Sam and Mary finally came back to their own solar system and landed in Iran.

6 MARS EXPLORER AND JOHNNY WALKER

Sam and Mary have made several shuttle services between Iran and Mars to carry more tent construction materials and other accessories for Iran's Mars colony.

After a few such trips, Mary requested, "Sam, I want to see my papa and mom. It looked ages since we left them. I feel very homesick. Please don't say No. Nobody will come to know if we go and meet them for a few minutes at least."

Sam was embarrassed to hear that. "It'll be risky to go to America now. Franklin or the Iran officials could come to know."

"But Sam, I can't resist the desire any more. If Franklin came to know, I'll convince him."

Sam has no other option. He agreed. "Ok, no worries. As you strongly desire to meet your parents, I can't deny it, sweet heart. I too want to see your papa and mamma."

While returning to Earth for the next trip, Sam made a small deviation to the flight path and took the spacecraft to America. They sent a message to the control centre in Iran saying there is a sandstorm in Mars at the Iran colony site and they will have to wait till it subsides.

This time Koshy ichayan was having a few alcoholic drinks sitting in the living room of his villa. Preetha was in the kitchen and Koshy ichayan was watching a thriller movie on the TV.

The movie was about aliens landing in a steep hilly area somewhere in an unchartered location along the India-China border. It was an inaccessible place due to hostile terrain and bad weather. The aliens came by a spacecraft and started building an artificial lake there. They have very powerful equipment and heavy Earthmoving machinery which are ejected as light beams from their spacecraft. Once the light beam touches the ground it grows into large heavy vehicles and construction equipments. The making of the lake and dam is going on at full steam.

Koshy ichayan was fully involved in the movie. Every second is thrilling. Their spacecraft is like a UFO suddenly appearing into view from nowhere and it also goes away with a sudden lightning flash.

As he was watching the movie and drinking Johnnie Walker, Koshy was in a dramatic world. Suddenly a light came through the window and swirled around a corner of the TV room. It suddenly became a spacecraft in the shape of a semi-transparent disc! Koshy was little bit frightened. He looked at the TV and then into the spacecraft and blinked his eyes. Seeing him embarrassed, the spacecraft suddenly disappeared, just as it was happening in the movie.

As the surprising sight repeated twice, Koshy ichayan called Preetha and narrated to her the wonderful thing happened in front of his eyes. But Preetha won't believe him as she thought ichayan was over drunk and is becoming intoxicated.

Koshy pleaded, "My dear better half, believe me! It really happened. I'm not under the influence of Johnny Walker, darling. The funny thing is that same spacecraft is shown in the movie too. It could be a 3D effect."

"Now, will you stop drinking, dear? And stop that movie too. On next visit to the doctor, we also need a check up for your eyes," Preetha snapped.

Koshy ichayan didn't know how to convince her, but he was sure that he saw something strange in the form of a spacecraft. "Look my sweet girl, I'll show you the magic. Look at the TV now, see that spacecraft lift up and just disappears? Now it's going to appear in our room. Wow, see for yourself, it came there near your money plant, by the side of the window."

As Preetha was looking in disbelief at the strange happening, Koshy continued, "But don't worry, it obeys me. Now see, 'tishyom' (he mimicked as if shooting the spacecraft)"

The spacecraft disappeared as Koshy shown his fingers at it. Next moment it appeared again in half light and half physical form.

Preetha shouted, "By Jove, this is really magic 3D, darling!"

Inside the spacecraft Mary laughed and said to Sam, "Now I think their fear is gone…let's end the 3D game and land."

As Koshy and Preetha were looking in awestruck eyes, lo, the spacecraft landed there in the room. The door opened and Sam and Mary alighted from it.

Koshy and Preetha couldn't understand what's happening, but they knew it's real as Mary came and hugged both of them.

"Oh, Mary and Sam, what a surprise!" Koshy and Preetha hugged them and said.

Then Mary and Sam faced a rush of questions from their parents to explain the miraculous happenings. They explained everything (without touching the commando operation and Iran) as Koshy ichayan watched them in disbelief. He asked, "The CIA people came here and enquired about you. Are you doing some risky operation in the Middle East? Now where are you coming from?"

Sam and Mary somehow convinced them that they are on the right track and they're doing it for helping humanity. They further explained that the light speed spacecraft is a new invention by NASA and currently on testing phase. They want to keep it a secret, so the flight testing is done on Mars only. They also assured their parents that they are safer than anybody on Earth.

Preetha brought some snacks for them. They shared happy moments for a while, and it's time for Sam and Mary to return. They promised to come back in the weekend and will spend more time with their parents as there will be more flights toward Mars in the coming days.

Sam and Mary boarded the spacecraft and went back to Satellite Control Centre in Iran. Next day there was meeting with a Nanotechnology specialist who had explained how their technology can help them to transport heavy machineries to space and Mars.

Actually machineries made of carbon Nano-tubes and other materials are very light ones but can take same load as heavy Earth moving and other construction equipments we use. In fact, the Nano specialist's company has already made those equipments and wanted to test them in Mars.

Franklin and the team felt that this will go a great way in extra fast and easy transportation of all the colony building structures and materials to Mars. So the Company producing Nano equipments have been given order for the equipments for trial run on Mars. Two of their technicians also have to be taken to space along with the futuristic tools and heavy-duty vehicles. The weekend was fixed for this breakthrough work.

All preparations and packing have been finished on war footing for the Nano technology equipment testing on Mars. And on Saturday, Sam and Mary picked the two Nano-tech technicians to space. After landing at the specified site for building the Iran colony, the technicians and their equipments were taken out safely. The Nano specialists said they need minimum three hours time to assemble all parts and do the trial runs of the heavy load Earth moving equipments on Mars. They also have a few spacesuits with Nanosensors and Nanorobots for serviceability testing on Mars.

Sam and Mary said they are going for a flying sortie to explore the surface of Mars while these project works are getting carried out. In case of emergency, they can send signal to the spacecraft through nanotech antennas developed by the same team. So, leaving the engineers at the colony site, they went straightway to their parents' villa in America.

Soon Mary and Sam reached their home in the US. Koshy ichayan and Preetha were very happy to see their children visiting them again as promised. While having refreshments, their talks mainly concentrated on climate change and its terrible consequences happening around the world. They shared deep concern about the possibility of the end of the world coming soon.

Mary told them about her efforts to transport life to another planet in case of destruction of life here through her large collection of DNA samples.

While discussing such matters, Koshy ichayan unexpectedly asked a question, "My lovely children, as there is no guarantee of continuation of life on Earth, we don't know how long we'll live. So could you please take us also to Mars for a small trip?"

The question was of course like a bolt out of the blue, but an equally surprising answer came from Sam.

"OK, sure. Get ready papa and mom. We have a couple of hours or more to spare while the nanotech team does their experimental works in the Mars colony. Here, we have two extra spacesuits with us, wear it now. And let's go."

Sam gave them the spacesuits.

Koshy ichayan and Preetha went to their room to change dress and wear the spacesuit. While going, Koshy ichayan looked very happy and thrilled.

Sam and Mary overheard him talking to preetha: "Get ready Preetha dear, fast. Wow, we're going to Mars!" He also hummed two lines of a love song:

"Once more you open the door
And you're here in my heart,
And my heart will go on and on..."

Sam laughed, hearing Koshy ichayan singing those lines, and Mary blushed. They wondered how their parents' favourite lines are same as theirs too!

Koshy ichayan and Preetha got ready quickly. All are in an excited mood. Soon the spacecraft took them to Mars. They have flown over the settlements on Mars and also revolved round the red planet twice.

They hovered around the Iran colony worksite and communicated with the engineers, and learnt that it'll take a few more hours for them to complete the task. The engineering team members are creating boundary walls for the colony and preparing the cave easily accessible for accommodating people.

Sam landed the spacecraft in a nearby hilly terrain where they saw a beautiful plane area with a cave. Everybody came out of the spacecraft. Koshy ichayan and Preetha are ecstatic to walk on Mars.

After a while, ichayan took out two gold rings from the pocket of his spacesuit...He gave one to Sam and the other one to Mary.

Sam wondered, "Rings?! Where have you got that from, uncle?"

Ichayan said, "I brought this with a purpose, my son. Now please exchange the rings and help each other to wear it."

As Mary and Sam put the rings on each other's fingers, Preetha and ichayan clapped their hands. Preetha also made a special acclamatory shouting using her tongue vibrating rapidly- this is customarily done during wedding ceremonies in South India.

Preetha explained, "Your dear Papa and I want to see this for our satisfaction. No idea when the auspicious occasion will materialize on Earth, but at least we're content that this marriage is made in Mars."

Papa and mamma blessed their children; a fantastic sight to see in Mars. Suddenly Koshy ichayan took out a full bottle of Johnny Walker and two small glasses from his spacesuit pocket. Everybody laughed aloud to see that.

Ichayan poured two tots and drank it stylishly, and shouted, "For the better married life of this young couple – cheers."

This might be the first time somebody carried brandy in a spacesuit, but achayan is different from the rest. And everybody joked about this added advantage of space jackets!

Koshy ichayan filled another drink and gave it to Sam, who declined the offer as he has to pilot the spacecraft.

Then ichayan said something awesome, "Today is a lovely day for us, and especially for both of you youngsters. We have approved your marriage this way and so it has to be celebrated. Sam, please let's go to Kottayam, my native place in Kerala where I'll have to share this joy with a couple of close friends. We'll have to take them here in Mars for the party."

After hearing this strange demand, Preetha scolded him, "Ichaya, don't ask such weird things, don't disturb Sam. This is Mars, not your villa in America."

But ichayan insisted, "Oh Preetha my sweet lady, keep quiet. Do you want to see? My smart boy Sam will not reject my request; will you, Sam?"

Sam was in a difficult situation. There are only two extra spacesuits and only four people can travel at a time on the spacecraft. If they want to bring two people from Kottayam, then Mary and Preetha will have to stay back on Mars- and also without spacesuits.

They checked inside the cave and found it to be a safe place to escape from radiation. Mary said they'll stay in the cave as Sam and ichayan go to Kottayam. After seeing Mary's confident face, Sam decided to take the risk. After all, these are once in a lifetime happenings, so it's ok to take such risks.

Finally it was decided that Preetha and Mary will remain inside the cave. It's just a matter of 15 or 20 minutes. Mary can utilise that time for cultivating her Manna plants inside the cave. Sam also gave them handguns for self defence.

Sam and Koshy ichayan soon started their flight to Kottayam.

On the way, Sam also sent message to Iran control centre that a couple of hours may be required for the testing of Nano equipment and further Mars exploration. So they have sufficient time for the marriage party on Mars.

It took only 15 minutes for Sam to reach Kottayam. It was great advantage that while travelling at light speed you don't get any harm even if you hit a hard object. You just get reflected as if you're a light beam.

How wonderful it would have been if we had something like that while driving on road! They could have put fire resistant rubber padding or something like that at suitable areas on the vehicle's body so that even on head-on collisions, the damage could be minimised.

Sam landed the spacecraft on the terrace of Koshy's house, which was in an isolated place. Time was around 9am and there was nobody around, so Sam could land peacefully without anybody watching it.

Sam sat on the spacecraft while ichayan went down from the terrace through the outer staircase. He rang the calling bell. There's a person appointed to look after the house building, who opened the door. His name is Mathan.

Mathan was embarrassed to see Koshy ichayan without any prior information. He cried, "Oh, God! Koshy Sir? How come you arrive this way without any message? Is everything ok? Where is your luggage?"

Ichayan said to the housekeeper, "Will explain everything later, now you go and bring Monayi sir from Maliyekkal house and Aavrachan from the nearby Kaithavalappil house. Go fast, take the car."

"Just a minute, I'll bring them straightaway, Sir."

Mathan came within 10 minutes with ichayan's friends. They were also astonished to see Koshy ichayan coming this way without informing them well in advance.

They used to get two weeks' prior info about his arrival…that means they have time for preparing and preserving the local liquor-arrack, made from home ingredients and local fruits, which was ichayan's favourite drink while they liked the US made foreign liquor achayan used to bring. So it's sort of give and take policy – a diplomatic exchange of US made whisky and Kerala's local arrack liquor.

As they were wondering what happened to their American achayan, Koshy made whisky tots for them and said, "Listen to me carefully… It's quite unbelievable thing I'm going to say, but truth is sometimes like that- quite enchanting than a drama! As people are now facing full of trouble to live on Earth, I got a chance to visit Mars, and I'm coming directly from there…Can you believe it?!

Everybody asked in a chorus, "What are you bluffing ichaya? Coming from Mars? How's it possible?"

Ichayan tried to convince them. "I was having a peg of Johnny Walker while blessing my daughter's marriage on Mars, and thought about you. Come to the terrace, the spacecraft and my son-in-law is there…I'll take you to Mars now."

Achayan took them to the terrace, and all were spellbound to see the disc-shaped spacecraft and Sam alighting from it.

Ichayan introduced Sam to his friends. "This is Sam, my son-in-law. I'm giving you party for their marriage which was solemnised today on Mars. Sam will take us to Mars. (to Mathan), You go back to the house now, and listen, don't tell about these happenings to anybody. People will tell you have gone mad."

But to Koshy ichayan's surprise, Monayi and Avarachan had already acquainted with Sam when he visited Kerala with Mary during their satellite launch program with ISRO. Koshy ichayan's friends were happy to see the young and vibrant Sam again. They narrated the story of Sam and Mary's visit last time and said they are very impressed to see them again. They also congratulated ichayan for getting such a smart boy as his son-in-law.

Ichayan said, "So, no need to introduce you to Mary too. Folks, now get into the spacecraft and you're going to have the thrill of flying at the speed of light."

Sam helped ichayan and his friends to wear the spacesuit and made them sit comfortably inside the spacecraft.

Mathan leaned from the staircase to see the spacecraft go up and then disappear like a flashing lightning- only a beam of light was visible for some time. He couldn't believe it and ran downstairs with fear.

Soon they reached Mars and saw Mary and Preetha waiting to receive them in happy mood. Sam feared that they would be affected with radiation or some other issues, but nothing happened as they were inside the cave.

Sam, ichayan and his friends wearing the spacesuit alighted from the vehicle while Mary and Preetha got in. It's safe inside the spacecraft, so they can stay there peacefully, while the men folks make party outside.

The drinkers sat inside the cave and enjoyed the Johnny Walker. They sang local Kerala songs and danced heartily there on Mars. It was such a sky-high feeling for all of them. They still didn't believe it fully and expect that anytime they may wake up from intoxicated sleep and find themselves in their house...

No wonder, it's a common thing to regular alcoholic drinkers that they always consider life as a half-dream and half-real entity.

Drinkers also deserve a place in the group of 'lunatic, the poet and the lover who act alike' as Theseus claims in Shakespeare's A Midsummer Night's Dream.

Mary has put her manna plants in the cave and they are floating there with their leaves having a slight halo in the darkness of the cave.

Looking at the plants, planter Avarachan asked, "Are there plants in Mars, Koshy ichaya? How awesome! I think we can then start making rubber plantation too on Mars."

Ichayan laughed and said, "No man! We pray to God that at least these plants, which are called Manna, grow and prosper on Mars.

"My daughter Mary had cultivated this in laboratory and it can withstand the harsh climate of Mars. It can be eaten raw and if it grows in plenty, then the settlers here can use it as food."

That time Monayi said in a sad voice, "The Earth which God gave us was so beautiful and there were abundant varieties of fruits and vegetables for us to eat and enjoy the life.

"But alas, our greedy nature has spoiled everything. We ruined the Nature by exploiting its resources and finally destroying the eco-balance. The beautiful Earth is slowly becoming a barren land – all due to the foolishness and false pride of the modern man.

Now, the next generations will have to live on such tiny plants in a hostile world."

Ichayan fully supported Monayi's viewpoint. "Compared to this desert Mars, Earth was like the Garden of Eden. And what we did!

"We were too proud of our scientific achievements and at some point we forgot God too!! It's our own making- we only have infected the Eden with poison! Now we'll have to face the consequences."

Planter Avarchen the asked Sam, "Do people live here in Mars?"

Sam said, "Yes, there are colonies of different countries. The settlements are about a few kilometres from here."

Ichayan's guests insisted on going to see the Indian settlers as they are now fully in the influence of liquor. Sam took ichayan and his friends on the spacecraft and went to the Indian colony. He landed behind a large rock so nobody will see the spacecraft.

Everybody got down and walked towards the tent. Avarachan, Monayi and Koshy ichayan all were thoroughly enjoying the Mars expedition.

Whilst they were walking slowly, Sam said, "Fearing the bad effects of radiation, normally people don't come out of the tents. Only the guards will be roaming here and there. We can give some of these Manna plants to the Indians."

In front of the Indian residential area, a North Indian security guard stopped them and enquired about the purpose of visit. Sam told the guard that they are from Kerala and work in the nearby Iranian colony which is getting constructed.

After hearing that, the guard smiled and said, "Oh, you Keralites staying in Mars? Glad to meet you. I was an airman in the Indian Air Force and had many Malayali friends. There was a saying that even if you go to the Mars, you'll be received by a Malayali fellow with tea there, ha haa. Now it has come true."

Ichayan greeted the guard, "Yeah, Mallus (Malayalis) are now going to be a helping hand for everybody on Mars." He then took out the Johnny Walker bottle and glass from the spacesuit and gave a large peg to the guard. The guard was very happy to meet such a jolly company.

Sam gave a bundle of Manna plants to the guard and guided him how to grow and look after it.

He added, "You can eat this plant as much as you want. It's very tasty and it gives you more energy. You Indians are the first one to receive it; even the Americans don't know about Manna. We're giving it for you to cultivate. It'll multiply quickly in the Martian weather. This will be an alternative food source for you."

They just had a peep inside the tents. It was like a military-barrack with no separate rooms; people were staying in cubicles installed in a spherical format. No idea how many years they'll be able to survive like that.

After some time, they returned back to the cave where Mary and Preetha were left alone. Mary was replanting some of the Manna shrubs there. Next time when they come, they can come to know the plant's growth pattern. Again, Sam, itchayan and his friends left the ladies there and went to Kerala. Sam also contacted the Nanotech engineers and they said everything was almost done, and they'll be ready to go back to Iran within an hour.

After dropping ichayan's friends at Kottayam, Sam and Koshy came back to pickup Mary and Preetha. They quickly flown to U.S. Mary and Sam had a short lunch with Koshy ichayan and Preetha at their villa. Soon they came back to Mars and landed at the Iran colony to join with the Nano tech engineers.

7 "IT'S FINISHED."

After testing the heavy equipment and other construction vehicles on Mars by the Nanotech engineers, Sam took a few more Mars flights with them shuttling supplies to build tents and other infrastructure set up for the Iran settlement.

Once everything was done perfectly, several flights were made to Mars to carry the passengers, who volunteered to stay on Mars till the rest of their lives. Around 20 Iranians were shifted thus to the Iran colony on the red planet. They already paid huge amounts for two years' stay on Mars. Provisions were made in the colony for storing basic food and other supply items for about two years. Then there will be shuttle service for every 3 months for additional supply from Earth.

One day, Franklin also decided to go with Sam and Mary to the outer space to see everything in person. He wants to visit the colonies on Mars and also desires to conduct some tests about micro-gravity, black matter and sun flares. Franklin's laptop which carries all the technical details about his discovery, and other CDs and storage devices related to the spacecraft and his future research plans have been shifted to the spacecraft.

Franklin also wanted to conduct some experiments on the Martian surface and Jupiter's atmosphere, so all their test equipments, tools and other laboratory items were also loaded into the spacecraft. Nanotech heavy load equipments like excavators, tent building materials and tools, Nano-suits and soil test instruments etc. were also uploaded into the spacecraft.

There is no restriction on the maximum load (cargo) the spacecraft can carry; only limitation is the availability of space. The Nano technology has helped greatly to make provisions for accommodating large items in one compact area.

Iran's Human Resource Development minister was also scheduled to travel with the team to Mars that day. The minister will be inspecting the setting up of the Iran colony and look into overall functioning of the settlement. He'll also be listening to the grievances of the Mars settlers.

All the pre-flight ground inspection has been carried out on the spacecraft. Franklin, Mary, Sam and the Minister boarded the spacecraft. Sam checked all flight instruments and gauges, and switched on the thrusters. He asked clearance from ground staff to take off.

Suddenly a police officer came to the tarmac and talked with the ground staff. There was an urgent message for Franklin from the defence minister. Franklin got down from the spacecraft and talked to the officer. The police officer said that the defence minister had called an immediate meeting with Prof. Franklin and the Chief of SAVAK.

Franklin said to Sam and Mary, "I have an urgent meeting with Defence Minister and Police Chief. No idea how much time it'll take. So you take the HRD Minister to Mars and show him our colony. Let him do his inspection there…By the time you return, my meeting will be over and we will directly go to Jupiter to conduct my research."

Franklin then went for the meeting with Defence Minister while Sam took off to Mars with Mary and the HRD minister. Landing on Mars after 15 minutes, Sam and Mary led the minister to the Iran colony there and explained to him the facilities available. The HRD minister conducted a meeting of the Iran settlers. He enquired about their well being and assured that all their genuine problems will be solved at the earliest.

The minister also said doctors and ambulance service will be made exclusively for the Martian settlers and it'll be shuttling to Mars every week or on emergency situations.

The minister told the Martians that if anybody falls sick, this ambulance service will be able to take him to a hospital in Iran within half an hour. And he emphasized that this facility is available only in the Iran colony as they have the light speed spacecraft. For other colonies, it'll take several days to get medical help.

The minister spent around one hour with the Martian settlers. He also secretly watched the arrangements in other countries' colonies while travelling at light speed around those tents. Because of the nanotech constructions, Iran colony looked the best among all the Martian settlements.

During the minister's meeting with Martians, Mary was busy with her Manna farming and research. When slight changes were made to the cell structure, the plants acquired the ability to withstand the harsh climate of Mars. They also started growing quickly after plucking the tender portion for food.

Sam was doing some technical checks on the spacecraft. The main advantage with the spacecraft is that it doesn't need much repair or maintenance. It develops no snags, may be because it's converted into energy ions while travelling at light speed. And Sam is confident of doing any repair works as he has handled the maintenance of larger aircraft.

The minister has finished the tour and told Sam to take him back to Iran. All the Iranian dwellers came to say good bye to the minister. The spacecraft soon took off from Mars. Halfway through the journey, Sam called the satellite control centre in Iran to inform their arrival. Strangely, no message came from the ground control centre.

Sam transferred the control of the spacecraft for a few seconds to the ground station, but nobody responded and no signal was received from the space antennas at the control centre in Iran.

This is the first time such an incident is happening to the communication network. Sam suspected that there is some grave issue at the ground station.

Sam informed the minister that they are not able to establish contact with the ground communication centre, but assured him that the spacecraft is working perfectly and they don't need ground support to land.

After 5 minutes they reached the satellite control centre, but Sam didn't land there, instead he went inside the ground station, revolving the spacecraft and checking if there was some trouble.

They were astonished to see that Iran police has sealed their office and the satellite control room. Franklin or other team members couldn't be found anywhere...

HRD minister said not to land there, and asked Sam to take the spacecraft to Police Headquarters to know what happened.

They went to police HQ and landed on the terrace. Keeping Mary inside, Sam and the minister got down from the spacecraft.

Soon the Deputy Police Chief came there and talked to the minister, "Sir, Two US helicopters attacked our space agency office. They wanted to get info about Professor Franklin's invention. They checked everything there but couldn't find Franklin's laptop and other documents. Also Franklin acted very courageously and didn't tell them anything about our spacecraft and the two Americans in our mission."

The Minister croaked, "Then what happened? Where are Franklin and his team members?"

"They fired at everybody in the satellite control centre and tried to kidnap Franklin, but our security guards also returned fire. Two Americans were killed, but others escaped with their helicopters. They also destroyed the satellite control systems and other equipments there. Franklin and his team members were shot at... they are now in the Govt Hospital ICU in Tehran. We fear all are in critical condition," Deputy Police Chief narrated.

Then he talked to the minister something seriously in Arabic (as if to hide the matter from Sam). They didn't know that Sam can understand Arabic.

Sam stood there listening carefully, but pretending that he doesn't know what they are talking in Arabic. Even though the police officer intently watched Sam while talking to the minister, he couldn't detect any suspicious expression on Sam's face.

Sam was kind of a breed much above the calibre of the Dy Police Chief to handle.

What the police told the minister is that Iran Govt is planning to revenge the American attack in their soil, but a clear decision is not yet taken. He added that one plan is to send nuclear missiles or bomb the New York City using the light speed spacecraft.

However, the Iran intelligence doubts that Sam, the pilot of the spacecraft, being a US citizen, may not agree to attack America. So they will keep Sam's fiancée, Dr. Mary, as a hostage in Iran and bargain with him.

The police chief further said that the defence minister had ordered to take out Franklin's laptop and other documents from the spacecraft, and also Dr. Mary is to be taken into police custody.

Sam realized that he has to act quickly. Now he shouldn't take side with Iran as it's going to be a war between Iran and America. He didn't hijack the satellite mission so far because of Franklin's commitment and greatness to achieve further discoveries to help humanity.

It's much applicable now because the world is in a critical situation due to climate change. But, Franklin may not be there to protect him and Mary at the moment, and it's turning out to be an ugly war which will further damage the grave situation Mother Earth and humans are facing currently.

In such a situation, Sam has decided not to go with Iran's plan for a nuclear attack. He also didn't justify American attack on Franklin, but the immediate thing needed is to stop Iran's revenge plan.

The minister looking at Sam said to the Deputy Police Chief in Arabic, "Do everything smartly without that man, the spacecraft pilot, getting suspicious about our plan. We don't have another pilot at the moment to fly the spacecraft. So handle him carefully."

The HRD minister then said to Sam, "Ok, police chief will tell you what to do further. I'm going now. Bye."

After the minister's departure, Deputy Police Chief approached Sam. "Our defence minister told me that we need to first take out Franklin's laptop and other items from the spacecraft. These important items have to be kept safe because there can be another American attack. Also tell the lady scientist with you that we'll now shelter her in a protected place, ok? These two guards will come with you to help you."

The Dy Police Chief called two inspectors and briefed them in Arabic. They accompanied Sam to the spacecraft.

The two minutes walk towards the spacecraft was sufficient for Sam to plan his operation. He helped the police inspectors to get into the spacecraft, and said to Mary, "Dr. Mary, Franklin is seriously injured in a US helicopter attack. Now these inspectors came to collect his laptop and other documents."

Mary shouted in disbelief, "God Almighty! How's Franklin? What happened to him?"

Sam replied hurriedly, "He's recovering, doctor; we'll discuss it later. Now please hand over Franklin's laptop and other items which are kept in the main capsule, there inside... Take these police officers to the main capsule while I prepare the spacecraft for safely parking somewhere here."

While talking to her Sam quickly started the thrusters and AbM motors of the spacecraft, and built up the pressure inside the main capsule. The police inspectors didn't suspect anything as Sam and Mary were behaving quite normally.

Mary was intelligent enough to detect something strange in Sam's behaviour. When Sam addressed her as Dr. Mary, something sparked in her mind. Then as Sam said Franklin's laptop is kept in the main capsule and asked her to take the police officers inside the main capsule, things clicked in her mind. She knew that Sam only kept the laptop safely in the human capsule drawer and locked it, keeping the key in his pocket.

Mary knew what to do in such a critical situation.

Without even a slight hesitation, she told the police inspectors to follow her.

"Please come this way, one at a time, and one behind the other. I'm following you."

She then turned the handle of the emergency exit corridor to the main capsule and signalled the officers to get in pretending that she is also following them. When the officers stepped in, they were pulled into the capsule by the huge pressure build up and the suction inside.

Mary closed the door of the main capsule.

The Deputy Police Chief and others standing outside were not knowing about the drama going on inside. It all happened within a few minutes' time.

Once the police inspectors are sucked in to the main capsule, Sam straightaway airlifted the spacecraft and disappeared into the thin air at light speed.

Nobody in the police team could react- they were completely taken aback to see the light speed spacecraft moving so fast and disappearing like a ray of light.

On the way, Sam told Mary about the US attack on the satellite control centre and Iran's plan to attack America using the spacecraft. He added that Franklin is admitted in the intensive care unit at Tehran Govt Hospital.

Mary first thanked Sam for cleverly managing the Iran police inspectors by sending them to the main capsule. She said, "That was a smart move Sam; I just could read your mind and act accordingly. Now, can we go to the hospital to see what happened to Franklin?"

"You too managed the tense situation pretty cool commando Mary! Ok, now let's see Franklin, we're going to his place. See there, we reached at the Govt Hospital, Tehran."

Sam took the spacecraft inside the ICU department of the hospital at light speed. The spacecraft can pass through glass and other transparent objects just like light rays. He revolved around the ICU ward to watch the situation and security arrangements there. There were only one doctor and two nurses in the ICU.

Sam quickly landed the spacecraft by the side of the door inside the ICU and they both got down. Mary rushed to the door and locked it while Sam raised the rifle and told the doctor and nurses not to move.

Mary then told the doctor that Franklin is their close friend and is the leader of their scientific team. Mary added that she is a medical doctor and assured them that they intend no harm; just they want to know the condition of Franklin.

The doctor replied, "It's a case of Traumatic brain injury (TBI). There was bullet injury- open head injury when Franklin was brought here. The patient was in a very serious situation. We removed the bullet and conducted operation. There was internal bleeding and brain suffered minor damages.

"Not sure whether there will be recovery from this comma stage. Everything now depends upon the injuries to the brain nerves and its healing, as you know the situation in such cases of TBI. Even if he recovers from the comma, there is less chance that he'll be able to pursue any scientific researches in the future."

Mary consulted with Sam. "Franklin's condition is hopeless. In such cases of TBI, the patient will lie unconsciously for several months or for years together, and finally die when the body become weak and thin."

Mary then suggested a strange thing, "Sam, why don't we take him to the spacecraft and do a trial by putting him inside the main capsule in energy form? Sometimes this could help regain his consciousness."

Sam was very happy to hear that innovative idea and readily agreed to it. He was very sorry to see the fate of Professor Franklin. If he lived his normal life, he would have made many more discoveries. What a loss for the whole humanity!

Sam thought that the U.S. Govt had done a blunder in conducting the raid at Iran's satellite control centre. What immediately provoked them to do this military operation is not known, but it was mistimed and led to the loss of a great scientist.

After getting Sam's consent to carry Franklin on the spacecraft, Mary said to the medical staff in the ICU, "We're taking Professor Franklin to the spacecraft for further treatment. As you know the result is very dim here."

But the medical staff objected to the move and said that they need to get approval from Iran Govt to take away the patient.

Sam and Mary had to keep the staff at gunpoint to take Franklin to the spacecraft. While getting into the spacecraft Mary tried to assure the medical staff, "Nothing will happen to you doctor, tell the authority that we took Franklin away forcibly and for further treatment."

Just as Sam and Mary stepped into the spacecraft with Franklin on their shoulders, Iran police came and knocked at the ICU door. The police broke in to stop Sam and Mary, but they could see only a flashlight going out through the glass window.

Sam directed the spacecraft to Mars and asked Mary to shift Franklin to the main capsule.

"The Iran police inspectors are inside the main capsule. Will it pose a problem if we put Franklin there without taking the police out?" Mary wondered.

"No, there shouldn't be any issues. While travelling with the speed of light, any object or person will be in energy form and so could not do any physical action. When the spacecraft is static on the ground or when we keep it in semi-transparent form, then only people inside the main capsule can do any work. Moreover, they won't harm Franklin; they have orders to arrest us only," Sam explained.

He pressed on, "Anyway we'll have to do more tests to authenticate the happenings inside the main capsule where the occupants are exposed to the effects of real light speed travel. However, we don't have much time to think about it considering the current medical situation of Franklin. So let's pray and take the Professor into the main capsule. Ensure that nobody comes out when you open the lever."

Mary checked Franklin's BP and overall medical condition. She strapped Franklin's body tightly to the hospital stretcher.

Mary then opened the NRV pathway to the corridor that goes to the main capsule.

"We'll reach Mars in 10 minutes; let's hope that something good will happen to Franklin by that time," Sam informed Mary while she transferred Franklin's body into the main capsule.

"May God bless him," Mary prayed.

"Amen," said a grief-stricken Sam.

They reached Mars as planned and orbited the red planet thrice. Sam then landed the spacecraft at the Iran colony and switched off the engines.

Mary has opened the passage to main capsule while Sam stood there with pointed rifle. Soon the police officers and Franklin tied on to the stretcher, flowed in front of them into the human capsule.

Mary attended Franklin while Sam and the police inspectors got down from the spacecraft, Sam pointing his rifle towards them.

Sam took the police inspectors to a corner of the Iran colony and told them that they are on Mars now and left with no chance to contact the police or Iran government. Sam added that if they behaved well, they can be inducted as guards for the Iran colony.

The police inspectors understood that they have no authority or power on Mars. In the new circumstances, they though it's better to obey the new commander who at the moment is Sam.

Sam was surprised to see their meek surrender and happily took the police inspectors to the Iran colony for introducing them as the security personnel.

Meanwhile, Mary was thrilled to see that Franklin has opened his eyes and started talking. Mary told him everything happened up to the moment.

Franklin murmured in a weak voice, "Mary, I had plans to conduct many scientific researches and tests that would have led to important discoveries. But all my energy has drained away. I lost my memory, and can't remember anything now; those formulas and theories which were at my fingertips- all vanished now...

"Achieving light speed was the first thing; once it's done, there are many things left to prove about black holes, space-time relations and their interchangeable nature, and even time-travel enigma. But alas, everything has been spoiled ..."

Mary consoled him, "Don't worry, Franklin. Nothing will happen to you; don't lose hope."

"No Mary, I know my brain is damaged...I'm getting this extra consciousness because of the energy transformation in the main capsule. You need to do more experiments with respect to the main capsule to check the possibility of converting people who're terminally ill into energy form and preserving their spirit...

"And for me, it's time to go. All data about my theory on crossing the light speed, and other research papers on time travel and black holes are kept in my laptop. The password to open it is my thumb impression, so preserve it for future reference...

"And Mary, you and Sam should try to prove all my hypotheses while travelling at light speed deep into the Milky Way Galaxy. My mind and wishes will be there with you as you move on to unknown star worlds with my spacecraft… Goodness gracious! Why did you allow this misfortune to fall on me at this crucial juncture? How I wish to complete my research! "

Franklin's condition gradually deteriorated. The energy he received from the light-speed travel slowly drained away. Mary checked his condition and knew that he is sinking. With a heavy heart, Mary realises the life-soul of Franklin slowly dripping from her grip as she held him with her hand.

Mary said to Franklin, "Listen Prof. Franklin, I give my word to you that you'll be resurrected, God willing! I'll use all my medical research and cloning technology to recreate you. Not only your thumb, but your brain also will be preserved. You won't go away from us forever; I'll bring you back from the valley of death with all your memories intact! Believe me dear; you'll be born again as the same Professor Franklin."

Mary whispered in his ear,

"Listen Franklin, when you come alive again, I promise to give you the Mary you loved to possess. Dear Franklin, I'll clone another Mary in the test tube and as she grows up, I'll resurrect you too, Insh allah! And both of you will travel with us through the shores of our Milky Way Galaxy, and we'll make our nests on another beautiful Earth."

There came a timid smile on Franklin's face as Mary spoke that lovely pledge from her heart and two drops of her tears fell on his face.

At that time Sam came inside. They both sat by the side of Prof. Franklin and said good bye as he breathed his last.

Mary collected the cells from Franklin's thumb, brain and internal organs and preserved them for her cloning experiments.

As Mary was doing all necessary things on Franklin's body, Sam quickly opened Franklin's laptop and pressed his thumb which was still warm enough for the computer to accept the password.

Sam checked some of the contents of the laptop and saw a file named, "Spacecraft moving at light-speed and its endless possibilities." Sam has just gone through it. It was a theoretical description of the superhuman capabilities one may get while travelling with the speed of light.

There are many interesting facts, and Sam was astonished to see Franklin's intellectual greatness to predict such things - only a genius can imagine like that. Sam thought they need to conduct tests to check all those assumptions and theories described by Franklin.

Sam realised that they have seen only the tip of the iceberg so far regarding the spacecraft and light speed travel. There are going to be full of adventures to be unfolded soon.

Sam and Mary have decided to preserve Franklin's body at the ice covered Martian pole using the advanced preservation method known as cryonic suspension. Mary has given some injections accordingly on Franklin's body and they took it to the South Pole where there are thick ice layers.

Sam used the Nanotech excavators and drills on the spacecraft to remove ice and make a burial spot some 20 feet below the surface. They kept Franklin's body in a medically prepared polyethylene bag and placed it inside the deep trench. They also prepared tombstones with electronic detectors and engraved Franklin's details on it - One stone was kept near the body while the other one was permanently placed on the surface as a marking. Ice tiles were cut to size and laid carefully to fill the trench.

Sam and Mary breathed a sigh of contentment and relief as they know Franklin's body will be kept safe indefinitely on the Martian pole. In case Mary needs any requirement in the future for her cloning work, they can come back and take out Franklin's body safely.

After preserving the body of their teammate and great scientist, Sam and Mary decided to go and visit Pentagon- Headquarters of the United States Department of Defense. They wanted to know why such a speedy Iran operation was carried out by the U.S. government.

At the same time, some major disaster happened on Earth. The world now faces the most unwanted thing – a 3rd World War! Nobody expected it to happen it at this difficult situation.

After the failure of Iran operation to hijack Franklin and his invention, the United States and their allies sent nuclear missiles and dropped powerful nuclear bombs at several places in China and Iran. This was as per their secret agreement to create a new world order. All major cities in China were completely destroyed. The attack was massive and was planned in such a manner that China should not get time to strike back. They used the world's biggest and most powerful nuclear bombs.

But, contrary to American belief, China has retaliated with full force. They have large nuclear stockpiles in the South China Sea and other secret places. Soon China's intercontinental ballistic missiles and submarine-launched ballistic missiles were fired at critical U.S. and European destinations.

It turned out to be global chaos and massive destruction. All countries were bleeding like hell. And to add to the fire, Russia and Iran jointly attacked US marine installations around the world. Russian strategic bomber fleet also singlehandedly destroyed majority of U.S. population on the eastern and western seaboards.

Within a short time of one or two hours, almost a major portion of nuclear-tipped cruise missiles and other nuclear weapons of mass destruction were exploded at every corner of Earth. The sea and land all are burning and exploding everywhere.

Mary and Sam came back to see this devastating face of a World War burning in front of them. The nuclear explosions also have triggered massive Earthquakes, Tsunami and volcano eruptions. They were stunned to see this dreadful sight. Yes, they are seeing the much talked about World War III and its monstrous effect just in front of their eyes. It was more devastating than the much hyped stories about it.

Mary suddenly thought about her Papa and Mamma. Sam quickly diverted the spacecraft to Koshy ichayan's villa. It was a deplorable sight they saw there. All the high-rise buildings were gutted down either by a missile or a massive Earthquake. The whole area was like a ploughed land. All the bricks and walls were shattered around.

On close examination, they located ichayan's villa amidst the desolation and piled debris. Mary couldn't control her sorrow. Sam drove the spacecraft on to the ground penetrating through the gaps of bricks and other building parts and scanned the area. They could finally locate ichayan and Preetha around 10ft below. They are lying unconsciously...

Mary is now crying loudly. Sam carefully landed the spacecraft on the ground. Using the earthmovers, Sam cleared the debris around the spot. Because of the high-tech nanotechnology, the equipments were very precise and easy to operate. The spacecraft's high magnetic field was used to lift heavy metal rods and other materials. Within 10 minutes Sam could remove broken walls, logs and other obstacles and clear the space where ichayan and Preetha are seen.

Mary quickly checked their pulse, sprayed some water on their face and shook them calling "Pappa, Mamma" repeatedly. Koshy ichayan and Preetha slowly opened their eyes and glanced at their children.

Mary told Sam to take them to the main capsule of the spacecraft. But unfortunately, it was found that their bones are all broken and they're not in a condition to move from the ground. They are half dead and just breathing their last.

In a feeble voice Koshy ichayan said to Mary, "Don't worry children, it's time for us to go…We're lucky to see you before departing…Also, we're happy to know that our Mary and Sam will survive the end of world. We, and all of the people in this locality, were expecting a catastrophe any moment. Do you know what's happening around?"

"It's the end of the world, papa. A world war is going on- the 3rd World War, which has almost destroyed everything on Earth. Huge disaster is taking place and it could be the wiping out of human civilization," Sam said.

Ichayan uttered his last words, "It's He who decides, amen. Good bye." Preetha also said good bye, and they are gone- together.

Earth started trembling again…Sam and Mary ran to the spacecraft and lifted it to light speed and looked at the terrible things happening around.

Sam and Mary have noticed that the main problem Earth is facing now is atmospheric pollution created by heavy nuclear explosions. A dust storm has gradually surrounded the Earth and it partially shadowed the Sun. Earth's surface temperature has alarmingly shot up due to the dust envelope reflecting back the heat emanated from its surface.

Sam just wanted to visit his orphanage and see the situation there, and flown to Kakkanad in Kerala, India. They were awestruck to see the situation there. Gigantic Tsunami waves have engulfed the area. The buildings are gutted and everything is under water now. There are no signs of any living persons around. With tears in his eyes, Sam plunged the spacecraft inside the water and collected some wet Earth from the orphanage compound using a drill.

India has so far not joined any fighting alliance and remained neutral. Nobody attacked them too, but natural calamities had taken their toll of large-scale casualties in India - the Tsunamis and bursting of dams wreaked havoc in South India and Bengal, while Himalayan Glacier melting and subsequent flooding destroyed many places in Northern parts of the country.

It was like doomsday dawned in the World!

Destruction and chaos are seen everywhere. Sam and Mary decided to meet the heads of state of countries around the world to offer help and try to diffuse the tension. They have the trump card in the guise of the light speed spacecraft, and there is slight chance that the leaders may agree for a truce.

From Kerala, they went to the Prime Minister's office in New Delhi to discuss what helps the country need urgently. They could see space rockets making last minute shuttle services for transporting people to Mars.

As they were trying to land at the Indian Parliament building or President's Office (Rashtrapati Bhavan), something amiss happened. The Earth shook violently with heavy seismic vibrations. They lifted up the spacecraft and watched the sudden development from a safe distance overhead.

With a heavy heart Mary and Sam watched the Earth suddenly sliding to one side. The instruments in their control panel showed that Earth has paused rotating in its axis for a moment and then tilted to 35.5 degree tilt position deviating from its normal axis tilt of 23.5 degrees. A ten degree tilt has affected the Earth's equilibrium and shaken it violently from within - and the result was unimaginable.

Huge explosions erupted and molten rocks and hot lava are seen spewed out from the Earth's centre. A big landmass of Earth has flown from the Earth's crust away into atmosphere.

The moon also zoomed past the Earth and escaped from its gravitational pull.

And Earth has turned into a ball of fire!

Mary and Sam have promptly flown away into the outer space. Carrying the DNA footprint of life on Earth from almost all species, they guided the spacecraft- the Noah's 2nd Ark- deep into the outer space.

They'll fly nonstop till they find a new young Earth God has in store for them to nestle and settle in. Travelling at the speed of light means their aging process will be very slow or almost nil. Physically moving into the main capsule of the spacecraft during certain periods and thereby becoming energy particles will allow them to completely stop the ageing process as long as they wanted.

By the time they find a new Earth, Mary and Sam could turn hundreds of years old as per the time calculation with respect to Earth's clock... and of course Franklin might have been cloned and brought to life on their way itself.

So there would be two pairs of Adam and Eve roaming on a new Earth – Sam and Mary, and resurrected Franklin and newly cloned Mary.

While galloping thus towards the shores of Milky Way galaxy, Mary and Sam just glanced back towards their Mother Earth with tears in their eyes. They saw Earth blazing like the Sun, burning and melting away the last traces of life. They couldn't watch it clearly as the tears have faded their vision!

Sam then asked Mary, "What's the date today?"

"14 August, 2050. Why?" Mary enquired.

"Nothing - Just trying to keep that fateful DATE in memory."

BIBLIOGRAPHY

1. IPCC reports on climate change from their website: IPCC's 43rd Session (Nairobi, Kenya, 11 - 13 April 2016). IPCC's report: "Climate Change 2007: Impacts, Adaptation and Vulnerability," published in Brussels on 6 April 2007.
2. The State of the Climate in 2015 report by The National Oceanic and Atmospheric Association (NOAA) published in August 2016.
3. Isaac Asimov's Foundation series of science fiction books – Two paragraphs quoted from: "Foundation (Foundation #1)(5)" by Isaac Asimov.
4. Mr. David Butler's Facebook post:
   [Link to the post dated August 5, 2014:
   www.facebook.com/davebutts7/posts/10152165382350044]
5. Titanic Movie theme song - "Every Night in My Dreams."

Please put your valuable comments and suggestions about this book at Amazon review – your constructive points, if needed, can be included in the ebook! Use this link: www.amazon.com/Matthew-Ilayathu/e/B01LW9PPTT/ or www.amazon.com/dp/B01LWB1G1U

ABOUT THE AUTHOR

Matthew ilayathu (Matthew Jr.), Kerala, India.
Mail to: sajiwrites@gmail.com.

DOB: 28 February 1966. Graduation in English Literature and PG in Journalism & Mass Communication, and Computer Applications.
About 15 years of journalistic and corporate copywriting career spanning India & the Middle East. Currently settled in Kochi and working as freelance Social Media Manager for companies in Australia, New Zealand and the U.S.

Having worked in the technical dept. of Indian Air Force for over 15 years, the author has profound knowledge in aeronautical engineering and the maintenance of a versatile fleet of aircraft. This might have helped him in envisioning a light-speed spacecraft with capabilities of time travel & hyperspace jumping.

Being a blogger, he's very active in social media handling global warming, climate change, and politico-social issues. Many skits of the same genre were written and directed on stage.

Done the proofing & editing of "World Bank and Beyond- a Memoir & a Proposal" by Stanley C P, publisher: P&B Corp, US.

Future plans include writing more about global warming & climate change for creating awareness.

Currently the book, The Coming of Noah's 2nd Ark, is being adapted for a movie screenplay.

Add COMMENTS & SUGGESTIONS on EBook:
www.amazon.com/dp/B01LWB1G1U

CONCLUSION

Global Warming and Climate Change

Are you aware that Earth's surface temperature is continuously increasing? When you see untimely rains, droughts, flash floods, massive earth quakes etc. pause for a moment and retrospect. The dangerous climate change of which the scientists used to warn us are happening now.

It may lead to some chain reactions and end up in a large-scale catastrophe that can threaten life on Earth. Our unreasonable ways of industrialization, deforestation and modern lifestyle etc. have given rise to huge CO2 emission, pollution and degeneration of Nature. This paved way for global warming & climate change. Starting in a low level, climate change gradually assumes alarming proportions. Melting of glaciers and polar ice has increased significantly. There are enough signs of climate change around us, and it's slowly growing beyond our control.

According to climate scientists, some tipping points will be crossed before they are recognized if we continue to wait for higher levels of scientific certainty on global warming & climate change. Transporting life from Earth to another planet will be the only option left now to save life because climate change might have gone beyond our control.

If we live in the hostile conditions of Mars for a week, then we'll know the blessings we have on Earth – even the air we breathe, the water we drink, the greenness and life giving environment around us will look like golden treasures!

The hardships we face to live on Mars will be an eye opener. After returning from Mars for a week's stay, you are sure to become an advocate for the protection of our environment and safeguarding of our planet.

Life is precious and Earth with its inhabitable condition is a very rare phenomenon in the Universe. So far scientists watching the Milky Way galaxy couldn't find any ideal planet like Earth. So, preserve it for the future generations to live here! Promote the concept of Peaceful Coexistence with the flora and fauna on Earth. Stop over exploitation of the Nature.

The Relevance of God/ the Spirit of Nature

Instead of blindly laughing at the scriptures, it's good to take the moral of the story (Noah's Ark in this case) and live a meaningful life. Defining or reasoning God and His acts are beyond our capacity. But the religious books, which describe God, are written by morally perfect personalities whose aim was to reduce sins and inhuman activities in the society. So, it's good to follow the scriptures as is, rather than interpreting it according to one's whimsical thinking.

If we can draw a line between science & religion, it'll be better for the mankind. We should not use one to despise the other; we need both. Sorrows and miseries are integral part of human life. And in difficult situations, believing in God gives hope and the strength to face misfortunes. Same way, science is also there to help us in physical advancements and make our lives more comfortable on Earth.

When you see the systematic way the planets are arranged and the orderly manner myriad forms of flora and fauna exists on Earth - when you feel the dream effects of innumerable stars scattered across the night sky twinkling at you and the shining moon enchanting you - when the life giving powers of the Sun lifts your spirits in the day - and when you watch our lives and the living things around us as a whole - it's quite reasonable to believe that a super intelligence is there behind everything and in the making of this Universe. There has to be a divine force controlling the maintenance of this Universe, even though we can't fully fathom its character or qualities.

But, it looks quite absurd to say that all these wonderful creations just came out from a Big Bang and no intelligence worked into its stunning formation and lay out - it's just like saying the Webster's

Dictionary came into being from an accidental explosion in some ink factory!

Even if you think strictly in a scientific manner, we can see that there was a special timing and fine-tuning for everything happened from the Big Bang to the creation of our Solar system and the formation of life on Earth. "If the rate of expansion one second after the big bang had been smaller by even one part in a hundred thousand million million, the universe would have re-collapsed before it ever reached its present size," says well known cosmologist, Stephen Hawking.

Similarly, there are several other factors that have happened in a precise and calculated manner for life to exist here. We can't reasonably expect that these are mere coincidences. It's thus sensible to think that there is some super intelligence behind the scenes that designed and created the universe.

Crossing the Light Speed Barrier
Now let's think about Franklin's theory and the possibility of crossing the speed of light...

According to Albert Einstein's observations, if a spacecraft travels with the speed of light, three phenomena will come into effect:
1. As per 'Time-Space-Mass' relation, when a spacecraft travels with the speed of light, time will remain standstill, that is, it won't change!
2. Length of the spacecraft will become zero, which means it'll disappear from our view.
3. And lastly, weight of the spacecraft will tend to become infinity!

The ultimate result will be that the spacecraft becomes an energy form. And as time doesn't change, people travelling in the spacecraft won't grow anymore - they won't become old!! Also there could be many such mindboggling results if we can achieve the speed of light...

It could be similar to The Time Machine and time travel stories. But not yet known what theory Franklin might have used - May be a 'wormhole' or 'Einstein–Rosen bridge' feature that would fundamentally be a shortcut connecting two separate points in space-time. However, all these stories and ideas are hypothetical, and Franklin would have found a practical solution to it...

Achieving the speed of light will be a dramatic moment for humanity. With our conventional rocket technology, we're just toddlers in our solar system - but with the speed of light capability, everything will change phenomenally... and we could expand our horizon not up to stars, but even up to galaxies and beyond! And who knows one day we might even reach the abode of almighty God!!...

The requirement to travel with the speed of light is also the need of the hour –the survival of human species depends on it. Climate change and global warming could make the Earth uninhabitable. So we need to find out another planet quite like Earth- and for that, it's a must to travel faster than light speed. If we travel with the current rocket speed in space (may be fifty times that of sound, Mach50), it will take thousands of years to reach even the nearest star. With our life expectancy a mere 100 years, we cannot possibly escape from the solar system alive! That means, only Mohammad Franklin's invention can help us in this predicament! So we want his invention at any cost!...

Even though Einstein had doubted man could break the speed of light, theories evolved later said otherwise. When new inventions and ideas like string theory, quantum mechanics, neutrinos, and Higgs boson or God particle were merged, it started dawning that Einstein's rules are limited. Isaac Newton's discoveries were limited to Earth and its gravity, and Einstein had stretched it beyond Earth. Now it seems that Einstein's theories and concepts might be limited to our solar system - perhaps our theory of gravitation needs upgrading! This may come as the theory of relativity advanced Newtonian gravitation. Principles governing the Universe are still beyond our reach at the moment…a new physics is to be evolved, and achieving the speed of light is the threshold point we should attain for further exploration of the Universe.

This book is found to be an eye opener- it's an appeal to the whole world to change our nature-abusive life style and start supporting the eco system. Our destiny is not on God's hands now; he has given it to our free will. If we don't conserve the environment, we'll perish.

Even with our higher intellectual capacity and the scientific advancements, if we fail to stop exploitation of nature and the ensuing environmental degradation, we'll be digging our own graves. God will punish us for sure. God as such is omnipotent and the owner of this universe, you can't expect him to come to our help for every misdeed we do. No meaning in asking questions like why god had created us if he can't protect us etc.

However, there is a little ray of hope as God had saved life during Noah's time when the great flooding occurred. He may also send another ark to preserve life in the event of a cataclysmic event leading to Earth's destruction in modern times. Just a small collection of DNA samples (of all species on earth to recreate them from their genetic information) will be preserved, rest all life forms, including humans and animals, on Earth will be annihilated.

Would like to emphasise the fact that the events happening in the story seems to be not mere imaginations of the author, rather they are part of a sequence of revelations from the unknown. We have every reason to think so, as we see signs of abrupt climate change around us,

Message by: A Well-wisher to Mankind & Nature.

www.ingramcontent.com/pod-product-compliance
Lightning Source LLC
LaVergne TN
LVHW091452170726
843492LV00001B/144